Praise For Bette Lee Crosby's Novels

When I La

D1235334

"There is nothing a mother will not do for he   novel, *When I Last Saw You*, proves that and more. Inspired by a true story, readers .... .ooting for Margaret Rose and Eliza Hobbs as you accompany them on their epic journey of life, love, and healing."

— Kay Bratt, International bestselling author of *Wish Me Home*

"A compelling and heart-warming story about loss and the long-kept secrets that tear a family apart. A memorable tale that instantly pulls you in."

— Alison Ragsdale, bestselling author of *Her Last Chance*

"Crosby has done it again! She has created wonderful characters who I fell in love with and a setting and time that captured my imagination."

— Susan, *The Book Bag*

A Million Little Lies

"Steeped in secrets and Southern charm, heartwarming and heartbreaking. A tale of forgiveness, family, and what it means to finally find your true home."

— Barbara Davis, bestselling author of *The Moon Girls*

"Crosby at her best! Masterful storytelling. A young mother builds her new life on a ladder of lies. Read it in one sitting."

— Marilyn Simon Rothstein, author of *Lift and Separate*

"Heart-wrenching and heartwarming. A novel to satisfy your soul and leave your heart feeling happier."

— *Linda's Book Obsession*

Emily, Gone

"Heart-wrenching and heartwarming. A page turner until the end."

— Ashley Farley, bestselling author of *Only One Life*

"An extraordinary book that raises questions about love, family, faith, and forgiveness. This one will stay with me for quite some time."

— Camille DiMaio, bestselling author of *The Way of Beauty*

"A beautiful story that will being you to tears! The writing is flawless! Definitely one of the most beautiful books I've read this year!"

— *Book Nerd*

A Year of Extraordinary Moments

"One of those rare books that makes you believe in the power of love. Filled with memorable characters and important life lessons, a Southern treat to the last page."

— Anita Hughes, author of *California Summer*

"Throughout this book, the author beautifully explores the theme of letting go of the past while preserving its best parts . . ."

— *Kirkus Reviews*

The Summer of New Beginnings

"This women's fiction novel is full of romance, the power of friendship and the bond of sisters."

— *The Charlotte Observer*

"A heartwarming story about family, forgiveness, and the magic of new beginnings."

— Christine Nolfi, bestselling author of *Sweet Lake*

"A heartwarming, captivating, and intriguing story about the importance of family . . . The colorful cast of characters are flawed, quirky, mostly loyal, determined and mostly likable."

— *Linda's Book Obsession*

"Crosby's Southern voice comes through in all of her books and lends a believable element to everything she writes. *The Summer of New Beginnings* is no exception."

— *Book Chat*

Spare Change

"Skillfully written, *Spare Change* clearly demonstrates Crosby's ability to engage her readers' rapt attention from beginning to end. A thoroughly entertaining work of immense literary merit."

— *Midwest Book Review*

"Love, loss and unexpected gifts ... Told from multiple points of view, this tale seeped from the pages and wrapped itself around my heart."

— Caffeinated Reviewer

"More than anything, *Spare Change* is a heartwarming book, which is simultaneously intriguing and just plain fun."

— Seattle Post-Intelligencer

Passing Through Perfect

"This is Southern fiction at its best: spiritually infused, warm, and family-oriented."

— Midwest Book Reviews

"Crosby's characters take on heartbreak and oppression with dignity, courage, and a shaken but still strong faith in a better tomorrow."

— IndieReader

The Twelfth Child

"Crosby's unique style of writing is timeless and her character building is inspirational."

— Layered Pages

"Crosby draws her characters with an emotional depth that compels the reader to care about their challenges, to root for their success, and to appreciate their bravery."

— Gayle Swift, author of ABC, Adoption & Me

"Crosby's talent lies in not only telling a good compelling story, but telling it from a unique perspective ... Characters stay with you because they are simply too endearing to go away."

— Reader Views

Baby Girl

"Crosby weaves this story together in a manner that feels like a huge patchwork quilt. All the pieces and tears come together to make something beautiful."

— Michele Randall, Readers' Favorite

"Crosby is a true storyteller, delving into the emotions, relationships, and human dynamics—the cracks which break us, and ultimately make us stronger."

—J. D. Collins, Top 1000 reviewer

Silver Threads

"*Silver Threads* is an amazing story of love, loss, family, and second chances that will simply stir your soul."

— *Jersey Girl Book Reviews*

"Crosby's books are filled with love of family and carry the theme of a sweetness for life ... You are pulled in by the story line and the characters."

— *Silver's Reviews*

"In *Silver Threads*, Crosby flawlessly merges the element of fantasy without interrupting the beauty of a solid love story ... Sure to stay with you beyond the last page."

— Lisa McCombs, *Readers' Favorite*

Cracks in the Sidewalk

"Crosby has penned a multidimensional scenario that should be read not only for entertainment but also to see how much, love, gentleness, and humanity matter."

— Gisela Hausmann, *Readers' Favorite*

To Susan

The Fault
Between Us

Enjoy!

Bette Lee Crosby

Also by Bette Lee Crosby

The Magnolia Grove Series
The Summer of New Beginnings
A Year of Extraordinary Moments

The Wyattsville Series
Spare Change
Jubilee's Journey
Passing Through Perfect
The Regrets of Cyrus Dodd
Beyond the Carousel

The Memory House Series
Memory House
The Loft
What the Heart Remembers
Baby Girl
Silver Threads

Serendipity Series
The Twelfth Child
Previously Loved Treasures

Stand-Alone Titles
When I Last Saw You
A Million Little Lies
Emily Gone
Cracks in the Sidewalk
What Matters Most
Wishing for Wonderful
Blueberry Hill
Life in the Land of IS: The Amazing True Story of Lani Deauville

The Fault
Between Us

A Novel

BETTE LEE CROSBY

BENT PINE PUBLISHING

Dedicated to all the families
Who are separated by too many miles

Templeton Whittier Morehouse

THE ONE THING YOU CAN be certain of in this life is that nothing is for certain. Nothing. Not even a future that once seemed as fixed in place and solid as the Rock of Gibraltar. Confident that you are in charge of your own destiny, you move forward with your feet firmly planted on the pathway you've laid out for yourself. Then fate steps in, and everything changes.

This change may bring you more happiness than you ever dreamed possible, or it may be a tragedy so horrible you fall to your knees scarcely able to breathe. Although you're powerless to change what has happened, you try. You plead and pray. Trying to strike a bargain with God, you swear that if He'll put the pieces of your life back together you'll never again ask for anything. When it seems as though your prayers have fallen on deaf ears, you curse Fate herself. When there's nothing more to say or do, then you're left with the endless waiting.

Then and only then, in that time of waiting, you look back on your life and see clearly the mistakes you've made.

I see my mistakes now, but I was blind to them when I first stepped onto the path I've traveled. It was many years ago. Before John. Before the child I'm carrying.

In the Beginning...

TEMPLETON WHITTIER WAS A LATE-IN-LIFE baby. She arrived in 1876, seven years after her sister, Clara, and a full ten years after Benjamin, the Whittiers' eldest boy. Her mother, Eleanor, had believed herself beyond child-bearing years until her stomach swelled to the size of a watermelon. Templeton came into the world just three months later.

When Albert saw his newborn daughter with her eyes wide open and a shock of flame red hair, he laughed aloud.

"Good Lord!" he exclaimed. "She looks exactly like my great-uncle Templeton."

Fortunate or unfortunate as the case may be, the child turned out to have a personality much like the great-uncle she'd been named after. She was smart as a whip but equally as headstrong and willful. Once she'd set her mind to go in a certain direction, nothing could stop her. As a toddler, she'd climb into her daddy's lap, tug the showy silk handkerchief from the breast of his jacket, then scream bloody murder if anyone tried to take it from her.

Initially they thought such behavior was because the child was overly attached to her daddy, but in time they came to realize it was the feel of the fabric that attracted her. By the time Templeton was four, she'd taken to raiding Eleanor's sewing basket for ribbons and scraps of lace. She'd stitch them onto a doll's dress, make bows for her hair, or weave a band that circled her waist or her arm. As soon as the project was finished she'd go in search of Clara or Eleanor, seeking approval. With her tiny shoulders squared back and her face radiant with pride, she'd ask, "Doesn't this look pretty?"

Eleanor believed such a fetish was a childish thing Templeton would eventually outgrow, but she didn't. She went from playing with scraps of fabric to sketching the dresses in magazines and then embellishing them in one way or another: a narrower skirt, broader shoulders, a leg-of-mutton sleeve. By the time she reached her last year of high school, she was designing and sewing almost every stitch of clothing she wore.

When Albert complained that she was spending entirely too much on the wools and linens she ordered from the dry goods shop, she claimed it was a necessity.

"I plan on becoming a fashion designer," she said.

Eleanor raised an eyebrow, and Albert stated unequivocally that such a thing was preposterous.

"I expect you to follow in your sister's footsteps," he said. "Marry a man with a promising career, and think about starting a family."

Confident that was the end of it, he turned back to his newspaper.

"I hate to disappoint you, Daddy, but I have no interest in marrying. Not now and perhaps not ever. This is 1895! There's nothing to stop a woman from having a career if she's a mind to do so."

"Poppycock! Making dresses isn't a career. Call it what you will, but the truth is that it's just a fancier way of saying seamstress."

Templeton glared at him with fire in her eyes. "That's not true! Haven't you heard of Jacques Doucet or Charles Frederick Worth? My designs can make me as famous as they are. Why, Mr. Darlington has already said I have a skilled eye for detailing, and if I apply myself—"

"Mr. Joseph C. Darlington? Proprietor of the very same shop where you've spent one hundred and twenty-seven dollars of my money these past two months?" His questions rippled with accusation. "Don't you realize he's simply encouraging you to make more of these extravagant purchases from his shop?"

"No. It's because he appreciates my talent."

"Well, then, since Mr. Darlington is such an admirer of your talent, he can also be the financier of it. As of this day, I will no longer be responsible for your purchases at his shop."

"Fine!"

Templeton stuck her nose in the air, turned on her heel, and walked away. As she was about to leave the room, she turned back and looked him square in the eye.

"I intend to continue my career as a designer."

"What career?" Albert mumbled beneath his breath, but by then she'd disappeared down the hallway.

The week Templeton graduated from high school, she set up a drawing board in her room, used her monthly allowance to buy a supply of charcoal pencils and drawing paper, and began sketching designs for everything from a ball gown to a tennis dress. When she closed her eyes, she could see each dress: a rustling silk swaying across the dance floor, a wool suit stepping smartly along Broad Street, a tennis skirt fluttering with the quick steps of its wearer. A dozen or more times she visited Mr. Darlington's fabric shop, soliciting tiny swatches of fabric to affix to the side of each sketch. When the time was right, she would point to the tiny samples and say, This design will be created in this fabric with this beading and an edging of this lace. At night when her eyelids grew so heavy she was forced to set aside the pencils, she climbed into bed, but even as she slept the images were there: a bit of smocking, a detail of embroidery, insets that narrowed the waist, a perfectly draped bustle.

When the weather turned blistering hot and perspiration beaded on her forehead, Eleanor begged her to give up such foolishness.

"You're wasting your youth," she said, but Templeton was not dissuaded—not by her mama's pleas and not by her daddy shaking his head woefully as he complained about such nonsense being a total waste of time.

"No, it's not," Templeton replied. "Soon enough you'll see my designs in the front window of Wanamaker's."

Their naysaying only served to increase her determination. That summer she didn't attend a single party or social gathering. When friends stopped by to ask if she'd join them for a game of lawn croquet or a picnic in the park, she shook her head and said she was too busy. Before the oaks lost their leaves in late September, she had a collection of over thirty drawings. Each was more exquisite than the other.

That Sunday Templeton fanned them out on the floor of her bedroom and studied each one with the critical eye of a buyer. After a moment, she smiled with satisfaction. The next morning she packaged them in a carrying case, took the streetcar into the city, and walked along Market Street, stopping in every dress shop to show her designs and explain how she could provide paper patterns for the shop seamstress to replicate the outfit right down to the last button. By the end of the day, she had two orders and the start of a business.

Refusing to acknowledge her success, Albert called it a flash in the pan.

Undaunted, Templeton continued on. Two weeks before Christmas, the women's wear buyer at Wanamaker's gave her a purchase order for sixteen exclusive designs, and even Albert had to admit that she'd accomplished what she'd set out to do.

THAT FIRST YEAR TEMPLETON RARELY left her room. She was at the drawing board from early morning until late night and only ventured out on days when she was delivering an armful of designs or trolling Broad Street in search of new customers. In the early spring, when tiny green buds were barely visible on the oaks, she signed her sixth client—seventh if she included Wanamaker's—and felt she was well on her way to the fame she was seeking.

That summer she once again found time to socialize. She joined the Women's Club, went to tea with friends, and started receiving gentlemen callers. With a cascade of red curls tumbling down her back and eyes the color of emeralds, she had no shortage of suitors.

The first was Roger Hawkins, a young law clerk from Albert's office. They kept company all summer, saw shows at the Chestnut Street Theatre, went to concerts in the park, attended her friend Sara's wedding together, and played dominoes with Clara and her husband. Yet the minute the young man hinted at marriage, Templeton ended the relationship.

"I don't understand why," Eleanor said glumly. "Roger seemed like such a lovely young man."

"He was," Templeton replied, "but there simply was no magic."

Eleanor stood there with a baffled expression on her face. "Roger is from a good family, he's got a promising career ahead of him, and he's obviously in love with you. What more could you possibly want?"

"When I fall in love, it'll be with someone who makes my heart race, someone who can kiss me and make the rest of the world disappear."

Templeton went on to liken poor Roger to one of her designs, claiming he was a frock without the shiny buttons or brocade ribbon that made it special, an outfit that was serviceable but too ordinary to wear forever.

Although Templeton felt sure of her feelings, Eleanor claimed they were frivolous. Albert agreed.

"With an attitude like that you'll never get married," he said then went back to reading his newspaper.

"Then so be it," Templeton replied.

As the years came and went, so did the gentlemen callers—seven in all, three of whom had spoken of marriage. The last one, Adam Marcus, a bookkeeper with a ship building firm, sent a bouquet of roses for her twenty-fifth birthday. Tucked inside was a card saying he would like to give their courtship another try if Templeton were willing.

Of course, she wasn't. She sent a lovely thank you note saying that as much as she enjoyed his company, her fashion design business was far too demanding to consider a serious involvement at this time.

"Are you certain of this?" Eleanor asked. "A gentleman such as Adam doesn't come along every day, and you're not getting any younger."

"Mama, I'm twenty-five, not ninety-five. I've got plenty of time."

"Not if you hope to someday have a family." Eleanor turned and walked away.

She almost gave up hope that her youngest daughter would ever get married, but in the spring of 1903 everything changed.

It happened on the first Tuesday of April. Templeton had just come from delivering her latest patterns to Wanamaker's when John Morehouse stepped onto the same streetcar. He was taller than most men, and with his bowler hat, fitted waistcoat, and jacket snug across his broad shoulders, she thought him the most attractive man she'd ever seen. From the corner of her eye, she watched as he moved to the bench opposite her, then pulled a copy of the *Philadelphia Inquirer* from his briefcase and began reading.

He didn't look up until the streetcar slowed at the corner of Madison and Broad. Then he lifted his head, glanced across, and smiled. Her heart did a funny little twisty thing, and a blush of color warmed her cheeks. Without a heartbeat of hesitation, she returned his smile.

Later on he would confide that his destination had been the Exchange Building on Market Street, but that morning, instead of getting off, he tucked his newspaper back into his briefcase, crossed the aisle, and asked if he might sit alongside her.

The Whittiers lived in a neighborhood west of the city proper, three blocks from the Main Line. By the time the trolley reached the Delaware River turnaround, John knew Templeton's name, her address, and that she was neither engaged nor married. On the return trip he asked if he might call on her that evening, and she immediately answered yes.

Despite how they'd already spent most of the day together and parted just two hours earlier, John was standing on the front porch at precisely 7 pm with a nosegay of roses.

When Templeton saw the flowers, her heart again skipped a beat. There was something special about him: the slightly crooked line of his smile, the way his dark eyes seemed to sparkle as if a secret were hidden inside, even the way he spoke her name. Hearing him say it, she no longer felt like a girl named after the now-dead great-uncle. John gave her name a musical sound, the L lingering and drawn out. Although it would be five days before he would profess his undying love for her, in that brief moment as they stood looking at one another, he gave her to understand he was as drawn to her as she was to him.

Later, as they sat on the front porch pushing back and forth in the swing, she told him of her design business and he told her of his life in San Francisco. He spoke of how ships sailed into the harbor laden with the latest European fashions and how people now called San Francisco the Paris of the West. He went on, describing the City of Paris department store that sat seven stories high on the corner of Grant and Geary Streets, the ladies who strolled the streets wearing tailored suits with cameo brooches pinned to their collars, and the Chinese workers who labored in factories to make dresses that were sent far and wide.

To Templeton, who'd never been outside of Philadelphia County, the world John spoke of seemed magical, a fashion designer's dream, a place where a woman could expand beyond herself and reach whatever goal she set her mind to. As she listened, she drew in every word. She was almost certain if she closed her eyes she would see herself marching into that department store with an air of certainty to her step and a jaunty little bonnet perched atop her head. She knew that tomorrow she would remember every word he'd spoken, but it wasn't just his words she was committing to memory. It was the depth of his eyes, the movement of his lips, the warmth of his hand on hers, and the way he seemed to reach into her soul and touch her heart.

Over the years Templeton had always maintained a certain reserve with her beaus, but that first evening she allowed John to kiss her, tilting her face to his in a way that was practically an invitation. Years later, when she thought back on it, she would remember that as the night she fell madly and forever in love with John Morehouse.

In the days that followed, they were seldom apart. Templeton pushed aside the fabric swatches and rough sketches waiting on her desk to spend every waking hour with John. They dined in the hotel restaurant, took long walks with her arm hooked to his, sat together on the park bench watching the swans on the lake, and twice rented a rowboat.

Templeton had never experienced an affair such as this; there was intensity in the thought of being with him, warmth in his touch, intimacy in the shared glances, and passion in every kiss. Knowing such a relationship could never be—the distance too great, their worlds too different—she tried to convince herself it was a fling, a temporary thing to enjoy for a short while then release, the way one releases a kite to float adrift on the wind. Yet day by day she fell more in love with him and he with her.

AS ONE WEEK TURNED INTO two, Eleanor noticed the glow that had suddenly appeared on her daughter's face. Pulling Albert aside, she told him that at long last it would seem their daughter had fallen in love.

"Then why haven't we met the young man?" he asked.

She hesitated, knowing how Templeton balked at the mention of marriage. She was reluctant to have it seem as though that was their thought, but Albert had a point.

"I'll invite him for Sunday dinner," she said, "but promise to treat him like her friend, not a prospective son-in-law."

He eyed her with a puzzled expression. "I thought you said—"

"I did," she cut in. "But you know how Templeton is. Until she makes that decision for herself, we'll do more harm than good by meddling."

With a grunt of annoyance, Albert turned away. "I hardly think concern over one's daughter should be considered meddling."

WHEN JOHN CAME FOR TEMPLETON that afternoon, Eleanor was sitting on the front porch with a book in her lap. With a carefully planned measure of casualness, she suggested he join the family for dinner on Sunday.

"We're having chicken and dumplings," she said. Noticeably absent was any mention of a beef roast, the customary fare for company dinners.

John said he'd be delighted, and Templeton seemed pleased with the invitation.

ON SUNDAY, SHERRY WAS SERVED before dinner, and the conversation moved along smoothly. After Templeton excused herself to give her mama a hand in the kitchen, the men spoke of books to read, plays to see, and how the political landscape had changed since McKinley's assassination.

"I like Roosevelt," Albert said. "He's young but got a solid head on his shoulders, which is what the GOP needs. He made quick work of the miners' strike and put a lid on something that was ready to explode."

"True enough," John replied. "That Square Deal of his keeps everybody happy."

With both men in favor of Roosevelt there was no argument to be had, and they moved on to talking about business. When John said he was a financier, Albert smiled.

"Glad to hear it," he said. "The investment business, now that's something solid, something a family can count on. You been in it for long?"

John nodded. "Nine years. I'm an independent now, but after I came over from London I spent two years with Cooper and Miles." He went on to say that he'd lost his mother, and his father was now remarried. "I'd heard tales of the opportunities to be had here in America, so I decided to try my hand."

"Brave fellow," Albert said and gave him a friendly pat on the shoulder. "Striking out on your own like that takes a lot of courage."

By the time they sat down at the table, both Eleanor and Albert were smiling. Halfway through dinner, he asked if John enjoyed baseball.

With his mouth now full of dumpling, John gave a nod, then mumbled, "Very much."

"Perfect. On the twenty-ninth, the Quakers are playing the New York Giants. I'm going with Templeton's brother, Ben. If you'd like to join us, I can get an extra ticket."

"I'd love to, but I won't be here. I head back to San Francisco the end of next week."

Albert gave an acknowledging nod. "I guess you've got business out there, huh?"

"My company is based in San Francisco. That's where I live."

Templeton cringed. She'd deliberately avoided the issue of John being an out-of-towner. Now there it was, a larger-than-life brick dropped square in the middle of an otherwise lovely chicken dinner.

Several beats passed with Albert saying nothing, then Eleanor stammered, "H-h-how did you and my daughter meet?"

Realizing there was no longer a way around it, Templeton jumped in.

"We met on the streetcar, Mama. I had just dropped off my newest sketches at Wanamaker's, and John was on his way to a meeting at the Exchange Building. We struck up a conversation, and before we knew what happened we'd both missed our stop."

"Lovely," Eleanor replied, but the look on her face indicated she thought otherwise.

Apparently no longer interested in John's opinion on politics, books, or baseball, Albert said, "You came here from San Francisco? Why?"

"Business. With cross-country commerce expanding as it is, I felt it necessary to have northeastern liaisons."

"So you're planning to relocate? Establish yourself in this area?"

Templeton felt the tension rolling in like a storm cloud, dark, menacing, threatening to ruin everything. Her father's voice, although not hostile, was no longer warm and friendly as it had been earlier.

John evidently did not sense the change. "Although I have no plans to open an office in this area, I expect these new contacts will necessitate a return trip every two or three years."

"Traveling back and forth to San Francisco," Eleanor said, "isn't that a terribly long and arduous journey?"

"Actually, Mama," Templeton cut in, "it's less than four days on the train. John says the Intercontinental Express even has a dining car and open-up beds where passengers can sleep. Isn't that amazing?"

Albert glared at her, then cut off a piece of chicken, put it into his mouth, and chewed slowly. His face gave away nothing. She had seen him at work in the courtroom, and this was the look he used when questioning an uncooperative witness.

After what seemed an eternity, he said, "Four days. Eight days back and forth. That's a lot of time to waste traveling."

He turned his gaze to John. "Philadelphia is a well-established business community. Given the number of banks and lending institutions in this area, wouldn't it be more advantageous for you to have your business here rather than San Francisco?"

"Not really. Philadelphia is a tight-knit community; they like dealing with their own, so new opportunities are far more difficult to come by. San Francisco is my home, and it's a city on the move. New opportunities open up every day. It's rare that a week goes by without some new shop opening or the cornerstone for a building being laid. We've got our own Stock and Bond Exchange building that just went up last year."

"I see." Albert bit into another piece of chicken and again busied himself with chewing.

The remainder of the dinner was a rather strained affair. The conversation that had once been lively and spirited grew flat with meaningless questions and single-word answers. Templeton tried to fill the awkward silences with chatter about her latest designs, the concert in the park, and the zoo's newest addition of a primate, but it was of little use. When her mama suggested they wait a short while then have cake and coffee, she shook her head claiming she couldn't manage another bite.

She glanced over at John with a look of desperation in her eyes. "I thought perhaps we could go for a walk, or would you prefer to stay and have cake?"

He smiled. "A walk sounds great."

ANXIOUS TO BE AWAY FROM the house and away from Spruce Street, Templeton looped her arm through John's and they walked toward the park. They strolled in silence for a while, then crossed over Belmont and entered the gardens. A light breeze had come up, and it was sweet with the scent of lilacs. A young mother pushing a baby carriage passed by, then two boys on bicycles, but Templeton barely noticed any of these things. Her mind was elsewhere.

"Let's sit by the lake," John suggested, and they left the pathway.

When they sat, Templeton didn't drop her head on his shoulder or turn her face to his as she had done previously. She looked off into the distance. In time the words came, but they were weighted with sorrow or possibly regret.

"I'm embarrassed about the way my parents behaved."

"There's no need—"

"Daddy still sees me as his little girl, so he's overly protective."

"He has every right to be. You're his daughter. He wants what's best for you." John tenderly placed his hand on her cheek and turned her face to his. "As do I," he said softly, then brought his lips to hers.

He lingered for a moment, pulled her into an embrace, and whispered, "I know how sudden all of this seems, Templeton, but I can't help myself. I have fallen completely and inescapably in love with you. Earlier, when I saw the concern on your father's face, I wanted to assure him that his worries were unfounded, that my intentions are most honorable, but I couldn't say anything to him without first speaking to you."

"It wouldn't have done any good," she replied. "I know Daddy, and he would have said the same thing I myself have thought."

John drew back and looked at her quizzically. "Which is…?"

"My love for you is every bit as great as the one you offer me, but the distance that separates us is greater still. Waiting two or three years for you to come back from San Francisco would be more than either of us could endure." Tears filled her eyes as she looked away.

Again, he brought her face back to his. "What you say is true. No love could withstand such a separation, so why would I suggest one? I'm asking you to marry me now, with your mother and father standing as witnesses, your sister by your side, and your brother there to wish us well. We can be married right here in Philadelphia and then return to San Francisco as husband and wife."

Although Templeton could think of nothing she wanted more, there was a moment of hesitancy as she weighed the distance from here to there.

"I have my business to think of," she stammered, "and my parents…"

Putting his finger to her lips, he hushed her. "San Francisco is full of business opportunities. For now, think only of our love. When there are bridges to be crossed, we'll cross them together."

He gathered her into his arms, brought his mouth to hers, and again she felt it: the quickening of her heartbeat, the urge to give herself completely, fully, with nothing held back. Feeling his hand firm against her back and his chest pressed to hers, Templeton knew this was the magic she'd hoped to find. Gone was the dread of spending her life with someone as boring as an unadorned dress; John was a ball gown with swirls of taffeta and lace and streamers of velvet ribbon. He was a man she would never tire of, and San Francisco was a city calling her name.

Templeton

FALLING IN LOVE FEELS LIKE an electric light bulb has been turned on inside your heart. You see things as never before, and your world suddenly comes alive. I never dreamed I could love someone the way I love John Morehouse. When we're apart I can think of nothing else, and when we're together I want to fall into his arms and have him hold me forever. Listening to him talk about us living in San Francisco, I can close my eyes and see a future that is as bright and sparkling as a diamond.

It's a given that Mama and Daddy won't look at it the same way. They'll count up the miles between here and California, then decide John is an outsider and not the right husband for me. They'll say I should make a more sensible choice, marry a Philadelphia mainliner, live nearby, and busy myself with raising children instead of being a designer.

The problem is love never takes sensibility into account. Your heart doesn't stop and ask questions before it plunges headlong into something so magical you're powerless to resist it. Love happens like a lightning bolt. It hits, and just like that your world is changed. His eyes meet yours, he smiles, and that's when you know this is your forever.

Right now I'm stuck between a rock and a hard place and honestly don't know what to do. John leaves in five days, and I either go with him as his wife or close that door and give up any hope of ever finding love again. The thought of losing him is as agonizing as the thought of disappointing Mama and Daddy. They want the best for me, but what they think is best is not what will make me happiest. John believes we can be happy together, and I agree. But if our happiness means robbing my parents of theirs, I don't know if I can do it.

Until this evening I thought my life was about as perfect as it could be; now I know how foolish that thought was. I have a horrible decision to make, and no matter what I decide I'll break someone's heart. Quite possibly it will be my own.

A Painful Choice

IT WAS ALMOST MIDNIGHT WHEN Templeton returned home and found the house dark. Upstairs the drapes were drawn, but in the center hall a single wall sconce had been left flickering. She turned the burner off, tiptoed up the stairs, and slipped silently into her room. Splinters of moonlight fell across the floor as she undressed and climbed into bed, her heart racing, skipping a few beats every so often, then starting up again with an even more frantic rhythm.

John loved her. He loved her and wanted to spend the rest of his life with her. And San Francisco was a city wide open with opportunities. Here she designed outfits for matronly women with little interest in couture styling. There she could reach for the stars, compete with the designers of European fashions, and be all she wanted to be. It was a thought so joyous, her heart could scarcely contain it. This was the magic she'd hoped to find one day, everything she'd ever wanted, all of it tied together with a silver ribbon, and yet…

She closed her eyes and tried to imagine the happiness of a life with John, but each time the picture came into view her family was standing in the shadows: Mama, Daddy, Benjamin and his brood, Clara with a toddler hanging to her skirt and another in her arms. The lot of them were bunched together like an angry mob with resentful scowls and no hint of compassion.

She buried her face in the pillow and cried. For years she'd thought it was the contentment of being a designer that made her reluctant to marry, but now it all seemed so perfectly understandable. She'd never fallen in love before. Not like this. Not truly and completely in love, and never to the point where she wanted to spend the rest of her life with someone. Templeton knew she loved John enough that she would have given up the business to be with him, but the beauty of this was that she didn't have to. In San Francisco she would have everything: him plus a golden opportunity.

Now that she could have everything she ever wanted, there was still one painful thought swirling inside of her head. Could she actually leave her family? As she imagined her parents growing old, nieces and nephews who would scarcely know her, and family dinners with her seat left empty, a new kind of sorrow settled into her chest. It was one thing to argue with her daddy or dismiss her mama's advice but quite another to move three thousand miles away knowing she might not see them for three long years.

A lot happens in three years. Babies are born, children become adults, and parents sometimes die. Not knowing if that thought was something she could live with, Templeton tossed and turned throughout most of the night.

Tomorrow she would meet John for lunch and give him an answer, but what would that answer be? She thought of the bronze figurine in her daddy's office, a woman blind to right or wrong yet holding the scale of justice in her hand. Now Templeton was faced with the same situation. She too held a scale with one side weighted by her love of family and the other side heavier still with a love of John and the vision of a future bright with success and the hope of someday having a family of her own.

A bright red sun was cresting the horizon when she finally fell asleep.

TEMPLETON SLEPT LATER THAN USUAL. When she went downstairs she expected her father to be gone off to work, but he was still sitting at the breakfast table. Fearing the worst, she gave a half-hearted smile and sat.

"I'm surprised you're still here. Aren't you going in today?"

"Of course I am, but first we need to have a talk."

All but certain the issue at hand would be John, she nonetheless asked, "About what?"

"I think you know." He stopped, called for Eleanor, and waited until she came from the kitchen and sat beside him. "Your mother and I are quite concerned about the young man you invited to dinner—"

"I didn't invite him, Mama did," Templeton cut in, knowing it was little more than a straw in the wind.

"That's neither here nor there. Your mama mistook him for a business associate, someone you'd been properly introduced to through one of your dress shops. You cannot imagine our surprise when we discovered he was a total stranger. A man you met on the streetcar, someone you know absolutely nothing about."

"I know one thing: he's a gentleman. One who was more courteous to you than you were to him. Not being born and bred in Philadelphia is hardly a sin. Until you discovered he was from California, you thought him just fine. In fact, you liked him well enough to ask if he'd go to the ballgame with you and Ben."

"What I do has no bearing on what I expect you to do. My reputation is not at stake. I'm an adult, capable of taking care of myself and—"

"I'm also an adult, Daddy. I know you still see me as the baby of the family, but I'm a grown woman, one who can be trusted to know right from wrong."

"Sweetheart, it's not that we don't trust you," Eleanor said. "It's just that men can sometimes be unscrupulous. They'll say anything to get a woman's attention, and then…"

Albert put his hand atop Eleanor's. "That's enough, dear. I'm quite sure she understands what you mean." He turned back to Templeton. "The problem here is that Mr. Morehouse lives three thousand miles away, and it's impossible to know whether what he says is true or not. Despite what he tells you, he could easily enough have a wife and kids back in San Francisco, and you'd be none the wiser."

With her eyes narrowed and her chin rigid, she leaned forward and folded her arms across her chest.

"John may not have a Philadelphia pedigree pinned to his chest, but I can assure you he doesn't have a wife in San Francisco or anywhere else for that matter."

"You don't know that."

"Yes, I do, Daddy. I know because he's asked me to marry him."

Eleanor gasped and slumped back in her chair. "You can't possibly…"

"Why can't I? For years you've said how you wanted to see me happily married, and now that I've found someone I genuinely care about, you want me to turn away from him?"

"Hold on here." Albert pushed his chair back and stood as if he were ready to give a courtroom summation. "This entire situation makes no sense. You're a smart girl, Templeton, smart enough to run your own business. Surely you're smart enough to see that marrying a man you've known for less than two weeks is pure foolishness. Give it time, wait and see if you both feel the same six months or a year from now, and then—"

"We don't have time, Daddy, and you know it. John's business is in California, and he has to go back next week. He wants us to be married here and now."

"Then what? He'll come back every few years to visit you?"

Templeton lowered her eyes and shook her head ever so slightly. "No, we'd go back to San Francisco together and live there."

Eleanor looked to Albert, her eyes wide. "Can't you do something?"

"Just what would you suggest I do?" he replied and dropped back down into the chair.

As Eleanor sat there looking helpless, he turned to Templeton and asked, "How much thought have you actually given this?"

"More than you might think, Daddy."

"Honestly? Do you realize moving to California means you might never see your family again? What you do affects us all—your mama, me, your sister, your brother, their children. If you leave, we all lose an important piece of our life."

"Don't you think I know that? Of course I'd like to be here to have Sunday dinners with you, to see my nieces and nephews grow up, but if I stay I'll be letting an important piece of my own life slip away."

She hesitated for a moment. When she spoke, her voice had an underpinning of sorrow.

"I see what Clara and Ben have, and I envy them. I want that same kind of happiness."

"Your father and I want you to have it," Eleanor said. "But you don't have to go clear across the country to find it. There are plenty of eligible young men right here in Philadelphia."

"Not for me there aren't, Mama. I've dated some wonderful men, but not one of them ever made me feel the way John does. I'm twenty-five years old now. Would you have me push aside this very real love and sit here hoping another one will come along before it's too late for me to have a family?"

"What about your business?" Albert asked. "Are you also willing to give up something you've worked so hard to build?"

"I don't have to give up my design work. Yes, I'll be calling on different stores, but the shops in San Francisco carry merchandise from all over the world, and I have to believe they'll welcome a designer with fresh, creative ideas. Here in Philadelphia my designs are stifled by tradition, but there I'll be able to create the kind of fashion that comes from the European houses. And in time, God willing, I'll be able to continue doing what I love while John and I raise a family of our own."

Albert sat with his shoulders hunched and his face cradled in his palms for several moments. He lifted his head and looked at Templeton.

"You're willing to walk away from your family and your home for Mr. Morehouse, but would he do the same for you?"

The thought hit hard, and it was several moments before Templeton answered.

"I think that's an unfair question, Daddy. Yes, I believe if circumstances were reversed, John would do the same for me. As you well know, his business is in San Francisco, and unlike fashion design, it's not a business that can be picked up and moved like a stick of furniture. When a man and woman get married it's accepted that he's to be the head of the household, the provider for the family. So, yes, John wants to stay where he's certain of making a good living, to stay where he knows he'll be able to give me a nice home and someone to help with the children. What kind of a wife would I be if I asked him to give that up to become, what, a clerk in a bank?"

"If he truly loves you—"

Templeton raised an eyebrow. "Daddy, you can't honestly believe giving up a business that makes a good living for your family is the measurement of love. You and Mama love each other, but if she wanted to move closer to Aunt Agatha in Ohio, would you be willing to leave your firm and start over?"

"That's different."

"It's not all that different."

Pushing back her chair, she stood. "I've got to get dressed. I'm meeting John for lunch in town, and I've promised to give him my answer."

As she climbed the stairs, her heart felt as though it had fallen into her stomach. The morning's discussion had pointed an accusing finger at the very same things that had troubled her throughout the night. A decision was at hand, but what it would be, she couldn't say. Regardless of her answer, someone would be hurt.

JOHN WAS WAITING IN THE lobby when Templeton arrived at the hotel. When he saw her, he smiled and started across the room. Noticing the look on her face, his smile faded.

"Is something wrong?" he asked.

She gave a reluctant nod. "Let's go somewhere and talk."

He led her over to a small alcove, and they sat side by side on the loveseat. She told him of all that had happened, then settled back with a sigh that seemed drawn up from the depth of her soul. For a while they sat silently, his fingers intertwined with hers, the weight of a decision heavy on both of their shoulders. After a time, he spoke.

"I know what I want, and you've told me what your family wants," he said. "But what about you, Templeton? What do you want? Do you want to marry me?"

Several beats went by before she answered. Perhaps she'd known all along it would come to this. At first, she'd lied to herself, allowed herself to believe it was only a fling, a few weeks of fun, after which he'd go back to California and she'd continue with her life as it had been. Now she'd come to realize that was never true. She'd fallen hopelessly in love with him the night he appeared on the porch with a nosegay of roses.

She started to speak; then a single thought flitted across her mind. If she'd known then what she knew now, would she still have allowed herself to fall in love with him? Knowing the answer was yes, she lifted her eyes and looked into his.

"I want to be with you; not just for a day or a week but always. I want us to have babies and grow old together. I want you to never leave my side."

"Is that a yes?" he asked playfully. Without waiting for an answer he pulled her into an embrace.

THAT EVENING WHEN TEMPLETON RETURNED to the house, John was with her. She feared the encounter was not going to be pleasant, but it was something that had to be done.

Albert was sitting in his big chair when they walked into the parlor.

"Evening," he said as he gave a slight nod, folded his newspaper, and stood as if to leave.

Templeton reached out and caught hold of his arm. "Please don't go. John wants to talk with you and Mama."

With a look of apprehension tugging at his face, he asked, "Is this going to be a continuation of the argument we had this morning?"

"Hopefully not," Templeton replied. Before she could say anything more, John took over.

"Mr. Whittier, I love your daughter as much as you do. I believe you and I both want the same thing: Templeton's happiness. For her sake, I'm hoping we can work things out."

Albert gave a half-hearted shrug and sat back down. He gave Templeton a quick glance.

"Call your mama," he said. "She'll want to hear this."

Once everyone was seated in the parlor, John stood and began the speech he'd rehearsed earlier in the afternoon.

"Templeton and I are in love and want to get married; however, neither of us wish to do so without your approval. You have certain concerns. We respect that, but hopefully we can work together and find a way to move past these problems. I realize that here in Philadelphia I'm an outlier, but back in San Francisco I'm a highly respected businessman."

He explained the operation of his business, the companies he worked with, his banking affiliations, and the reasons why a move to Philadelphia was not feasible. After he'd gone through all of that, he pulled a sheet of note paper from his jacket and handed it to Albert.

"This is a list of men I've done business with for almost ten years. You can contact any of these people, and they will assure you that I am an upstanding member of the community with no history of unseemly behavior."

"All fine and good," Albert said. "But even if we acknowledge that you're a man of credibility, there is still the issue of distance. Templeton is a member of our family. She has a brother, sister, nieces, and nephews. To have her taken away would leave a hole in our midst."

"And to lose her would leave a hole in my heart," John replied. "That's why I'm going to offer a compromise. If you willingly agree to our marriage, Templeton and I will return to Philadelphia every summer. I'll stay for three weeks, as I am now doing, and when I leave she will stay on for another three weeks to spend time with your family."

"That sounds good now," Eleanor said, "but what will happen once you have children?"

"They will accompany us and stay on with Templeton."

Eleanor shook her head sorrowfully. "Six weeks is such a little bit of time to spend with one's grandchildren. We see Clara's girls once or twice a week."

"I know you think this a less than ideal situation, Mrs. Whittier, but please be assured that I am very much in love with your daughter. I promise you she will have a lovely home and the best of everything. She will want for nothing."

"She wants for nothing now. Besides which, Albert and I get a great deal of pleasure from having her here. And the thought of only seeing my grandchildren—"

Templeton cut in. "Mama, if you and Daddy insist I stay here in Philadelphia, I may never even have any children!"

John gave her a nervous smile, then turned back to Albert. "I know we're asking a lot, sir, but I trust that you love your daughter enough to give her, to give both of us, this chance at happiness."

With a polite nod, he turned and sat next to Templeton on the sofa. As they awaited her father's response, Templeton was certain she could hear the pounding of her own heart.

It seemed an eternity before Albert looked at her and said, "What you are getting into is not going to be easy. You think you can just move out there and start over, but most of your work is from Wanamaker's, and I doubt you'll find a store like that in California. If you do, they may not be interested in your design work. Do you realize that?"

"The City of Paris Dry Goods Shop is half again as large as Wanamaker's, and if they don't want my designs, that's okay because there are dozens of other shops I can approach. I'll be doing the kind of design work I enjoy, and when we do have a family I may decide I don't want to be working all the time anyway."

"When the children come along, your mother won't be there to lend a hand the way she did with Clara and Ben's babies. You'll be all alone, on your own, without—"

"She won't be alone," John said. "I'll be there right there beside her, and we'll hire a woman to help out with the children."

Looking square into her daddy's face, Templeton said, "I know how much I'm going to miss you and Mama, how much I'll miss everyone. But I also know that I love John with all my heart. Allowing him to walk out of my life would be a mistake I'd regret forever."

"Two weeks of courting someone is hardly time enough for you to make such a big decision. Your mama and I kept company for well over a year before we were married."

"Times are different now, Daddy, and this situation is different."

"So you say." Albert gave a weary sigh. "You're a smart girl, Templeton, and I guess we'll have to trust that you know your own mind. If you are absolutely certain…"

"I'm as sure of this as I am of breathing."

"Well, then," he said solemnly, "you and John have our blessing."

Templeton gave a shriek of delight, jumped up to hug her daddy, then turned to embrace her mama.

John rose and crossed over to shake Albert's hand. As their hands met, Albert pulled him into a fatherly hug and whispered, "I've given you my blessing, son, but you need to know that if you harm or do wrong by my daughter, I'll be on the next train to San Francisco, and I'll be carrying a Colt forty-five."

"I understand, sir, and, believe me, I'll give you no cause to do so."

Albert Whittier

I MEANT WHAT I SAID to John Morehouse. If he so much as harms a hair on her head, I will follow him out to California and make him sorry he ever met me. Templeton is my baby girl, and that's not going to change just because he puts a ring on her finger. She's my daughter now, and she will forever be my daughter.

I know it's wrong for a parent to favor one child over the others, but with Templeton I can't help myself. The other two take after their mother in appearance and also their temperament. They're both easy-going and dependable like Eleanor, but Templeton, she's more like me. Full of sass and vinegar, fiery as the great-uncle she was named after, and as determined as the day is long. If Benjamin had half of her spunk, I'd be grooming him to take over the practice when I'm ready to retire.

I'm proud of the way Templeton has made a success of that design business, but I'll not give her the satisfaction of saying so. She's independent-minded enough without my encouraging her. This may be 1903, but I assure you the world is not ready for women to be taking over businesses. I doubt that it ever will be, but try telling that to Templeton and you're in for an argument. Eleanor and I both hoped that once she'd done what she set out to do, she'd forget this nonsense about being a designer, find a good husband, and think about starting a family.

She may well do that with John, but it won't be here where we can enjoy watching our grandchildren grow up. That breaks my heart.

It's never easy for a father to give his daughter to another man, but when you know that man is going to take her clear across the country with the possibility you may never see her again, it is excruciating. The only reason I'm agreeing to it is that I know if I didn't, we'd lose Templeton forever. John has promised to bring her and the family, when there is one, back for a visit every summer. I hope to God he's a man of his word.

Honeymoon Trip

ONCE HER PARENTS HAD AGREED to the marriage, Templeton was happier than she'd ever thought possible. That night she went to bed filled with visions of their future. When she closed her eyes, she could almost feel John beside her. Drifting on the edge of sleep, she imagined how it would be once they were man and wife, his hands warm against her naked skin, his kiss filled with passion, his body pressed to hers, and the mingling of their souls as they became one.

She pictured a bedroom where the sun woke them in the morning and the stars looked down on them as they slept. Day after day, they would wake still wrapped in the pleasures of the night before, then dress and go into town together, him to his office and her with a fat package of sketches beneath her arm. She'd wear one of her very best creations, and when the buyers admired it she'd offer to design something similar for their line.

IT IS SAID THAT FOR people in love time moves more swiftly, and so it seemed to Templeton and John. With a mere five days before the Intercontinental Express left for San Francisco, there was no time to waste. They immediately applied for a marriage license and arranged for the chapel, then set about the task of notifying the handful of people who would be invited.

Clara was at the top of Templeton's list.

"I know it's short notice," she said apologetically, "but I'm hoping you'll be my maid of honor."

Clara laughed. "With two toddlers and another on the way, I think I'd be considered your matron of honor."

"Then you'll do it?"

"Of course I will!" Clara pulled her baby sister into an embrace, then kissed John's cheek and gushed about how happy she was for them.

With Benjamin, it was quite different. He frowned at the idea of his sister marrying a man she'd known for just two weeks and grumbled about already having plans for Saturday.

Thinking he might speak one man to another, John said, "Our timing may not be the greatest, but we have no alternative. I have to get back to California because of business."

All but ignoring John, Ben glared at his sister. "I find it hard to believe Mom and Dad are going along with this nonsense."

"Well, they are. They've already given us their blessing."

For a while Templeton tried to placate her brother with various explanations, but when he didn't come around she squared her shoulders and looked him in the eye.

"We can't force you to come, but I think Mama and Daddy are going to be pretty put out if you don't."

"Okay. I'll do it because of Mom and Dad," Benjamin said begrudgingly, "but I still think rushing things this much is asking for trouble."

After her siblings, there were a few family friends to invite and then letters telling the shop owners that she was relocating her business to San Francisco. In each letter she thanked the buyer for having done business with her and promised to be in touch once her new location was operational.

Up until Thursday, there was little time for thinking about anything other than what absolutely had to be done. But that morning as Templeton stood in front of her closet deciding what to pack in the trunk she'd carry with her, a sudden sadness sprang up in her chest. She began missing the things she'd leave behind: the sound of her mama's voice, the doll she'd had since childhood, the glass perfume bottle on her dresser, the drawing desk her daddy built. As the thought of not designing her own wedding dress rose in her chest, she lowered herself onto the side of her bed and tears filled her eyes.

For what seemed a long time, she sat there thinking of things that would be forever lost. There would be no goodbye parties with friends or the shop owners she sold to, no more Mr. Darlington and his wonderful fabric shop. There would be no wedding festivities and no one to whom she could toss the bridal bouquet. The hastily arranged wedding would be a simple ceremony at the chapel; then they'd go directly to the train station.

Every minute was accounted for. Even if she'd had time to design and sew her own wedding dress, there wasn't time enough to change from the gown into a traveling dress. After the ceremony, there would be a few minutes for coffee and cake in the church vestibule. Then they'd climb into the carriage and travel crosstown to the train station.

Templeton lowered her face into her palms and closed her eyes. There, behind the darkness of her lids, she saw herself in the wedding gown she would have designed: a slender skirt made of taffeta, the bodice fitted with a high collar and tiny seed pearls tracing the edges of the flowers in a lace inset.

The knock on the door was unexpected and a bit startling. She sucked in a raspy breath and tried to brush away the dampness on her cheeks.

"Templeton?" Eleanor called. "Are you okay?"

The sound of her mama's voice was as welcome as hot chocolate on a wintery day. Templeton jumped up, pulled back the door, and threw her arms around Eleanor. Burying her face in the hollow of Eleanor's neck, she sniffled.

"Mama, I'm going to miss you so much!"

"I'm going to miss you also," Eleanor said. Unaccustomed to such a display of emotion, she drew back and eyed her daughter's face. "Have you been crying?"

Templeton gave a feeble nod. "A little."

"If you're having second thoughts about this marriage, now is the time to say so. This is a huge move, and if you have any doubts whatsoever—"

"It's not that. I'm absolutely certain about marrying John…" With a tiny flicker of hesitation, Templeton added, "It just feels sad to be leaving things behind and not designing my own wedding gown."

Eleanor wrapped her arms around Templeton and held her close. When she spoke, her voice was soft and filled with compassion.

"When you have to let go of something you want so badly, it hurts. That's how life is. It doesn't matter whether it's the joy of designing your own wedding dress or the realization that someone you love is moving away; losing a thing you've held dear always hurts." A tiny sigh floated up from her chest as she traced her fingers along the edge of Templeton's cheek. "It's seldom easy, but we forge ahead because we know a greater happiness at stake."

Templeton lifted her face and eyed Eleanor quizzically. "I don't understand."

"Life is full of give-and-take situations, so you learn to look at both sides of the issue. For instance, I'm glad for the happiness marrying John will give you, but I'm sad to see you moving away, so I make myself forget about my sadness because your happiness is more important. Now you have to do the same."

"Do the same how?"

"I understand you're sad about not designing your wedding gown, but measure it against the happiness of marrying John and going off to California with him. Does that happiness outweigh the sorrow of not having the chance to make your own gown?"

"Well, of course it does."

"Then stop fretting about the gown, because you've got something far better."

Templeton smiled. "I don't know how you do it, Mama, but it seems you can always find a way to lift my spirits, even when I have to get married in some old thing I've had for ages."

Eleanor chuckled. "Your closet is full of fashionable clothes, but you're right, a bride should have something special to wear on her wedding day. Perhaps if we spend tomorrow afternoon at Wanamaker's, we can find you a nice traveling suit and a few things for your trousseau."

Peering out from under her damp lashes, Templeton smiled. The gloomy thoughts that had plagued her earlier were buried under the anticipation of a new outfit and the things that awaited her in San

Francisco: an exciting new start to her career, a life with John, and, someday soon, a family of their own.

On Friday, Templeton and her mother spent the day shopping. As they strolled through Wanamaker's browsing the counters of kid gloves and silk stockings, thoughts of the wedding gown that would never be were all but forgotten. As she went from one department to the next, trying on dresses and finding the right bonnet to wear, she never once noticed the sorrowful look on Eleanor's face. While she was busy admiring the elegant brocade of the traveling suit, her mama's eyes were fixed on her. You could almost see Eleanor missing her daughter before the girl was even gone.

ON SATURDAY MORNING TEMPLETON DRESSED in her new suit, a ruffled shirtwaist, and a narrow-brimmed hat with grosgrain ribbon trim. Were it not for the glow on her face and the small nosegay she carried, you would have thought her an ordinary traveler rather than a bride. Albert had hired a carriage for the occasion, and before the clock struck nine the driver had her trunk strapped to the rear of the carriage and was ready to go.

With her earlier concerns forgotten, Templeton appeared almost radiant. Her hair was swirled into a chignon at the base of her neck, and her cheeks reflected the rose color of the brocade trim on her suit. As the carriage pulled away from the house, she smoothed her skirt, arranging it just so, then settled back with a sigh.

Looking across at her mama, she said, "This truly is the happiest day of my life."

Eleanor's smile appeared so fragile, it could have shattered at any moment.

"You might think that now," she replied, "but wait until you're a mother."

Skepticism caused Templeton to raise an eyebrow. "I don't know about that, Mama. Although John and I are looking forward to having a family of our own, I doubt that a baby could make me feel happier than I do right now."

"You never know. I thought the same when your father and I got married. Then Benjamin came along and changed everything."

"You mean he changed things between you and Daddy?"

Albert, who'd been listening, gave a nod and smiled at Eleanor. The glance they exchanged was like a shared secret. With the corners of her eyes crinkling, Eleanor said, "He certainly did. All three of our children changed our lives in different ways, and with each new baby we discovered a happiness that was even bigger and better than what we'd known before."

"Who changed your life the most?" Templeton asked.

The corners of Eleanor's mouth lifted, and a slightly amused expression lit her face.

"Well, I suppose you did. When you happened along, Benjamin was already in the fifth grade and Clara in the second, so we didn't think we'd have any more children." She paused, gave a chuckle, then continued. "The first few months I thought you were just an upset tummy, but before the summer was out, there you were with your eyes wide open and your tiny little feet kicking at the air."

"And hair as red as Great-Uncle Templeton," Albert added. With a touch of melancholy threaded through his voice, he went on to say that perhaps naming her after an unconventional rogue was not such a good idea after all.

With an exchange of thoughts going back and forth, Eleanor and Albert reminisced about the early years of her childhood.

"You were the most challenging of all three," Eleanor said. "But you were also the most fun. You walked early, talked early, and wouldn't sit still for a minute. I chased after you from early morning until late at night but loved every minute of it."

Templeton smiled. "I can't wait until John and I start our own family. We've already talked about having three or maybe four babies…" She continued on, saying that he'd promised that before the year was out they'd have a house on the hill overlooking the bay with bedrooms enough for a housekeeper and any number of children.

WHEN THEY ARRIVED AT THE chapel, the handful of attendees were already inside. While Templeton waited in the back, Albert walked Eleanor to her seat in the front row. As he turned and started back, he gave a nod to Ruth Trent, the pianist. Moments later the music began.

Templeton slid her hand through the crook of her daddy's arm, and they started down the aisle. Although she'd had to forego the gown and veil, she relished this small touch of tradition.

As they neared the alter, she saw John standing to the side with a smile stretched across the full width of his face. If Templeton ever had any doubts, they vanished then and there. She looked at him and knew he was all the happiness she could ever wish for.

The ceremony was a pared down version of what might have been. A Bible reading, an exchange of vows, a narrow gold band slipped onto her finger, a single kiss, and then it was done. Afterward two girls from the Bible study group served coffee and cake in the vestibule, and Templeton's siblings embraced her and wished her happiness. They congratulated John, shook his hand, and chatted for a brief moment. Then it was time to go. The newlyweds, along with Albert and Eleanor, returned to the waiting carriage and headed crosstown toward the railroad station.

AS THE DRIVER WAS UNLOADING her trunk, Templeton heard the distant whistle. Moments later the train chugged into the station belching billows of black smoke. She noticed the crowd milling about the station and sensed a need to hurry.

Giving John a quick glance, she said, "Maybe you should go ahead and buy the tickets; we don't want to miss the train."

"No need. We've got a Pullman sleeping cabin reserved."

"Sleeping cabin? I don't understand what—"

Before she could get to the question, he bent, kissed her cheek, and whispered, "It's a private room where I'll have you all to myself."

Although she'd never heard of trains having such a thing, the thought of them being secluded for almost four days sent a delicious shiver down her spine. Had her parents not been standing there, she would have thrown her arms around his neck and pressed her mouth to his, but she maintained her decorum.

"All the same," she said, "I think we should hurry."

Almost fifteen minutes ticked by before the porter came and carried their trunks off to the baggage car, but with Templeton now eager to see this magical sleeping cabin it seemed as if half a day had passed. Once the trunks were gone, she and John lingered over last-minute goodbyes until the conductor stepped onto the platform, waved his arm, and hollered, "All aboard!"

She gave her father a quick hug, then touched her mama's cheek and brushed back a tear.

"Don't be sad, Mama," she said. "It's not as if we'll never see each other again. I'll write to you every single day. Long letters. Pages and pages telling you all about our life in San Francisco. Why, you'll be so busy reading all those letters that before you know it the year will be gone, and we'll be back for a visit. I'll even write you a letter while we're still on the train and have it ready to post the minute we get to San Francisco."

"Last call!" the conductor yelled. "All aboard. Departure, five minutes!"

Eleanor hugged her daughter for one last time and kissed John's cheek.

"Take good care of her," she whispered.

"I will," he promised. After shaking Albert's hand, he wrapped his arm around Templeton's waist and gave a gentle nudge.

"Sweetheart, we've got to get going."

She kissed her mama's cheek one last time, then turned and stepped onto the train. Just before she disappeared into the coach, she turned back and waved. In that last moment, she saw the misery on her mama's face, and her heart seized.

John edged past her and led the way through the coach to the far end of the car where the sleeping cabin was located. As she followed along, Templeton was no longer thinking about the four romantic days that lay ahead. She was fixed on the haunting look she'd seen on her mama's face.

The whistle blew again, this time louder and longer. As the train rumbled to life, a queasy feeling settled in her stomach.

"I hope Mama's okay," she mumbled, but John was too far ahead to hear.

THE SLEEPING CABIN WAS JUST as John had said: a private room, compact but not cramped. One half of the room was like a miniature living room with a sofa bench of burgundy velvet; across from it sat two comfortable chairs and a tiny table attached to the wood paneled wall. On the table she saw a bud vase with a single red rose, two glasses, and an ice bucket with a bottle of champagne. At the far end of the cabin there was an alcove for changing, a hook for hanging clothes, and a washbasin.

John dropped Templeton's train case on the chair and scooped her into his arms.

"I hope you like it," he said and covered her mouth with his.

When the kiss ended, she turned toward the window and asked, "Did you see the terrible look on Mama's face?"

Taken aback by her not noticing the sleeping cabin that had cost him a small fortune, John looked at her quizzically. "Do you not like it?"

"Well, of course I don't. How could I possibly like seeing my mama so distraught?"

"I meant do you not like the sleeping cabin? I thought since this trip will be somewhat of a honeymoon, it should be—"

"I like the room just fine."

With her nose pressed up against the glass, she caught one last glimpse of her mama as the train began to move forward. She waved again, but by then her parents had turned and started toward the waiting carriage. She was struck by the way they walked, clinging to one another with their steps so slow it was as if there had been a death in the family.

After the railroad station was gone from view, Templeton dropped down on the velvet bench and watched the remainder of Philadelphia slide by. First there were the brick buildings of the city and beyond that neighborhoods with tree-lined streets not unlike the one she'd lived on all her life. She'd always considered Spruce Street her home, but now that was no longer true. The familiar-looking neighborhoods soon disappeared, and there was only a scattering of farms dotting the countryside. In time, they too were gone, followed by vast stretches of nothingness.

As Templeton sat at the window, she felt a great longing for the things left behind: the Tea Room with its fruit-filled pastries, the sound of hooves striking the cobblestone streets, the gas lamp that lit the corner of Spruce Street, the neighbor's dog that barked at every coming and going. In the past she'd barely noticed some of these things, and yet having them gone from her life seemed somehow wrong.

Turning to John, she asked, "Is there nothing between here and California?"

He lifted her hand into his. "I understand how you're feeling. I felt the same after I left London. During the crossing, there were times when I'd stand on the deck, look at the endless ocean, and believe I'd never again see dry land."

"Did you ever wonder if you should have stayed in London? Think perhaps coming here was a mistake?"

"Only a thousand or more times." He chuckled. "Once I even walked down to the steamship office, intending to buy a ticket on the next ship headed back to London."

"Why'd you change your mind?"

Several beats went by before John answered, but when he finally did his voice was steady and certain. "That would be admitting defeat. If I remained in London, I'd forever be a clerk in my father's lending house, whereas in San Francisco I had the opportunity to build a life of my own, go places and do things that otherwise wouldn't have been possible."

"Oh," Templeton replied absently as she turned back to the passing landscape.

A beat passed, and for a few moments there was only the chug of the locomotive and the clatter of wheels carrying her further and further away. Then she asked, "But what about your father? Didn't you feel bad leaving him?"

The question sat there for several seconds before John answered. "At first I did. At one point, I almost decided not to go, but he convinced me otherwise. He said if I didn't have the courage of my convictions, then I wasn't the person he raised me to be."

Templeton turned with a look of surprise. "He wanted you to leave?"

"I don't think he saw it as simply staying or going; he wanted what was best for me."

The worried look on her face softened slightly. "That's almost the same as my mama. She said I had to weigh the happiness of one thing against the sorrow of another, and if marrying you gave me the happiness I wanted then I should follow my heart."

John smiled. "Well, Mrs. Morehouse, perhaps we should drink a toast to our future happiness and the advice of our very wise parents." He stood, poured the champagne, then sat beside her and touched his glass to hers. "To a lifetime of happiness with my beautiful bride."

As the train sped past rolling hills, thick pinelands, and an occasional farm, they spoke of the future, their plans for a big house overlooking the bay, and the family that would one day fill it. With the sweetness of his words in her ear and the giddiness of champagne swirling about her head, Templeton found her memories of the things left behind growing dimmer.

When the sun disappeared and the sky darkened, they made their way to the dining car and sat at a table covered with a starched cloth and lit by candles. They ate roasted chicken and drank wine before dinner and coffee afterward. The waiter, who said his name was Abraham, brought chocolates artfully arranged on a silver plate and refilled their water glasses after every sip. Looking into one another's eyes, they held hands across the table and spoke as though no one else were in the room.

Later on, when they returned to the sleeping cabin, they found the chairs moved aside and the sofa made into a bed. Overhead hung a second bed that had been unfolded from the wall. The lower bunk was perhaps wider than a single bed, but not nearly as wide as a double.

John laughed. "Well, now, this presents somewhat of a problem doesn't it."

Templeton blushed, not knowing what to say.

As it turned out, there was no need to say anything. John bent and covered her mouth with his. Everything else happened just as it was supposed to, and they made love for the first time on that tiny bed. Afterward they curled themselves around one another and remained together so close that she could feel the thump of his heart alongside of hers. With the sway of the train rocking them to sleep and the feeling of oneness settling over her, she whispered, "Will it always be this way, John?"

"No, sweetheart," he answered. "It will get even better with time."

As she drifted off to sleep, Templeton could see the future stretched out in front of her. Within the year, she'd have a successful business up and running. Before long there would be a baby and in time a second one with the toddler tugging at her skirt, asking for a candy or to be lifted into her arms. She imagined a boy dark-eyed like John with his smile and his sense of sureness; a girl would be fair and delicate-boned like herself. When the picture was fully formed, she began to understand what her mama had meant when she said, *Wait until you're a mother.*

Templeton

MAMA ONCE TOLD ME THAT if you try hard enough, you can always find something to regret and I can see now she was right. Here I am with exactly what I wished for, and yet there's a part of me regretting that I've had to leave so much of my life behind. When I made the decision to move to San Francisco I knew I'd be living thousands of miles from my friends and family, but I didn't feel the true weight of it until the train pulled out and I watched Mama and Daddy walk away.

Moments before I got on the train, Daddy said he loved me. Then he hugged me tight and whispered in my ear that I was always going to be his baby girl and for me not to forget it. It was the first time he'd ever said it that way, and his voice sounded almost teary.

I expected something like that from Mama but not Daddy.

I've already written three letters home. In all three of them I told my parents how much I loved them and said Daddy needn't worry about me forgetting I'm his daughter. I couldn't even if I wanted to, because he's the one I got my stubbornness from. Then I wrote "ha ha" so they'd know I was saying it in the spirit of good humor. I mailed the first letter from somewhere in Kentucky, the second from Oklahoma, and the last one in Arizona. Tomorrow we'll be arriving in San Francisco, and as soon as we get to the house I plan to write another letter telling them all about the city or at least what I've seen in a single afternoon.

I do regret that we didn't have more time to plan for the wedding. I missed not having a wedding gown and a reception with friends and family to wish us well. Most brides toss their bouquet to see who'll be next to marry, but I handed mine to Clara who just stood there looking at it. With two toddlers and another one on the way, Clara's about as married as a woman can be.

Of course, I have a few regrets, but marrying John is not one of them. Being with him in this tiny sleeping cabin these past three days has made me love him even more, as if that were possible. At night when we climb into bed and I rest my head in the crook of his arm, it's as if I've found my spot in heaven. I am happy beyond belief, and a woman can't ask for anything more than that.

San Francisco

WHEN TEMPLETON STEPPED ONTO THE station platform, she was still feeling the motion of the train, her legs wobbly and her chest throbbing with anticipation. After four glorious days of romantic dinners and talk of the exciting future that lay before them, she was more than ready to plunge headlong into this new life.

Leading her to a bench inside the station, John said, "Wait here, and I'll arrange for your trunk to be brought to the carriage."

The wait was long, and as she sat there Templeton watched the bustling crowd moving about the station. She'd never before been in a place where so many different languages were spoken. As the porters hurried by, shouting words that were strange to her ear, a longing for home set in. She wished for the home she'd grown up in and the parents who'd watched over her and guided her through life right up until that fateful day John Morehouse stepped on to the streetcar.

As she recalled that last glimpse of her mama and daddy walking away, a feeling of apprehension rose in her chest. She'd always been such an impulsive person, strong-willed and determined to do things her own way. She'd always trusted her own judgment instead of asking advice from her parents, and so far she'd been right. But what if this time she wasn't?

She thought of all the things she'd left behind: a career, a thriving business, a family who loved her. At first the longing felt like a tiny pebble in her chest, but as the minutes ticked by it swelled and grew to the size of a boulder. By the time John returned, a worried look was pinching her brow and tugging at the corner of her mouth.

His smile faded. "Is something wrong?"

It seemed foolish to be having these thoughts now. If she had concerns, she should have voiced them before she climbed aboard a train and left everything behind.

"Nothing's wrong," she said and stood.

"Good, then we're ready to go." He offered out his hand. She took it and squeezed.

As they left the station, she leaned in to whisper, "I'm surprised at how different this place is. I thought it would be more like—"

He laughed before she could finish her thought. "You haven't seen the city yet, but you will and I'm certain you'll fall in love with it just as I have."

Templeton had begun to wonder if such a thing were actually true, but his reassurances did make the boulder feel a tiny bit lighter.

With her trunk now strapped to the back of the carriage, she climbed in and they began the journey to what would be her new home. Templeton had believed that once she arrived in San Francisco she would be overcome with happiness, but that was not the case. She simply couldn't dismiss the feeling of apprehension clawing at her chest.

The afternoon was unseasonably hot and the air heavy with the salty smell of the ocean. The traveling dress that earlier felt comfortable now seemed scratchy and overly warm. She brushed a wisp of perspiration from her forehead and nudged John's shoulder.

"I'm anxious to freshen up and change into something more comfortable. Are we far from the house?"

"Not very," he answered. "We should be there in fifteen or twenty minutes."

Eyeing the street with its narrow houses crowded one on top of another and nothing more than an alleyway in between, she wrinkled her brow. Was this the kind of area he lived in? It looked more like North Philadelphia than Philadelphia proper, not at all like she'd pictured.

For the past four days they'd spoken of the things they'd do, the places they'd go, and how they would one day have a big house on the hill overlooking the bay, but not once had he described the house they'd be living in now. She hadn't thought to ask, but after seeing the houses that lined Third Street a new level of concern had risen.

"The house," she said hesitantly, "is it like these? No porch? No front yard? No trees or flowers?"

"I'm afraid so. It's a little bigger and newer but no front yard. Land is at a premium here in the city. Most of the houses are built close to one another—"

"Really?" Her voice was weighted with disappointment. "So if you want to sit outside on a summer evening, where do you go?"

"The house has a small back yard and a back patio. The park is nearby, less than a ten-minute walk away."

"Oh," she said. Still examining the tight-knit row of houses on Third Street, she nodded and gave an almost imperceptible smile.

"San Francisco is not like Philadelphia. Everything here is different. The houses, the lifestyle, the people…" He touched her cheek and turned her face to his. "I want you to be happy here, and I honestly think you will be once you have a chance to—"

The carriage swayed as it turned onto Market Street.

Templeton looked up and gave a gasp. Suddenly there it was, the city she'd imagined: important looking buildings that stood several stories high with colonnade facades and elaborate entranceways, grander than many of the buildings in Philadelphia. Glass-fronted shops with breathtakingly beautiful window displays of fashions, footwear, and almost anything a woman could wish for.

"This is amazing," she said. "Exactly as I thought it would be."

A grin lifted the corner of John's mouth. "This is why the houses are built on such small lots. Everyone wants to live in town, close to shops, offices, the restaurants, and—"

"Well, no wonder; just look at these stores!" As the carriage moved past the milliner's shop, Templeton turned around admiring a wide-brimmed hat covered with pink roses.

When she turned back and caught sight of the Emporium, she gave John's arm an affectionate squeeze.

"I suppose a house is just a house," she said. "But a city like this is a marvel! I'm going to love living here, I know I am." She was already picturing herself with a portfolio of sketches tucked beneath her arm as she went from shop to shop presenting them.

John leaned forward and tapped the back of the driver's seat. "Please turn on Stockton and take us around Union Square. It's the missus's first time in San Francisco, and I'd like to show her the Ville de Paris."

The driver nodded and tugged on the reins.

"The department store you told me about?" Templeton said. "Didn't we just pass it?"

John shook his head. "That was the Emporium. I was planning to take you there for supper this evening."

"Supper at a dress shop?"

"Not just a dress shop, it's a department store. You name it, they've got a department for it: clothing, tools, gourmet foods, French wines, a restaurant, even a bandstand right there in the atrium."

Templeton laughed. "Go on, you're just teasing, aren't you?"

Her laughter caused John to laugh; although he insisted it was the God's honest truth about the bandstand, she refused to believe him.

As they rounded Union Square, John asked the driver to stop for a moment. When the carriage pulled to the side, Templeton sat there memorizing the style and cut of the black gown featured in the front window. It would be a month, perhaps longer, before the crate with her drawing table, portfolio, and art supplies arrived from Philadelphia, and she doubted she could wait that long. For now, she'd get a sketch pad and begin accumulating ideas: create more fashionable silhouettes, rethink her use of decorative trims, do away with the fussy Philadelphia styles, and adapt her drawings to the sleeker Paris couture look. A swarm of ideas started buzzing inside her head, and her fingers itched to hold colored chalks and pencils again.

Twice the driver circled Union Square. Then he continued down Geary and turned onto Jones Street. Four blocks later he eased the carriage to the curb.

John stepped down and turned back to take Templeton's hand.

"This is home," he said, pointing to a brick house with bay windows and an entranceway flanked by decorative columns.

Templeton looked up. The house was elegant in its appearance, three stories high with crisp white trim, but with only a pencil-thin walkway between it and its neighbors. It was far grander than the boarding houses they'd passed on Third Street and definitely bigger.

"It's quite large," she said. "Does anyone else live here?"

"No, I'm afraid it's just me. May Ling comes twice a week to take care of the laundry, change the beds, and clean, but she doesn't stay. Right now, the third-floor rooms are closed off, but once we start a family that would be the perfect place for a nursery and nanny."

"What's up there now?"

"Nothing. They're empty. I haven't done much in the house, because I've been busy focusing on the business." He gave a soft smile. "Now that you're here, you can decorate the place any way you like."

Before she had time to answer, he scooped her into his arms, carried her across the threshold, and pressed his mouth to hers.

"Welcome to your new home, Mrs. Morehouse."

INSIDE THE LOWER FLOORS CONTAINED furniture that reflected the simple classic architecture of the house, the wood lighter than what her mama had, a color that reflected the sun and warmed the room. Along the wall opposite the fireplace was an overstuffed sofa with the pillows plumped as if they had yet to be sat on, and over by the bay window sat a pair of soft blue wingback chairs with a table between them. The dining table was polished to a shine and surrounded by eight chairs. Behind it was a matching sideboard. There were no paintings, wall sconces, or bric-a-brac. The bedroom was much the same, the furniture a slightly lighter oak color but with the same luster as the dining room table. There was a candlestick lamp on the nightstand and little else.

That afternoon as Templeton followed John through the house, she began to relish the task that lay ahead of her, imagining the rooms as they'd look after she'd added the finishing touches. In the dining room, she pictured a crystal chandelier above the table and the sideboard with a silver candelabra alongside a vase of flowers. In the bedroom, she saw their bed covered with a rose-colored throw and matching pillow shams.

As they went from room to room, she narrowed her eyes and tilted her head to an angle where she could see things not as they were but as they would be. On the third floor, she pushed open the door and carefully inspected both rooms, tracing her finger along the curlicued mantle above the fireplace and standing at the window long enough to study the northern light that fell across the far end of the room.

Long before she changed and dressed for dinner, she'd decided the third floor would be her design studio. She would set her drawing table to the right of the window where the light was best and place a long cutting table against the side wall. With two spacious rooms, there would be space enough to store bolts of fabric and have a sewing table and a dressmaker's form. She could have separate bins for buttons and rolls of braid, and rather than simply creating a pattern for a design she could stitch it herself. She'd create a smart day outfit to wear when she called on the buyer at the Ville de Paris and after that a ball gown worthy of display in the front window.

Swept away with thoughts of such a grand design studio, she had somehow forgotten John's earlier mention of the space being used for a nursery and nanny.

THAT EVENING THEY DINED AT the Emporium, and it was every bit as grand as John had promised it would be. He ordered a bottle of champagne and toasted the start of their life together in San Francisco. He spoke of how they would raise their family here and someday have a house on Telegraph Hill with an expansive back porch overlooking the bay and a yard big enough for any number of children to run and play.

"Once we have little ones to consider, that would be wonderful," Templeton replied. "But there's no hurry. We don't need a bigger house right now, and living on Jones Street is perfect. Why, I can practically walk to the Ville de Paris or the Emporium. What could be better than that?"

"I was thinking ahead to when you might want to give up working and stay at home with the children."

"Give up working? Why would I do that?" She gave a lighthearted pearly-sounding laugh that floated off and disappeared into the music coming from the bandstand.

After dinner, they walked back to the house, browsing the shop windows as they strolled along Market Street. When she stopped to again study the gown in the front window of the Ville de Paris, Templeton was humming the Mister Dooley song that was stuck in her head. She'd hum a few bars then switch back to the chorus and sing, "Mister Dooley-ooley-ooley-oo."

THAT FIRST WEEK IN SAN Francisco, Templeton could easily believe she were still on a honeymoon, one that quite possibly could last forever. It was far more wonderful than anything she might have anticipated or expected. John was at her side for most of the day, his hand touching hers, his breath warm against her cheek, his lips whispering intimacies that brought a blush to her face.

This new life was very unlike her mama's; there were no household chores to oversee, no supper menus to plan. There was only togetherness and lovemaking. That week John spent very little time at the office. He'd hurry off before she was fully awake, spend an hour or two taking care of business, then be back at the house by the time she was dressed.

On days when the sun broke through the early morning fog, they'd take a leisurely stroll along Market Street, browse the shops for a time, then stop for lunch and linger over coffee with thoughts of what to do for the remainder of the afternoon. If the gray mist that rolled in from the bay still hung heavy in the air, he'd arrange for a carriage to spirit them off to some new attraction he wanted her to see.

Like many San Franciscans, they dined out every evening. With an abundance of restaurants offering everything from a simple ragout to an elaborate five-course supper, there was no need to be fussing about the kitchen. Wine was served with every meal, and one could always find an entertainment that carried them into the wee hours of morning. This was a city that bristled with an unexplainable fervor, and Templeton took to it as a duck takes to water.

At night when she fell into bed, exhausted and deliriously happy, she snuggled close to John and whispered of how she'd never been happier in all her life.

She'd fallen in love with him from the very start but never imagined a love as big and exciting as what she now felt. Years earlier, when she was dating men like Adam Marcus, her mama had suggested she might be in love and simply too preoccupied to realize it. Back then, Templeton had wondered if perhaps her mama was right, but now she knew for certain she'd never loved before. As they strolled arm in arm through the city, she found it impossible to regret the decision she'd made. She'd not only fallen in love with John, she'd also fallen in love with San Francisco.

Before the second week was out, John went back to spending long days at the office, and the house suddenly seemed bigger and emptier. Templeton missed her family more than ever; she missed her friends, missed the shopkeepers she'd visit with, and missed the small drawing table she'd left behind on Spruce Street. She walked listlessly from room to room thinking she might straighten things as her mama did, but there was nothing to straighten. May Ling had done it all.

When it began to seem as though a single day could drag on forever, she tried to fill the hours by writing long letters. Without skipping over even the tiniest detail, she told her mama of the places they'd gone and the things she'd seen. She told of May Ling, the woman who came on Monday and Thursday but seldom spoke and moved about the house as silently as a shadow. She ended each letter saying that she missed everyone and asking her mama to send her yet another thing she was missing; her childhood doll, a book she'd forgotten to pack, a scrap of lace she needed to edge a collar.

With her earlier letters telling all there was to tell, she soon ran dry of things to write about and began including sketches that could show the rooms of the house. As her pen scratched out an image of the sitting room, what she noticed most were the things that were missing: doilies on the table, a feathered pillow on the sofa, a patterned carpet in the entranceway. As lovely as the furniture was, the room seemed somehow unfinished almost as if the person decorating it had suddenly been called away. Too many things were missing; things that made a place look lived in, a place you wanted to be.

She closed her eyes, and the picture that came to mind was of their house in Philadelphia. Remembering how she and her mama had gone through Wanamaker's in search of that blue patterned carpet left a lump of sadness in her chest. A tiny tear slid from her eye and splattered against the page, blurring the ink.

Blotting the smudge away, she wrote, *Mama, I miss you so much. Do you remember how we used to go shopping together?* Trying to push back the loneliness that had settled in her heart, she folded the letter and slid it into an envelope.

That afternoon she carefully analyzed each room of the house, trying to look past what was there and see what was missing. When a more complete picture of the sitting room began to form in her mind, Templeton took a sheet of stationery and with her fountain pen drew a sketch of the way she imagined it to be. She repositioned the sofa so that it faced the fireplace then added a tea cart along the side wall and a painting above the mantle. After doodling a vase of flowers on the lamp table, she added a footstool in front of the velvet chair.

Once the sketch was finished, she studied it and smiled. Not only was she pleased with how the room might look, it felt right to be holding a drawing instrument in her hand. Instead of the graceful swirls of her fashion illustrations, she'd focused on perspective and spatial relationships, and it had worked. A fountain pen could never replicate the subtle shading of a charcoal pencil, and without rainbow-hued pastels or chalk sticks the drawing seemed colorless, but she'd done something she hadn't done before. She'd designed a living space.

That evening she and John dined at the Old Poodle Dog. After they'd shared a plate of buttery sweet cod and settled back with a second glass of port, Templeton pulled the drawing from her bag and handed it to him.

"This is how I see the sitting room," she said apprehensively. "What do you think?"

He took the drawing in his hand, studied it for a few moments, then smiled. "When did you do this?"

"This afternoon. Do you like it?"

"I do. Very much. I'm glad your design supplies arrived."

"They didn't. Not yet. Hopefully in another week or—"

He glanced down at the sketch then back to her. "Then how did you…"

"Fountain pen," she said. "It's very rudimentary, I know. There's no shading or color and—"

"Rudimentary?" Again glancing at the sketch, he shook his head and smiled. "Not at all. I'm awed by the fact that you did this with only a fountain pen. There seems to be no end to your talents. You, sweetheart, are an amazing woman. A woman destined for great things." He suggested she start shopping for whatever she felt the room needed.

"Tomorrow I'll arrange for you to have an account at both the

Emporium and City of Paris. Buy whatever supplies you need and anything else you want. Have them deliver it."

"Anything?" she echoed. "Furniture? Carpets? Paintings? You don't want to have a say in it?"

She'd expected that, like her father, he'd want to accompany her, be on hand to offer an opinion on what she chose and pay for the purchases. Instead, he'd given her carte blanche. He leaned forward, touching her hand.

"I'd like to be there with you, but I can't take time away from the business right now. With the commitment I have from Philadelphia Trust, I've got a shot at financing the Argonauts' new office building along with a stretch of construction on Hyde Street. An opportunity like this disappears in a flash. If I don't jump on it right away, it'll be gone." He lifted her hand to his mouth and pressed his lips to her knuckles. "Besides, after seeing that sketch, I'm certain I'll love whatever you select."

As he spoke, Templeton felt a sense of pride swelling inside her heart. If she were not already his wife, she would have fallen in love with him right then and there. No one had ever trusted her abilities as he did. Not her father, not her mother, and certainly not Benjamin or Clara. Later that night, when the house was still and John had surrendered to sleep, she thought back on his words…

Destined for great things.

For the first time ever, she began to believe she was within striking distance of what she'd always dreamed of: her own design label. As she drifted off to sleep, she could picture it in her mind, a cloth label painstakingly sewn into the collar of a woolen cape with TM Designs, the T larger and crossed with a line that resembled the swirl of a skirt.

TWO DAYS LATER, TEMPLETON LEFT the house a short while after John. It was early June, and although traces of mist still hung in the air there was no threat of rain. She hurried across to Powell Street, climbed aboard the cable car, and took it to the end of the line. Once on Market Street, she walked down to the Emporium.

The street was lined with shops. The grocer and the shoe repair were already open, but the barber shop was still dark inside. As luck would have it, the owner of the stationery shop was unlocking his door just as she passed by. With the confidence of John's words still buzzing in her head, she turned and followed him inside. Studying the display on the counter, she selected a font that was neither too flowery nor too stark and ordered calling cards with "Templeton Whittier Morehouse" printed in the center. Beneath her name, she added the two words she would soon lay claim to: Fashion Designer.

The hard part would be waiting three weeks for the cards to be delivered and almost as long for the crate to arrive from Pennsylvania. Anxious as she was to get started, a day felt like a week and weeks felt like years, but it was what it was. Thinking back on her mama's adage about a watched pot, she vowed to keep herself busy. It wouldn't be hard to do; she had a house to decorate and while she was roaming about the stores, she could study the European fashions they were showing. She would make note of the folds in a skirt, the fit of the bodice, and the fabrics they used to create something far more stunning.

The Fabric Shop

BEFORE INDEPENDENCE DAY, TEMPLETON'S CALLING cards arrived and she'd accessorized almost every room in the house. There were lace curtains at the bedroom window, an Axminister carpet in the foyer, and a colorful landscape hanging above the mantle. By then she was able to find her way around the city as if she'd been born there.

Despite John's warning, she ventured into Chinatown for porcelains and wandered through the narrow back streets south of Market where little shops were crowded together and a person could find almost anything they wanted. On Mission Street she'd gone looking for lamps and found a furniture maker to build the cutting table for her design studio, and on Howard Street she happened upon a fabric shop that had a collection of brocades, the likes of which she'd never seen. There she met Denise Laurent.

It wasn't until her third visit to the shop that Templeton discovered Denise was the owner and lived five doors down from her. The first time she stopped in, she was simply browsing; the second time the Venetian broadcloth she wanted was on display in the front of the store. Once she'd fingered the fabric and was satisfied with the weight of it, she simply asked for the five yards she needed and carried it home with her.

Denise, a narrow-faced woman with a look of sadness, was tending the shop both times. The first time she'd offered up a weak smile and said she hoped Templeton would visit again. The second time she'd hefted the bolt of fabric from the rack, carried it to the cutting table, and measured off the five yards.

At the time Templeton had thought lifting bolts of fabric a rather strenuous task for such a frail woman, but she'd said nothing. She reasoned that it could have been an isolated incident, a time when the stock boy was unloading a wagon or off on a delivery.

On the third visit, she found the woman alone in the shop again. This time she appeared wearier than before, her eyes reddened and a cloak of sadness wrapped around her. When Templeton asked for a pale yellow messaline, she burst into tears.

"Is something wrong...?" Templeton stammered.

"Mon dieu," the woman moaned. "You are asking for a cloth I know nothing of."

"I'm sorry, I didn't mean to upset you. There's no rush. I'll come back tomorrow—"

The woman swiped her hand across her eyes to brush back the tears. "No, no, not you. It is I who must apologize for my foolish behavior. Please, come with me, there are more fabrics in the back, perhaps if you show me..."

"Honestly, there's no need to bother. I can come back another time, perhaps when the owner is in."

The woman pressed her hand to her chest and sucked in a deep breath. "I am the owner."

"Oh." Taken aback, Templeton stood there a moment wondering how a person who knew so little about fabrics came to own a shop such as this.

"Well, I suppose I could help you look around back there," she finally said. "Messaline is very satiny, it has a subtle shine but is lighter weight than..." Noticing the way the woman's eyes had glassed over at the description, she stopped. "Should you be working?" She touched the woman's arm. "You don't look well."

The tears started up again. "I do what I must do."

Templeton tightened her grip on the woman's arm. "Come, sit for a moment and rest."

The woman gave an obedient nod and moved to the back of the store where she lowered herself into a small wooden chair. For several moments, she sat with her eyes downcast and hands twisted together in her lap. Without looking up, she murmured, "I apologize—"

"You've no reason to," Templeton said. "Being a woman in the workplace is not easy. You're very brave to take on a business like this, especially with so much to learn."

The woman shook her head and looked up. "Not brave, only desperate. I try to learn the differences in these cloths from a book, but a book cannot teach your eye to recognize weave or your hand to know the feel of…"

"If you have no love for fabrics, then why did you open a shop like this?"

"I didn't. Jacques did. He was the one who understood fabrics. Blindfolded, he could touch his fingers to a piece of cloth, know where it came from, and how it was made."

"Jacques?"

"My late husband. His papa was a tailor as was his grandpapa. From the time he was a boy, Jacques had a feel for this business. It is why we came to America. It is why…"

Her words thinned and faltered then, giving way to her sorrow. Her face crumpled, and she started to sob. These were not the sad wispy tears she'd had earlier but heaving, heart-wrenching cries.

Templeton remained there, at first bewildered then feeling awkward as though she were intruding on a private moment of grief. Hoping to offer a measure of comfort, she reached out and wrapped her arm around the woman's shoulders.

"You're probably exhausted. No one can deal with problems when they're exhausted. You need to take a break and give yourself time to see things for what they are. If you close the store, I'll take you to the bake shop for coffee and pastries."

"That is most kind…" Her tears slowed, but her breath was still ragged and thin. She shook her head wearily. "I cannot. There might be customers—"

"It's late in the day for customers. If someone does show up, they can come back tomorrow."

With a look of doubt still clinging to her face, the woman shrugged. "I do not know. Jacques never closed the shop before six and—"

"Jacques isn't the one who needs a break, you are. Come on, join me for coffee, then tomorrow I'll come to help you go through the material in the back. I'll give you the name for each bolt of fabric, and you can pin a note to it."

The woman finally agreed, and the two of them left together. They spent the remainder of the afternoon at a small table in the corner of the pastry shop. That's when Templeton learned the woman's name was Denise Laurent, that she and her husband had come to America seven years earlier, had a five-year-old daughter, and lived on Jones Street, five doors down. When she spoke of Jacques who died two months earlier, Denise again grew teary.

Templeton studied her face as she told of how they had planned to have two, maybe three more children. She was young, at most a year or two older than Templeton herself, and yet the sorrow in her eyes made it seem as though she had lived a thousand years. There were no laugh lines, only worry-weighted furrows stretched across her forehead.

"He died in the middle of night," she said. "The angel of death came and carried him off without a sound. We made love, he kissed me goodnight, and then he went to sleep. In the morning he was gone."

"With no warning?" Templeton said. "With no pain, no sickness?"

"None," Denise said flatly. "How do you tell a five-year-old child that her papa is gone? Now she has me; that is all. When I tuck her in bed at night, she cries for me to stay beside her. She is afraid the death angel will take me too."

"That's not likely to happen. You're young yet and—"

"I thought the same of Jacques, and look what happened. He carried Isabelle on his shoulders the very day he died! How can a man who is healthy and strong enough to carry his daughter on his shoulders one day be dead the next?"

"It seems terribly unjust," Templeton said.

That afternoon as they sat and talked, a small chunk of Denise's sorrow seeped into Templeton's heart and she felt the weight of such a terrible loss.

They remained there until the bakery closed, then took the Powell Street cable car home. As Denise turned into the small gray house, Templeton glanced up and saw a small face in the window. *Isabelle.* The little girl's eyes were opened wide and her tiny brows pinched tight.

The fear Denise had spoken of was visible in the child's eyes.

THAT IMAGE OF THE CHILD'S face stayed with Templeton. Denise's sorrow was not hers, and yet she'd taken on a piece of it and wasn't certain why. Later on that evening, as she and John sat across from one another at the Pot de Poisson, she said, "Today I met the owner of that fabric shop I've been going to."

"Great." John sipped his wine and set the glass back in place. "Is he the one you're going to work with?"

"It's not a he, it's a she. The owner's a woman."

His lip curled ever so slightly. "It's wonderful that you'll have another woman to work with. I imagine she has a better eye for fabrics than a man might."

"Actually, she doesn't. She's in way over her head, trying to identify fabrics based on the descriptions in a book."

John raised an eyebrow. "And she's the owner?"

Templeton nodded. "It was her husband's shop. He died, and she had to take over running it. She lives on our street, that small gray house on the opposite side. It's the one close to the corner."

"I know the house you mean, but I think it belongs to a young couple with a child."

"That's Denise. It's just her and her daughter now."

"Really? He looked healthy enough the last time I saw him. What happened?"

Templeton shrugged. "Denise said he died in his sleep. I'm guessing it was his heart, because she told me he wasn't sick beforehand." As she spoke, she absently scooped three spoons of sugar into her coffee then stirred. "I can't even imagine what it would be like to suddenly have to take over a shop when you know nothing of the business."

"Doesn't she have family to help out?"

"In France. Not here." Templeton scooped another spoonful of sugar into her cup. "The poor woman looks frightful, as if she's ready to fall over dead herself."

As she sat there stirring her coffee, her thoughts strayed. She shuddered when she began wondering if someday she could find herself in the same situation. She too was far from family. John was the only one she had in San Francisco, and were she to have a child…

That night, long after the moon had risen high in the sky and John had drifted off to sleep, Templeton lay awake thinking of Denise and the possibility that she could be thrust into a similar situation. At some point in time she hoped to have a thriving design business, but now all she had were the thoughts in her head and a handful of thumbnail sketches. John was strong and healthy right now, and, God willing, he'd stay that way. But if something were to happen tomorrow, or next week, or next year? What then?

She cringed at the thought. Losing him would be devastating. It would be the end of everything. There would be no house on the hill, no trips back to Philadelphia, no design business. It would be a struggle to simply move from one day to the next; how could she possibly take care of a child? Alone, she might be able to hang on for a while, pinch pennies, and work to make a go of the business. But once there was a child, that would be impossible.

She again pictured Isabelle's face at the window. Fearful. Anxious.

No, she couldn't do that to a child.

She climbed from the bed and stood at the window for a long while, thinking of what she would do in such a situation. The early light of morning was creasing the horizon when she came to a decision that she would keep to herself. Until she'd built a following and established herself as a designer, there would be no baby. It would take a year or two, maybe three. They could surely wait that long to start a family.

Templeton

FOR A LONG WHILE I thought about whether or not I should tell John what I am doing; then I decided not to. Yes, I feel guilty keeping this to myself, especially since I know how much he wants children. I do too, just not now. What harm can it do to wait a few years? By then I'll have established myself as a designer, and when we do have a child I'll be able to work from home doing what I love.

The truth is I'm frightened to death of finding myself in a situation like Denise's; of being alone with a child to provide for and no way in which to do it. She doesn't say anything about working at the shop, but you can tell by the look in her eyes she's not happy. How can she be with a job that keeps her from her daughter? The fabric shop was her husband's choice, not hers; yet she's the one stuck there morning 'til night. What kind of a life is that for her or for Isabelle?

I can assure you there's a huge difference in a career and a job. With a career, you do the kind of work that satisfies your soul and makes you feel good about yourself. With a job, you work at whatever you can get; do what someone else wants you to do, not what you want to do. A career gives a woman pride in herself; a job drains her soul dry.

John thinks me brave for wanting a business of my own, but I'm nowhere near as brave as Denise. It takes far more courage to do what she's doing and face each day.

This past Tuesday, I spent the day at her shop. We went through the aisles and tagged almost every bolt of fabric. There were only a few I couldn't identify; most I remembered from the hundreds of hours I spent at Mr. Darlington's shop back in Philadelphia.

While we were working, I asked if she had ever thought of selling the shop and taking Isabelle back to France so she'd have family to help out. She shook her head and said knowing how much the business meant to Jacques, she could never let go of it.

Without thinking, I blurted out, "That's crazy! Jacques is no longer here."

She gave me the saddest smile I've ever seen and placed her hand over her heart.

"He is still in here," she said, "inside of me and inside of Isabelle."

You can't argue with a love that powerful.

The Design Studio

THE FOLLOWING WEEK TEMPLETON'S DRAWING table and portfolios arrived, and she went about the task of setting up the design studio. Since she'd visualized the room in her mind a dozen or more times, she knew exactly where each thing belonged.

The delivery men had carried the crates up to the third floor, but they'd stacked the cartons one atop the other and left the drawing table in the far corner of the room. Templeton stood looking at the haphazard arrangement for a moment then gave a sigh, threw open the window, and pulled a smock over her dress. Anxious to sit once again at the table and feel a charcoal pencil in her hand, she began shoving the boxes aside.

With a firm grip on the edge of the drawing table, she tried tugging it away from the wall but it didn't budge. She circled around to the other side, put her back against the table top, braced her feet, and tried pushing. The first time, it didn't move. The second time it felt as though it started to give a bit, but by then beads of perspiration were rising up on her brow. She stopped, pulled in a long breath, and pushed as hard as she could. The table moved, and there was a thunderous crash.

The table was tipped over onto the boxes and Templeton sprawled on the floor when May Ling appeared in the doorway.

"What happen?"

She hurried over. Latching onto the woman's offered hand, Templeton forced a smile.

"I was trying to move the drawing table over by the window, and it toppled over."

Once she'd pulled Templeton back to her feet, May Ling gave a nod toward the table and said, "I very strong, I help."

"No, May Ling, I think we need—"

Templeton was going to say they needed a man for the job, but before she got the words out, May Ling had squatted with her shoulders up against the top of the table. She gave one shove, and the table righted itself.

"We move boxes, then move table," she said. "You push top, I push bottom. Table no fall on side."

The idea made sense, but May Ling was considerably older and smaller than Templeton herself. If she couldn't even budge the table, it seemed unlikely the two of them would fare much better.

"I think maybe we should wait for Mr. Morehouse to come home. He's a lot stronger. He can move it tonight."

"You no believe I strong? I do, easy. More easy than two peoples."

Templeton had to hold back a grin when she caught May Ling's look of indignation.

Although she had her doubts, once they got into position and started pushing it worked as May Ling predicted. Inching along, they slid the table across the room and into a spot slightly right of the window.

As soon as the drawing table was in place, May Ling hefted a carton onto the long cutting table and popped it open. That afternoon the two women worked side by side unpacking boxes, arranging the sketch pads and portfolio drawings in the cupboard, and scouring the pantry for ceramic jars to hold the assortment of pens, pencils, and chalks. Once she'd gotten started May Ling chattered on like a magpie, telling tales of her four sons and how she had to be strong to stop the roughhousing of those four rambunctious youngsters. At times she would stop working, look at one of the sketches, then shake her head and return to what she was doing.

When she happened upon the sketch of an elaborate day dress with puffed sleeves and a ruffled hem, she examined it carefully, then asked, "This, you draw?"

Templeton nodded. "Wanamaker's featured it in last spring's collection."

May Ling studied it a moment longer. "This much work for iron."

"That it is," Templeton replied and laughed. May Ling laughed along with her.

Before the day was over, the matronly shadow that had floated from room to room washing windowsills and wiping dust from the furniture was gone, replaced by a woman who was friendly, pleasant to be with, and unbelievably strong.

THAT SUMMER TEMPLETON WENT FROM writing long letters to sending picture postcards that said little more than *Thinking of you.* There were no more visits to the Emporium, the City of Paris, or any of the shops along Market Street. When the sun was barely cresting the horizon, she would climb from the bed and head for the third floor, not bothering with breakfast or even a quick cup of coffee. Before the morning fog lifted, her fingers would be smudged with charcoal and another new sketch would be stuck to the wall with one of her drawing pins.

With his newly acquired Philadelphia banking affiliations, John was busier than ever. He spent long days at the office, and often when returned home late in the evening he would find her at the drawing table.

"Still working?" he'd say then ask if she wanted to go to dinner.

She inevitably shook her head, said something about May Ling leaving a cold supper on the butler's table, and claimed she'd be down as soon as she'd finished this last suit or day dress she was working on. If it wasn't a dress, it was a motoring outfit or a dinner gown or an evening cape. As soon as one sketch was off her table, she'd start thinking of the next one.

When Templeton finally arrived downstairs, there was usually a chill in the night air, so they'd eat at the butler's table then settle on the sofa in front of the fireplace with a brandy or glass of port. He'd tell her of the deals he'd been working on and how he'd arranged financing for this or that building. Although she appeared to be listening, Templeton's thoughts were often on narrowing the line of a skirt, adding a row of buttons to a military-style jacket, or creating a look that could rival Paul Poiret's high-waisted gown and do away with the need for a corset.

Later on, when they lay side by side in the bed, she tried to push back thoughts of work and allow herself to enjoy him as she had in the early days, but even then her reverie would sometimes slip back to what lay waiting on the drawing board. As John traced his finger along her bare shoulder or touched his lips to the hollow of her collarbone, she'd remember their time in the train's tiny sleeping cabin and yearn to recapture the feeling.

On nights when she could revel in some new design she'd rendered or the second glass of port they'd shared, she'd give in to the passion of their lovemaking. Once on just such a night, he snuggled close to her and whispered the hope that this would be the night they'd started their family. His words sent a tremor through her, and she wondered if perhaps he had somehow learned of her plan.

The calendar where she marked her monthlies was safely hidden upstairs in the design studio buried beneath a stack of drawings. John seldom came up there, and on the few occasions when he did it was only to kiss her goodbye or call her down for supper. For two weeks after that night she shied away from his touch, claiming she was overtired, having a headache, or coming down with something.

May Ling came every day that summer. She prepared lunch and carried it up to Templeton, but more often than not it remained uneaten. When she returned for the tray and saw the sandwich still there, she'd make a tsking sound but Templeton ignored it, just as she'd ignored the food on the tray.

ON A BALMY DAY IN late September, everything changed. The morning began with a bright blue sky, the wind was little more than a soft breeze, and the fog remained offshore. It was the kind of day when people threw open their windows, forgot their chores, and sat on the porch reading a book or took a long walk in Golden Gate Park. Apparently caught up in the mood of the day, John arrived home early and found Templeton in the sitting room. She was dressed in a green silk tea dress and had rouged her cheeks, which was something she hadn't done for months.

"You look lovely," he said and smiled. "Too lovely to spend an evening at home. Would you like to go for an early supper?

"Yes, I would." She looked at him in the same flirtatious way she had that first day on the trolley in Philadelphia. "Perhaps we could go dancing afterward? Maybe have a glass of champagne at the Palace Hotel or the Regency Room?"

His smile broadened. "That sounds wonderful. Are we celebrating something?"

"Indeed, we are. This morning I finished the drawings for my collection. Tomorrow I'll visit Denise's shop to select fabric samples for each outfit and after that start talking to buyers."

That evening it was as it had been that first week after her arrival in San Francisco. John ordered a bottle of champagne, and she laughed at the bubbles tickling her nose. Sitting opposite one another at the dinner table, she stretched her leg across and playfully rubbed the toe of her boot along the inside of his calf. Afterward they lingered over a second glass of champagne, then drained the bottle.

Perhaps because she had held him at bay for so long or felt the surge of relief that came with the completion of a task that often seemed daunting, or quite possibly it was the magic of the music, but Templeton felt as though she were falling in love all over again. That evening as they danced to the soft strains of a string quartet, the sound of the violins swept her away. The rest of the world disappeared into the distance and there was only the two of them, her head on his shoulder, his words warm and tantalizing in her ear.

That night they made love as they had not in many months, and afterward she fell asleep in his arms, feeling as she did when the gentle rocking of the train was beneath her. Not until the following morning did she realize she had forgotten to check the calendar of her monthlies. Before John was fully awake, she darted up the stairs, pulled the calendar from beneath a stack of sketches, and counted off the days.

She repeated the count three times, and each time the result was the same. Last night was smack in the middle of the week she should have abstained.

"No," she whispered. "It can't be."

A queasy feeling rose in her chest as she lowered herself into the chair. For months she'd diligently kept track of when it was safe to make love and when it was not. In one night, she'd stupidly thrown caution to the wind in a moment of passion.

A pregnancy would ruin everything she'd worked for, everything she'd planned. She thought back, remembering Clara's pregnancies. How she'd been nauseous for months then grown so plump she'd waddled like a duck. Templeton had planned to make the tailored suit in her collection and wear it when she went to call on buyers. How could she possibly do that in such a misshapen state?

For a brief moment the thought of ending an unwanted pregnancy flickered across her mind, but it was too terrible to even consider. John would never forgive her for killing the baby he was wishing for, and in all honesty she'd never be able to forgive herself.

No, if the pregnancy happened, it happened. She had no one to blame but herself.

FOR TWO DAYS TEMPLETON MOPED around the house and didn't even step foot in the studio. Several times John asked if she were sick or needed to see a doctor, but the only response he got was a shake of her head and a disheartened sigh. On the third morning, he met May Ling arriving just as he was leaving for the office.

"Templeton is still in bed," he said. "She might be coming down with something; will you keep an eye on her?"

May Ling nodded. "I make Chinese tea. Chinese tea fix good."

Fifteen minutes later, she carried the tray of tea and biscuits upstairs and rapped on the bedroom door. When there was no answer, she rapped again. Still getting no answer, she called out, "Mister say you sick. You sick?"

"Go away. I'm not sick."

May Ling pushed the door open, carried the tray in, and set it on the bureau. "If you not sick, why you talk sick?"

Templeton lifted her head from the pillow and swiped the back of her hand across her eyes. "I'm not sick. I'm sad and discouraged. It's better if you just leave me alone."

"Sad?" May Ling tilted her head in confusion. "What you got for sad?"

"No reason. Just forget it." Templeton dropped back down onto the pillow.

May Ling crossed the room and stood at the foot of the bed, arms folded across her chest. "If you sick, I get doctor. If you no sick, get up. Sad no reason for stay in bed. Go do work, then you get happy."

Templeton sat up again, her eyes filling with tears.

"Work won't help," she said tearfully. "I've about killed myself trying to get these designs done, and now that I'm ready to launch the collection I've probably gotten myself pregnant."

May Ling smiled. "Baby good, no?"

"In a few years yes, but not now. It would ruin everything."

May Ling didn't need words. She raised an eyebrow, obviously wanting to know more.

"I can't have a baby right now. I just can't. It's almost impossible for a woman to get a buyer to take her seriously, and a pregnant woman doesn't have a prayer. If I can't even wear the suit I designed, how can I expect a shop to buy it?" She sniffed back another sob. "And afterward, what then? I can't work once I have a baby—"

"Why not?" May Ling cut in. "Plenty women have baby then work. You more lucky than most. You got good man, good house. May Ling watch baby, you do drawing."

"You make it sound easy, but it's not…"

"Plenty easy." May Ling tapped a finger against the side of her head. "Too much thinking make hard, but it not hard."

Templeton wanted to believe it could work that way, that she could have a child, be a good mother, and still pursue the dream she'd held in her heart for so many years. She knew the odds were against her, but the truth was the odds had always been against her. She'd just been too stubborn to accept it.

THAT AFTERNOON, TEMPLETON GOT OUT of bed, dressed, and went upstairs to the studio. She sorted through the designs one last time and selected the twelve she believed best. Inserting a sheet of tissue between the pages to prevent smudging, she carefully slid the sketches into her portfolio and snapped it shut. Tomorrow she would visit Denise's shop to select the fabrics.

Even if she were pregnant, it would be three, four, maybe even five months before it became obvious. If she stuck to a rigid schedule and made every hour of the day count, it was possible that by then she could have a handful of clients.

Possible; not necessarily probable.

DENISE WAS ARRANGING A DISPLAY of silk threads when she saw Templeton enter the store. She gave a cheerful wave, then walked to the front of the shop and wrapped her arm around her new friend's shoulder.

"I have been wishing you would come, so I could again thank you."

"For what?"

"Helping me with fabric names." She chuckled. "It is much easier to learn from a friend than from a book. Now when I speak to a customer, I know what I am talking about."

"Actually, I enjoyed that day. It was fun for me too."

Denise went on to say that business had picked up, and she was no longer quite so intimidated talking to customers. She gave a shy smile.

"Instead of worrying about Isabelle, I keep myself busy in the back of the shop. I have already sewn three dresses for her. All from scraps of fabric, remnants that would not put one extra penny in the cash box."

"You keep a sewing machine here?"

"Jacques did. It is old but works well. Come, see what I am working on."

Templeton followed her back through the store and was pleasantly surprised when Denise held up an exquisitely detailed taffeta dress with lace edging the neckline and velvet ties at the waist. The bodice was a pale yellow and the skirt a darker shade of gold.

"This is absolutely beautiful! Wherever did you learn to sew like this?"

"I have been sewing since I was a very small child. My mama taught me just as her mama taught her. To the women of our family, sewing is a joyful thing."

"I get the same feeling when I'm sketching something." Templeton smiled. "Perhaps we could help one another."

She explained how she would soon be presenting her collection to the stores and if they placed orders, she would have to provide them with finished samples rather quickly. Without saying why, she said she'd need to maximize her time for the next three to five months.

"I know I'll need help if I'm to get the samples done that quickly." She went on to say it would be a huge favor and she would pay Denise for her help.

They talked for a while longer then spread the designs on the cutting table and began selecting fabric samples and attaching swatches to the designs. It turned out that Denise, who originally claimed to know nothing of fabrics, actually had a good eye for what worked. When she suggested gold braid and jet-colored guipure lace to trim the boldly striped tea dress, Templeton turned with a grin.

"Great idea! You'd make a terrific designer."

Denise laughed. "With a needle and thread perhaps, but not with a pencil."

That afternoon the two women worked side by side as they clipped swatches of fabric and attached them to the appropriate designs. It was nearing the end of the day when Templeton asked if Denise wished Jacques had taught her the business before they started a family.

"Non." She shook her head and sighed. "Life is a seesaw. When one end goes up, the other goes down. To get this, you must give up that. Although I would wish to be like you, wise in the ways of business, I would never give up my sweet Isabelle."

"Not give up Isabelle, but maybe waited two or three years before having her, until you'd learned the business."

"God decides when it is time to have a child, and who are we to argue with God?"

"True, but perhaps if you'd planned to wait—"

Denise was already shaking her head. "If we had waited, Isabelle would have been a baby when she lost her papa, too young to remember how he carried her on his shoulders, how his stories made her laugh, how he sang songs for her, and told her she was the fairest princess in all the land. Those memories are all Isabelle has left of her papa; had we waited, she would not have even those."

"But isn't it terribly hard, running a business and trying to raise a child on your own?"

"It is difficult to not be with her as much as I wish, but to be without her would be far worse. Isabelle is my reason for living. Without reason to live, a person is the same as dead."

Believing there was nothing more she could say, Templeton switched to talking about the lining for a velvet evening cape.

"Raw silk or perhaps moiré…"

Templeton

SOMETIMES YOU GET LUCKY AND stumble onto the very thing you need before you even realize you needed it. That's what happened yesterday. I've always been so protective of my designs that I never once considered allowing anyone else to make the samples. Now I've changed my mind. The truth is Denise sews every bit as well as I do, maybe better. Her seams are straight and flat, not a single pucker. And the lace collar she hand-stitched into place is better than anything I could have done.

Having her do the samples will work for both of us. She'll get to earn extra money without taking time away from her daughter, and I'll be able to spend all of my time calling on buyers. Hopefully within the next few months I can get started with three or four clients. It's not much, but it'll be a foot in the door. Once you're working with one or two shops in the area, it's a bit easier getting the others to listen. At least that's how it was in Philadelphia. Wanamaker's wouldn't give me the time of day until after Madame Clare's salon began featuring my designs, and then it was another six months before they finally placed an order.

Given the way everything is starting to fall into place makes me feel much better about this pregnancy. May Ling was right; with her to watch the baby and Denise willing to make the samples, I can do it. I can have both a baby and a career.

John is going to be deliriously happy about this, I know he will. A dozen or more times he's talked about us starting a family, and up until now I've always switched over to another subject without saying yes or no. I'm going to wait until the next time he brings it up, then smile and say, "Well, guess what..." That's when I'll tell him about the baby.

I just hope he doesn't bring it up again for a few weeks, not until I'm absolutely certain. It would be devastating to make him think I'm expecting a baby then discover I'm not.

Patterns & Problems

AFTER TEMPLETON LEFT DENISE, SHE stopped at the art supply store to buy two large rolls of tracing paper and three blue copying pencils. Although the shop owner offered to deliver the bulky rolls of paper, Templeton claimed it not necessary and walked out with the package tucked under her arm.

That same afternoon she spread the paper across the long cutting table and went to work outlining the pattern pieces for each outfit. She began with the tennis dress, a design that required only a handful of pattern pieces, all of them so simple she could have laid them out in her sleep: a gathered sleeve, a loose bodice, flared skirt panels, a waistband. Before three hours had passed, she was done. Every piece was marked with both a cutting line and a stitching line, arrows to show how the pattern had to be positioned to align with the grain of the fabric, a rendering of the finished outfit, and detailed instructions for assembly.

Satisfied with the tennis dress, Templeton moved on to the tailored suit she would be wearing to call on the buyers. This was one of the more complex designs with tapered insets to narrow the waist of the jacket, fitted sleeves with multi-layered cuffs, and a double-breasted bodice that had to be just so. She worked on the pattern for eight hours then grew too bleary-eyed to finish the markings. She was just about ready to quit when she looked up and saw John standing in the doorway.

"You startled me," she said and laughed.

He didn't laugh. Instead he pulled the watch from his pocket, glanced at it, then looked back to her. "Templeton, it's ten o'clock! You told me you'd be down for supper two hours ago."

"Oh dear, I didn't realize the time—"

"Lately it seems there are a number of things you fail to realize. Your father called my office today asking about you. Apparently, you haven't written home in almost two months. Albert claims the last they heard from you was two weeks ago, a postcard where you wrote 'missing you' and didn't even bother to sign your name. Your parents were worried and justifiably so."

"I've been busy working. I planned to write last week, but it slipped my mind."

"Did it also slip your mind that you have a husband waiting downstairs?"

"John, I hardly think—"

"That's right, you hardly think about anything other than those damn designs. I've always appreciated the fact that you have a talent and want to have a business of your own, but now it's almost an obsession. It's all you talk about, all you think about. What happened to the plans we had for us? Is that something else that's slipped your mind?"

With his expression as somber as that of a gravedigger, he turned and started down the stairs.

"John, wait—"

There was no answer, and she stood listening to the sound of his footsteps as he stepped onto the second-floor landing and disappeared. Moments later the front door opened and closed. Leaving the suit pattern yet to be marked, she turned off the light and hurried downstairs.

AS TEMPLETON SAT IN THE parlor waiting for John to return, a million thoughts raced through her head and not one of them was about the patterns waiting to be finished. She thought back to the early days, before she met John, when she'd sold designs to Wanamaker's and a dozen other shops. She remembered how good it felt to walk out of a store, order in hand, head held high and shoulders pushed back.

Then she moved on to thinking of the day everything changed, that day on the trolley when John Morehouse glanced over and smiled at her. From that moment forward, other happiness—the joy of a new client, the fun of a day spent with friends, even the thrill of seeing her dress in the front window of Strawbridge and Clothier—they all paled in comparison to what she'd felt when he first held her in his arms.

Now she'd jeopardized that happiness, letting herself be drawn in by the glitter and glamour of San Francisco. How could she have been so blind? She didn't leave her family and travel all this way just to have her own design house. She came because more than anything else in the world she wanted to be with John. He was her reason for being here, and yet she'd let him fall to the very bottom of her priority list behind her need to create a new fashion, to be successful, even to have her name be famous.

As the tears came, so did the memories of how they'd talked of having a family and how she'd gone out of her way to avoid doing so. Along with the memories came a sense of shame and the lingering question of whether or not he had known all along what she was doing. Her breath grew ragged, and the tears continued. She cried as she had never cried before, pining for what she feared lost, and chastising herself for being the cause of it. The minutes limped by like a wounded bird until in the wee hours of morning she heard the door click open.

"John?" she called out.

She lifted her head and saw him standing in the doorway.

"I'm surprised you're down here," he said. "I thought you'd be upstairs in the studio."

Templeton caught the sarcasm in his tone. "I realize you're angry, John, and—"

"I'm not just angry, I'm disappointed. Disappointed in you and disappointed in what I expected our marriage to be. I knew you wanted to be a designer, and I respected that, but I never thought I'd have to take a back seat to this obsessive drive you now have."

"I'm sorry, I'm—"

He raised his hand with the palm out. "Hear me out, Templeton, before you say anything more."

Silent tears filled her eyes, and she gave an almost imperceptible nod.

"I've waited, hoping you'd soon find your footing with this project and we'd get back to the kind of relationship we originally had. But I realize now it's never going to happen. When one project ends, there will always be another and another…"

"No, John, that's not what—"

Again, he held out his palm. "Please, Templeton, I'm not looking for empty promises. Take time to think about it, then decide whether you want the most important thing in your life to be your husband or your business."

She stood and moved closer to him. "I don't need time. Without question, John, you are the most important thing in my life. I fell in love with you the day we met, and I love you still. For a moment I got frightened and lost sight of—"

"Frightened of what?"

"Being in a situation like Denise's. Alone, with a child to take care of, no one to help and no way to earn a living. I thought if—"

"Do you think me a fool? How could you not know I'd provide for you? I was not overly anxious to bring up the subject of death, but I'm realistic enough to know that it will one day happen, and when it does my family will be more than adequately provided for." He turned away and looked up at the ceiling. "If you had trusted me enough to ask, Templeton, I would have told you."

Templeton felt her heart break into a million little pieces as she stood there with tears overflowing her eyes. For a moment she considered telling him about the pregnancy. If he knew she was with child, he would not only forgive her but fall to his knees and apologize for judging her so harshly. But if she were wrong and there was no baby? What then? Would he believe it an honest mistake or think she'd used it as a ruse to soften his anger?

She bit her lip and made the decision. She would speak to him from her heart. It was what she'd done in the early days, and he'd loved her then. She could only pray that he'd again love her.

Reaching for his shoulder, she turned him around to face her.

"Please believe me, John, I am sorrier than you can possibly imagine. You're right when you say I've put the design business ahead of you, but I assure you it will never happen again. You are and always will be the most important thing in my life. If I have to give up being a designer to keep your love, I'll do so without regret. You can chop the drawing table into firewood, and I'll put all my efforts into being nothing more than a good wife and mother."

He smiled ever so slightly. "Chop the drawing table into firewood? Don't you think that's a bit dramatic, Templeton?"

"Dramatic?" she snapped, the fiery spirit of her great-uncle rising to the surface. "I'm speaking from my heart and you think I'm just..."

He moved closer, touched his fingers to her chin, and lifted it so their lips were only a whisper apart.

"I'm not asking that you give up your love for design, only that you have your love for me be greater."

Her voice wavered as she said, "It already is greater; it always has been."

His mouth came down on hers before she could say anything more.

IT WAS NEAR DAWN WHEN THEY climbed into bed together and made love. His touch was soft and gentle, his fingers teasing her neck and shoulders then sliding slowly down to her breast. He whispered of a love that would last beyond eternity, his breath warm in her ear, his hand pressed to the small of her back, bringing her to him. When their bodies came together, she drew in the sweetness of his scent and held on to it. Afterward they collapsed into each other's arms, and Templeton wished the moment to never end.

THE FOLLOWING MORNING, TEMPLETON RETURNED to the third-floor studio a few minutes after John left for the office. She finished marking the suit pattern then unrolled the drawing paper and began laying out a tea dress. As she penciled in the cutting line and marked arrows indicating the pattern placement on the fabric, her thoughts strayed back to last night and the altercation she'd had with John.

She cringed at the memory of her saying he could chop her drawing table into firewood. Luckily, he'd seen the foolish gesture for exactly what it was: a dramatic overstatement. The thought of losing him had thrown her into a tizzy, and in a moment of desperation she'd offered to give up something she loved.

Ordinarily she'd never dream of saying a thing like that, but the way he'd put it to her, as if she'd chosen her work over him, was like a bee sting to her heart. He'd made her feel terribly guilty when there was nothing to feel guilty about. He loved his work, so why shouldn't she?

When Templeton finished marking the tea dress pattern, she moved on to the morning outfit, a simple gored skirt and blouson top with lace trimmed collar and rows of pin-tucking down the front. Penciling in the rows of stitching lines for the tucks, she thought of how John had complained of her endless talking about the design business, but she felt that was an exaggeration. Yes, she spoke of it often, but no more than he spoke of his financing deals or banking affiliations. Loving their businesses, wasn't that something they had in common?

As she moved from one pattern to the next, Templeton came to the realization that if she were to have a happy marriage, she would have to downplay her love of being a designer and lessen the visibility of it in John's eyes.

When the clock struck five, she left the pieces of a motoring coat half-finished and hurried downstairs. By the time John arrived home she had rouged her cheeks, changed into a pale blue dinner dress, and had two glasses of sherry waiting.

She handed him a glass. "I thought perhaps you'd enjoy a drink before we go to dinner."

"I would indeed," he said, and the smile that lit his face was what she'd hoped to see.

That evening they dined at the Gold Crown and when John spoke of a factory to be built over on Duncan Street, she leaned into the conversation as if it were the most interesting thing she'd ever heard. That evening she said nothing about the fact that she'd finished cutting and marking five new patterns.

Later that night, after they'd again made love and John drifted off to sleep, Templeton lay awake thinking through all that had happened. The truth was she loved John, loved him as she could never love another man. She'd thought him bigger than most men, big enough to accept that work was as important to her as it was to him. He was a good husband and she knew he'd make a wonderful father, but he was also a man of the times.

The world simply was not ready for working women; someday,

perhaps, but not now. While John's ideas were nowhere near as stodgy as most men, he'd made it obvious that she was to be a wife first and a designer second. Although it wasn't precisely as she'd like it to be, with a bit of finesse she could easily enough keep that pot from boiling over.

As she lay there waiting for sleep to come, she placed her hand on her stomach and again wondered if there was a baby on the way.

TWO DAYS LATER, TEMPLETON BUNDLED up the finished patterns and headed off to Howard Street. A feeling of anticipation, excitement almost, settled in her chest. For weeks she'd been a woman alone at a drawing table, but today...well, this was the start of a business. She would ask Denise to start with the tailored suit since that was the outfit she'd wear to call on buyers. She'd been planning this since the day she first arrived in San Francisco, and now her dream was about to come true.

When she arrived at the fabric shop, Templeton found Denise at the sewing machine behind the counter. She was adding a ruffle to a piece of organdy no larger than a tea towel. After a quick hello, Templeton leaned over and asked what Denise was working on.

"A doll dress. This Sunday is Isabelle's birthday, so I have made her and the doll she named Sister matching dresses." Denise stood and lifted a somewhat larger version of the dress from beneath the folded tissue paper. Holding it up, she asked, "What do you think?"

Templeton gave a wide grin. "It's beautiful. She is a lucky little girl to have such a loving and talented mama."

Denise laughed, claiming she was the lucky one, then suggested Templeton join them for a small birthday party on Sunday.

"It is but a small group of neighbors, and Isabelle would be thrilled if you and Monsieur Morehouse could join us. This will be her first birthday celebration without her papa, so I must warn you she is likely to ask Monsieur Morehouse to swing her in the air or ride her on his shoulders as her papa did."

"John is anxious to start a family of our own, so I think he'd love filling in for Isabelle's papa." Templeton continued on telling of how she half-suspected that she might be already be pregnant, then added, "It'll be a few weeks before I can say for sure."

That afternoon as Templeton went through the intricacies of each pattern, the women talked of many different things but mostly about the families and friends they'd left behind. The hours flew by, and when the sky grew hazy Templeton said she had to be going.

With a conspiratorial giggle she said, "You know how husbands can be when you keep them waiting."

"Oui." Denise nodded. "That I remember."

AS DENISE HAD INDICATED, THE party was a small affair with a handful of adults sipping tea and Isabelle wearing her new organdy dress. There were the usual gifts—picture books, a teddy bear, and tea set—but the gift that brought the brightest smile to Isabelle's face was the magic lantern John brought. At first she'd been a bit shy, apparently not knowing what to do with it, but when John slid the picture strip into place and began turning the wheel, she became fascinated. Before the party ended, she was sitting on his lap asking that he play it again.

As Templeton watched, she knew that he would indeed make a wonderful father. Perhaps it would be sooner than he thought.

Templeton

MAMA ALWAYS SAID A LADY never tattles about her troubles at home, but I told Denise about my altercation with John and I'm glad I did. She understood completely, and it felt good to have someone to talk to. I adore John and I'm happy, truly happy, with him, but regardless of how much you love your husband there are times when you simply need another woman to talk with.

Women see things differently than men. How can they not? I would bet my last dime no one ever told a man that he shouldn't have a job simply because he's married.

I didn't argue the point with John because he was already angry enough, and I really had kept him waiting for too long. When it comes to my career he's more understanding than most men would be, but he's still a man and he definitely has his limits.

When Denise and I were going through the patterns, she told me that at times Jacques also got peevish because she fussed over Isabelle and paid little attention to him. She said men were like *petits bébés*, and we both had a good laugh over that.

Of course, I imagine it's hard not to dote on a child such as Isabelle. She truly is a darling. John has all but fallen in love with her. I could see the happiness in his smile when she kept asking him to play the magic *lantern picture show over again. Right then and there, I could see what a wonderful daddy he would be.*

Given how important my career is to me, you might think I'd be more upset about the possibility of being pregnant, but the idea has begun to grow on me. Now I think I might actually be looking forward to it, especially after seeing John with Isabelle.

With Denise to do the sewing and May Ling here to care for the child, we could have the family we want and I could continue with the work I love. A situation like that is about as perfect as it gets.

More Than a Designer

THE FOLLOWING WEEK, TEMPLETON BEGAN calling on the ladies' wear shops along Market Street. Early in the morning she dressed in the tailored suit, tucked her portfolio under her arm, then climbed aboard the trolley and rode it all the way out to the ferry building. From there, she walked back along Market Street, stopping in every ladies' wear shop along the way. Some shops were not much bigger than a pantry, and others stretched out for half a block.

That first day she concentrated on the smaller shops, using them as a testing ground to gauge buyer response to her designs. The smaller shops were less intimidating with many of them managed by a woman. All were willing to offer opinions on how a design could be improved.

The buyer at Clara's Fashions suggested the blue tea dress would be smarter without the pleated hemline, while the buyer at Le Femme Frocks thought the same dress could use a double row of ruching and a band of braid at the top. A few of the buyers declared the designs pleasant enough but said they were not prepared to purchase just now.

It was the same day after day as she carried her portfolio from one store to another. On occasion one of the buyers offered a word or two of encouragement, but there was little to be happy about and by the end of the week she was exhausted both mentally and physically. It seemed they all asked the same question: "What other shops are showing TWM designs?" When she answered none, they inevitably turned away.

"Imagine the prestige of being the first on Market Street to feature the collection," she said, but it made no difference.

Madame Michelle's Fine Fashions was her last stop on Friday afternoon. The fair-skinned woman with hair the color of corn silk was taller than Templeton by at least a foot and had a certain haughtiness about her. She leafed through the sketches quickly and handed them back to Templeton.

"Check back after Christmas," she said and turned away.

"Did you care for anything in the collection?" Templeton asked.

Madame Michelle gave an almost imperceptible shrug then went on to say while she liked the narrower lines of the tea dress, her customers were society matrons who demanded exclusivity, so she required more customized patterns.

"You know what I mean," she said. "A simple design such as this is good, but I would need to see variations of it. A side drape perhaps, a cuffed sleeve, or a lace cutaway. Although some of my customers are not from the wealthiest of families, they still insist on purchasing a dress created expressly for them."

Templeton nodded even though she found it difficult to buy into the woman's description of a single style with that much flexibility. Changing the design of a dress meant it became a different dress, and a different pattern was needed to make it. She thanked the woman for her time and left the shop feeling more than a little bit discouraged.

It had been a long day and an even longer week. She'd called on a dozen different shops, and not one had expressed an interest in buying. She'd offered them options of buying the patterns outright so they could use their own manufacturer for ready-to-wear fashions or having her provide the patterns for custom-made dresses, but it seemed as though her suggestions didn't matter. She could not solicit even an order for a sample dress.

It was near the end of the day, the stack-heeled boots she'd worn were pinching her toes, and the thought of talking to yet another opinionated buyer made her head ache. With the designs folded back into her portfolio, she started for the trolley, then changed her mind and decided to visit Denise's shop.

As soon as Templeton pushed through the door, she heard the

clickety-clack of the sewing machine and knew Denise was busy at work behind the counter. Hurrying toward the back of the shop she called out a greeting. Denise looked up with a smile.

"Good you have come," she said and pulled a box from beneath the counter. "Your tea dress is finished." She took the blue dress from the box and held it up for inspection.

Templeton gave a weary sigh. "It's beautiful as is, but it seems everyone wants to change it in some way, which is terribly discouraging."

"Before they see the dress, they want to change it?"

"Yes and no." Templeton went on to explain her conversation with Madame Michelle. "What she wants is impossible. I'd be making ten different patterns for the cost of one."

Denise studied the dress for a moment. "Perhaps the idea is not so foolish as you might think."

Without taking time for an explanation, she scrambled through the aisles and returned with several pieces of cloth. Sliding the dress onto a hanger, she placed it on a wall hook behind the counter, then draped a boldly striped piece of silk across the front of what had been a flat-fronted skirt.

"See what I mean? A scrap added here or there and, voila, a different dress."

Templeton laughed. "True but that only—"

"No, we can do many things with this same dress."

Denise removed the striped fabric and stretched a narrow band of green taffeta around the waist then added two panels of the same green trailing down the back. This continued for several minutes. With ruffles, bits of lace, and scraps of fabric pinned, tucked, or draped in different spots, the dress took on a totally new look.

As Templeton watched, an idea began to take shape inside her head. It churned and roiled through her brain, one moment arguing that such an endeavor would be too expensive and risky, and the next second reasoning that it would give her an edge never before seen in the market-place. Ladies could order a custom-made dress for pennies more than a readymade.

"Once the basic dress is made, how long do you think it would take to customize it?"

Denise wrinkled her brow.

"Two hours," she finally said. "That is for something simple, like the belted waist or a lace collar. Three for a ruffled hem and four if we are adding cuffs or pleats."

A dozen more questions followed on the heels of that first one. Could Denise teach someone else to do what she'd done? Would they be able to find a manufacturer willing to make the basic dress? How long would it take? What would the manufactured cost be? What would they sell it for? Could Denise place a wholesale order for enough fabric? Did they do the basic dress in one color, two, or three?

The longer they talked, the bigger and more realistic the idea became. It took on a life of its own and danced around them like a garden sprite sprinkling great handfuls of hope and promise. At six o'clock the two women left the shop together, and on the trolley ride home they continued to talk about how much help they would need and what the investment would be. Denise had no cash to invest but was willing to do the work. Templeton had no ready cash but she did have two sources who might be willing to finance them. Only one of those sources was viable—John.

AFTER SUPPER THAT EVENING, TEMPLETON sat beside John on the sofa and explained her idea. At first his brow was furrowed and his expression doubtful, but once she got to the part where she said it would be impossible to do without his help, he smiled ever so slightly. He leaned in and asked her to run through the concept one more time.

"I'll show you what I mean. It's easier than explaining."

Before he could say no, she headed up the stairs. Moments later she returned with a handful of drawings and a sketch pad. Handing him the sketch of the tea dress, she said, "This is what we start with…"

As she spoke her pencil flew across the paper, first creating a silhouette of the dress, then quickly penciling in extras like a draped apron, a folded back cuff, a ruffled hem.

"See, we can take a simple dress and with a few tricks turn it into a custom-made garment. This will enable women of more modest means to choose and pick the look they want just as those who frequent expensive dressmakers do."

John listened intently then smiled and gave a nod. "You're right, the idea is revolutionary, but whether or not the shops will buy into it is still a question."

It was the glimmer of interest Templeton had hoped for. "If I can get three shops to feature the line, would you be willing to finance the initial production?"

John leaned back, his hands cupped behind his head, and sat there looking up at the ceiling. For what seemed like an eternity, he said nothing. When Templeton could stand the silence no longer, she spoke.

"Is this a no, or are you considering it?"

"I'm considering it. But you're going to need more than just financing. Let's say the program takes off and becomes as successful as you think it will be. Then there's no way you and Denise could handle the finishing work for hundreds of dresses."

"Denise said it would take two or three hours—"

John was already shaking his head. "Templeton, you're a wife and before too long I'd like to start a family. That won't happen if you're working ten or twelve hours a day. And what about Denise? Good grief, she's a mother!"

"It would only be for a short while. Once we get established—"

Again, John shook his head. "No, Templeton, I won't do it that way. But if you can come up with three shops willing to carry the line and a logistically sound plan for the production, finishing, and distribution of the dresses, I will arrange the financing."

IT TOOK ALMOST THREE WEEKS to pull everything together, but somehow they did it. Templeton had initial orders for 40 dresses, which left them with another 110 to sell, but she felt confident those would move quickly once they were in the stores. Acorn Manufacturing, which for the past two years had been sewing men's shirts, agreed to produce 50 dresses in each of three different colors, and a family with three generations of women living under one roof would handle the finishing. It was a small start, but it was a start.

True to his word, John obtained the financing for the venture. It was enough to cover the first production run and subsequent follow-up orders.

In the weeks that followed, the two women dedicated themselves to making the program a success. While Denise stitched samples of each design and trained the five women to finish the garments, Templeton prepared posters to be hung in the stores. Each poster featured 12 watercolor illustrations showing different versions of the dress, and beneath the illustrations were rows of fabric samples. The posters were placed in gilt frames, covered with glass, and hand delivered to the shops.

With John now squarely behind the venture, Templeton set about assuring him that their home life took priority over the business. During the hectic day she seldom took time for even a cup of coffee, but at the stroke of six she stopped whatever she was doing, slipped into a fresh frock, and made certain she was in the sitting room when he arrived home.

As they dined, it would appear her thoughts were on nothing more than the bouillabaisse they'd ordered or the glass of wine in her hand, but most of the time she was pondering a lace inset or a plaid ruffle she'd not thought of earlier.

With so many things circling through her mind, she totally forgot about the calendar where she kept track of her monthlies. When she finally did remember to check it, she was already three weeks overdue.

Templeton

I FEEL LIKE AN ABSOLUTE fool. A brainless idiot. Why did I not check that calendar? I knew there was the possibility I might be pregnant, but I got caught up in the excitement of getting the business started and ignored everything else. Had I known I was carrying a child, I certainly would have done things differently.

I'm not saying I would have given up the business, but I would have held back on the production of those dresses. Maybe waited until spring until after the baby was born. Then I could have approached the project a bit more leisurely, taken my time with the illustrations. We could have chosen a different fabric, had all of the samples ready, and presented it as a fall-winter collection.

Now that's no longer an option. John has already arranged the financing, Denise has ordered nineteen bolts of a summer-weight cotton fabric, and I've signed the contract with Acorn Manufacturing to produce the dresses. This is going to be a summer collection, and come hell or high water I have got to get it out there on the market.

Don't misunderstand me, I'm happy about this baby, and I think John will be also. It's just the timing that's bad. If this were to happen next summer we'd both be dancing for joy, but with all that's going on right now, I think it's best that I say nothing and keep it to myself, at least for a few more months. Once the merchandise is in the stores, then I can tell him.

No doubt John will be thrilled to find out we're having a baby, but once he knows I can almost guarantee you that he'll insist I slow down and get more rest. Right now, that simply is not possible. We've got orders for 40 dresses, but we're producing 150. If the merchandise isn't in the stores by early spring, we're sunk. I can't let that happen. Too many people are counting on me. If I fail, John will lose the money he's invested, Denise will have done all that work for nothing, the Pulaski women will lose the finishing work they're counting on, and I can forget any hope of ever being a designer. It's hard enough to get people to accept a woman in business, but if she's got failure stamped across her forehead, she won't have so much as a prayer.

I hate the thought of keeping secrets from John, but in this case I've got no choice. I just pray to God I'm doing the right thing.

Long Days

TEMPLETON HAD SUSPECTED SHE WAS pregnant a few days before she confirmed it on the calendar, but she'd ignored the tenderness in her breasts and blamed her fatigue on such a hectic schedule. Now that she knew the truth, her sense of desperation became greater than ever. She left the house without taking time for breakfast and was waiting at the door when the shopkeeper arrived. Making a second and then third call on many of the shops that had originally turned her away, she'd place the illustration showing a dozen variations of the same dress on the counter and immediately segue into telling how the shop's patrons could purchase the exact dress they wanted for far less than the price of one that was custom-made.

If the shop owner remained hesitant or suggested they might wait a few weeks to see if this new concept was something customers would take to, Templeton gave a nonchalant shrug and said, "If we're not sold out by then."

Apparently, no shop owner wanted to be without what was being touted as the latest trend in women's fashion, so more often than not they placed a small order. At the end of a long day, she'd come home with orders for another fifteen or twenty dresses.

The days were long, and she often returned home frustrated with such slow progress. Her back had begun to ache, and by the time she arrived home her ankles were inevitably swollen. John noticed and more than once suggested she slow down a bit.

"There's no rush on this," he said. "You've got production underway and can continue to write orders through the end of April."

"I'm really not that tired," Templeton said, "and I'll rest easier knowing the entire production run is sold out."

Denise knew about the baby. She'd guessed it even before Templeton had confided in her, and she too seemed concerned. One afternoon in mid-December, Templeton stopped by the fabric shop to check on the delivery of ribbon trims.

"Are they in yet?" she asked.

Denise looked at her and did a double-take. "Mon dieu! Have you not eaten for a month?"

Although her suit jacket barely fastened across her swollen breasts, Templeton's face had grown thin, her wrists spindly, and her collarbone more prominent than ever.

"I'm trying to watch what I eat. It's only three months, and already my clothes are like the skin on a sausage."

Denise stood there shaking her head. "This is not good for the babe. The little one needs food to grow, milk to build bones—"

"It's only for a short while longer. Next week I have an appointment to meet with the ladies' wear manager at the Emporium. If I can convince them to take the last forty dresses, then I'll feel a lot more relaxed."

"And then you will tell John he is going to be a papa?"

Templeton nodded. "I'll tell John and my family. I haven't even mentioned it in my letters to Mama for fear that she'd tell Daddy and he'd call John up to congratulate him." She laughed. "For years Daddy has said I should forget about designing and think about raising a family. Once he hears the news, I think he'll be as happy as John."

"And what about you?" Denise asked. "Will you also be happy?"

There was a flicker of hesitation; then Templeton smiled. "Actually, I will be. Early on I thought I'd like to wait a few years, establish myself as a designer, then have a baby, but watching you with Isabelle has changed my mind. I've come to realize having a baby isn't an interruption of life, it's a reason for living it to the fullest."

Denise clapped her hands gleefully, leaned in, and kissed Templeton's cheek.

"Your little one is going to be a very lucky babe."

ON THE MONDAY TEMPLETON WAS to meet with Mildred Kent, the manager of the Emporium ladies' wear department, she woke feeling queasy. Figuring it to be simply a case of nerves, she reminded herself that she had spoken to Miss Kent on two previous occasions and both times found the middle-aged woman approachable and not at all intimidating. Chiding herself for worrying needlessly, she packed up her portfolio and fabric samples and hurried off to catch the trolley. By the time she arrived at the Emporium, she felt considerably more confident and was stepping lively.

Once inside the store, Templeton hurried through the ladies' wear department and back to lingerie where Kent had a closet-sized office. Before she made it to the door, a shop girl stopped her and said the meeting had been moved to Mr. Bellingham's office.

She'd heard the store manager's name bandied about from time to time but had never met the man, nor did she have any desire to do so today.

"Did Miss Kent say why?" she asked apprehensively.

"No, ma'am. Only that I'm to show you to his office as soon as you arrive."

The nervous feeling she'd had earlier was back. This was not good.

BELLINGHAM'S OFFICE WAS NOTHING LIKE Kent's. It was ten times larger with mahogany-paneled walls, bookcases, and paintings that stood as tall as a man. His desk was massive, but the chair behind it empty. Both he and Mildred Kent were sitting at a small round table in the corner. When Templeton entered the room, he stood and pulled out a chair.

"Please," he said and gestured to the seat.

Bellingham had a narrow face, thick beard, and a mustache that obliterated his upper lip. He did not look like a man who smiled often, and he certainly wasn't smiling now. Templeton had the sickening feeling he was here to squelch whatever buy Kent had in mind. Pushing past the fear that she might throw up on his plush oriental carpet, she smiled, stepped forward, and offered her hand to him.

"I'm delighted you could join us today, Mr. Bellingham."

He hesitated a fraction of a second, almost as though the gesture had taken him by surprise, then shook the offered hand and returned to his seat. Ignoring Bellingham's unrelenting expression and thinking only of the 40 dresses she had to sell, Templeton pulled the presentation sketch from her portfolio and placed it on the table.

"What you see here is not simply a dress design but a concept that is going to revolutionize the fashion industry."

Templeton couldn't say where the words came from, but they flowed freely and confidently as she spoke about a basic style that could be customized to accommodate any woman's taste.

"And we can do this at a price considerably below that of a custom-made garment."

As she turned to pull the fabric samples from her case, she saw Kent smile and give Bellingham a nod.

Spreading the fan of fabric samples across the table, Templeton said, "The dress is available in three basic colors, but with a range of accessorizing trims such as this you can offer your customers an almost endless array of fashions."

Bellingham said nothing, but Kent had a number of questions on minimum order, pricing, delivery time, and warehousing. One by one Templeton answered the questions, apparently to everyone's satisfaction. Once she'd finished, Kent turned to Bellingham and suggested they order 25 units to try the program.

He sat there, fingering his beard and eyeing the sketch with his brows pinched tight.

After what seemed an eternity, he looked over at Templeton and asked, "Have you sold this program to the City of Paris?"

"Not yet. Some of the smaller specialty shops along Market Street have already placed orders, but I haven't spoken to the City of Paris buyer."

"What about I. Magnin, have they bought it?"

Afraid that he was losing interest because none of the other department stores would be showing it, Templeton could almost feel the floor giving way beneath her.

"Not at the moment, but in all fairness, sir—"

"Good," he snapped cutting her off. "I like the program, but I want an exclusive on it."

Templeton's heart thudded against her chest, and for a moment she thought maybe she'd misunderstood him.

"For me to give an exclusive on it, you'd have to order forty units. And while I can promise you the other department stores will not have it, there would be exceptions with the specialty shops that already bought into the program."

Looking to Bellingham, Kent gave a nod. "We can handle forty units."

He shook his head then leaned back in his chair and looked across to Templeton. "Not forty. I want two hundred, and I want the dress in five basic colors. The three you've got here plus a black and white. The last two colors will be exclusive to the Emporium."

Templeton swallowed back the lump in her throat. "Before I can commit to an order that size, I'd have to check our production capacity and fabric inventory." She searched her mind trying to recall the bolts of fabric she'd seen lined up along the walls of Denise's shop. "On the black, we'd like to do that in a dressier fabric, a raw silk perhaps or taffeta."

"Better yet." He stood, walked over to his desk, shuffled through a pile of papers, and looked back at Kent. "I want this to go big. Posters in every department, newspaper ads, a fashion show, play up *only at the Emporium*." He turned to Templeton. "We're going to need six—no, make that ten samples for the window displays."

THE MEETING LASTED FOR ALMOST three hours, and when Templeton left the store she was still trying to grasp the reality of what had happened. She'd walked in hoping to sell 40 dresses and walked out with an order that would double the size of their production run. For the last 45 minutes she'd sat there with her fingers crossed, praying that Acorn could handle a job this big.

As she counted up all the things that had to happen to get the job done, she began to wonder if it had been a foolish move to accept a job this big. Possibly so, but how could she not? With the Emporium promoting the dresses as Bellingham suggested, the TWM brand would be established here in San Francisco, and that was something she'd thought would take three, maybe four years.

Her first stop was the fabric shop. After she'd explained the shock of what happened, she and Denise spent the next three hours estimating the amount of material needed for an additional 160 dresses. By then it was too late to start on going over the trim fabrics.

Denise sighed. "What have we gotten ourselves into?"

"Don't worry. We'll be fine." Templeton waved away the troublesome thought with a flick of her fingers, but a strange new rumbling was swirling through her stomach.

FOR THE NEXT FOUR DAYS, Templeton did not sit still for a single minute. Acorn went back and forth, first agreeing they could handle the additional 160 dresses, then saying such a task would be impossible. Templeton could do little but watch as the factory owner and the Chinese foreman argued back and forth. In the end, the owner admitted the only way they could handle the job would be to deliver the last 100 dresses in mid-August.

With the Emporium's promotion scheduled for May, she had to find a second manufacturer. That took a full two days of running from one place to another and more haggling over price. With all of the hopping on and off of trolleys, walking up long flights of stairs, and carrying around the bulky package of patterns, Templeton went home both days with her back aching, a raging headache, and very little appetite.

On top of all the production problems she was encountering, John was in a foul mood and had been since the night she told him about the Emporium's order. Rather than celebrating what she considered a huge success, he said she looked like a shadow of herself and had no business working such long hours. Instead of going to dinner, they'd remained in the sitting room and argued about it for hours. As he stood looking out the window, his back turned to her, he said she'd gone back on her promise.

"You said when the financing was in place, you'd slow down, we'd spend more time together, try to start a family. That was not two months ago, and now this! It's not getting better, Templeton, it's getting worse.

You care more about that business than you do—"

"That's not true," she snapped. "I'm as anxious as you are to start a family, but there's no reason I can't do both. These problems are temporary. Once I've got a new manufacturing plant, that's it. I won't be—"

"Don't be so damn naïve. If you've got a business, you're going to have problems. That's the nature of the beast. You solve one problem, another one crops up. It's not something you can control. What you can control are your choices."

"What choice did I have? None, that's what! Bellingham told me what he wanted and how he planned to run this big promotion. I didn't ask for it!"

"But you didn't turn it down, and that was your choice."

Templeton was at a loss for words. It *had* been a choice. She could have told Bellingham they couldn't fulfill such a large order in time for a spring showing. She could have suggested they introduce it in spring and then offer the Emporium an absolute exclusive on the winter collection. Why hadn't she thought of that then?

As they stood apart, neither of them speaking, she could sense a wall of invisible bricks rising up between them, separating them perhaps forever. She was on the verge of telling him about the baby when he spoke.

"In another year I'll be thirty, Templeton. That's old for fathering a child. I want to make sure I'm around and young enough to enjoy our children, when or if we ever have any. I thought you wanted the same thing, but perhaps I was mistaken."

As he turned and walked away, Templeton felt as if he'd set the last brick in place, sealing them off one from another.

"John, wait…"

Her voice was thin and trailed after him like a lame dog. Had he waited, she would have told him about the baby. She would have explained that the very reason she was hurrying to get everything done was that so she could ready herself for motherhood.

She listened to his footsteps click across the foyer and heard the front door slam. By the time he returned, she was in bed but not yet asleep. He undressed in the dark, climbed into the bed, and turned his back to her.

Templeton remained still for a long while, hoping he would turn and pull her to him. When he did not, a huge sorrow swept over her and settled in her heart. In time she heard the muffled sound of his snore. She buried her face in the pillow and sobbed. When she woke the next morning, he was gone.

A Time of Sorrow

IN THE DAYS THAT FOLLOWED, the sadness that had settled in Templeton's heart seemed to grow larger and heavier. It caused her to wander away from any thoughts of business and grow teary at the least little thing. She pushed through the days thinking each evening she'd tell John of the baby, explain that this was what she had wanted all along, and she'd not said anything sooner only because she wanted to wait and be sure it was true. She was almost certain that once he realized there was a baby on the way, he would love her as he had before.

Desperate to repair the bond that had been broken, Templeton kept a sharp eye on the clock. Regardless of where she was or what she was doing, when it neared six she'd hurry back to the house. For days she waited, hopeful of sharing her news, but by the time John arrived home she was always in bed. He'd now found reasons to work late or have dinner with a client, and at such an ungodly hour she'd lost the desire to talk.

On Friday she arrived home with her back feeling as though someone had pummeled it with a sledgehammer. So weary that she could barely drag herself up the stairs, she crawled into bed and didn't bother waiting for John that night. The next day was Saturday; he never worked on Saturday. They could have a leisurely breakfast together then go for a walk or a carriage ride; that's when she would tell him.

As she tried to imagine the easy curl of his smile, the pain in her back spread across her hips, sliding down into her stomach and kicking like a mule. She rolled onto her side and swore that once this project was over, she would never again take on such an effort. John was right, it had been too much for her. She'd been foolish in thinking of the business first. She was nearing the end of her child-bearing years. That's what should have been her first consideration; perhaps her only consideration. The thought of walking away from Bellingham's offer was on the edge of her mind when a pain worse than any of the others cramped her stomach, and she curled into a ball. Moments later she felt wetness between her legs.

Pulling back the blanket, Templeton saw a crimson stain on her gown and the sheets.

"Oh God!" she screamed. "This can't be happening, no, no..."

Pushing up with her arms, she forced herself to stand, trying to make her way to the commode. Her steps were small and her body folded over. She grasped whatever was within reach to steady her as she moved, but before she could cross the room she collapsed and fell to the floor.

How long she was there, Templeton couldn't say. She could do nothing but lie there, unable to help herself until she heard the front door click open. Knowing it would be John, she called out for him.

There was a rush of footsteps on the stair, and then he appeared at the bedroom door.

She looked up, her face ashen, her voice whisper-thin. "John, I'm sick. Get May Ling."

He hurried over and kneeled beside her. "Templeton, you need a doctor." He slid his arms beneath her body, lifted her, and carried her to the bed.

"No doctor. Get May Ling. She knows how to—"

John made a soft shushing sound; he bent and kissed her forehead. "Rest, my darling. I'll get help and hurry back."

The pains continued, a sharp stab, then a moment of calm, then another stab. Templeton feared she was going to lose the baby.

"Not now," she prayed. "Please, God, not now."

If John brought the doctor instead of May Ling, he would know she was with child. May Ling had kept her secret all this time; she would not give it away now. May Ling had been through this herself; she would have Chinese medicines to stop the bleeding before…

Templeton arched her back as another pain ricocheted through her body. She cried out but could not say what hurt more, the pain in her body or the shattering of her heart. Once John knew she had deceived him, it would be the end of everything.

Another pain and then another; then she heard voices. John. The doctor. Tears filled her eyes, and she turned her face to the pillow.

Doctor Presley was a man with white hair, a bulbous nose, and a ruddy complexion. He had a kindly manner about him and suggested John wait downstairs while he conducted his examination. For that Templeton was grateful.

He sat on the bed beside her, saw the crimson stain on her gown, then prodded her stomach, moving his fingers across her stomach slowly and methodically. He asked if this or that hurt and she answered honestly until he asked if she thought herself pregnant.

Templeton had heard of instances where a young mother gave birth without ever realizing she was pregnant. She herself had never known any such person but was desperate, and that seemed the only way out.

"I don't see how I could be. I haven't missed a monthly."

"Hmm. What about your breasts, any swelling or tenderness?"

She shook her head. "No, not that I've noticed."

He nodded knowingly. "And your monthlies, have they been the same as usual?"

Templeton again hesitated. Did he suspect she was lying? A sharp stab hit her back, and she gasped.

"I think so," she said, then closed her eyes and surrendered to the pain. When she looked up, May Ling was standing beside the doctor.

When Templeton stretched her hand and reached for May Ling, the doctor stood and moved back. He turned to John who had followed May Ling upstairs.

"Mr. Morehouse, unfortunately, I do not have good news. It looks as though your wife has a cryptic pregnancy—"

John stared at the doctor with a wide-eyed expression. "She has a what?"

"A cryptic or, for lack of a better word, unrecognized pregnancy. It's a pregnancy without any of the normal symptoms but a pregnancy all the same. Such pregnancies are unusual, and without the proper care a woman can easily miscarry, which seems to be what is happening here."

"How could Templeton not know she's expecting a baby?"

"As I said, she had none of the symptoms. No morning sickness, no breast tenderness. Your wife is a thin woman and with almost no weight gain, it's understandable—"

John scrubbed his hand across his forehead. "I don't get it. We just find out she's pregnant, and now you're saying she's going to lose the baby?"

"Without a small miracle, I'm afraid that's what will happen. Once a woman's bleeding reaches this point, there is nothing anyone can do. It's in God's hands."

John's shoulders slumped. "I don't understand what would cause…"

"It could be any number of things: emotional stress, overwork, heavy lifting, a traumatic injury…" He continued on, listing everything, emphasizing nothing.

May Ling's eyes flicked back and forth. Templeton, John, the doctor, John again.

"This business of hers, that's what caused it. She's been working crazy hours because of this damned business. I know that's what—"

"Missy sick because she fall on stair."

John turned and glared at May Ling. "Templeton fell? When?"

"Yesterday. She come home early, go up to dress. Then I hear thump, and she lying at bottom of stair."

"Why didn't you call a doctor?"

"I say call doctor but Missy say no. She waiting for you."

"Then what?" John asked. "Didn't anyone check to see if she was hurt?"

"No want check. Missy sit by window and wait, then I go home."

Templeton grasped May Ling's hand and held on as another pain rumbled through her body. In that moment, a surge of emotion passed from one hand to the other and a bond was formed between the two women, a bond that would never be broken. May Ling knew the truth, and she had lied to protect their secret.

John stood dumbfounded for a moment, then looked to the doctor. "There's nothing you can do? *Nothing*?"

The doctor shook his head and touched John's arm. "I understand your grief, and I'm truly sorry. I can give your wife some laudanum to

ease the pain, but there is nothing anyone can do to stop the bleeding."
He pulled a bottle of brown liquid from his bag and handed it to May Ling.
"One tablespoon each hour until the pain lessens, but someone will need
to stay with her."

"I stay," May Ling said and squeezed Templeton's hand.

JOHN FOLLOWED THE DOCTOR DOWN the stairs. They stopped in
the foyer, and as they shook hands he assured John that Templeton
would make a full recovery.

"But it would be best if she remained in bed for a few days, even
after the pain is gone. Her body has suffered a trauma and needs time to
rebuild itself."

The muscles in John's face were rigid, his lips stretched thin and his
forehead a washboard of wrinkles.

"This type of unrecognized pregnancy," he asked, "does it always
end in miscarriage?"

"Not really. It is often a tenuous situation, but once a woman reaches
her fifth month the signs of pregnancy usually become more visible and
she starts to feel the baby's movement. That's generally when she consults
a doctor and gets the care she needs."

"Was there any way she could have known? Anything I should have
noticed?"

The doctor shook his head. "I doubt it. Her only symptom was
extreme fatigue, and that could have been caused by most anything." He
placed his hand on John's shoulder. "I know things seem pretty bleak
right now, but look to the future. Remember, this is a rarity. Once your
wife is healed, there is no reason for her not to have children."

AFTER SHOWING THE DOCTOR OUT, John sank onto the sofa and
dropped his head into his hands. As a million questions rolled through
his brain, he thought back to the night she told him about her deal with
the Emporium. He should have been happy for her, but instead he was
angry.

Angry or jealous?

He pushed the thought from his mind and labeled it ridiculous. Why would he be jealous? True, she'd been preoccupied with business and come home late, but hadn't he done the same from time to time? That night he'd noticed how stressed she seemed, but instead of offering help he'd said how terrible she looked.

The doctor's words came back to him.

"A miscarriage can be brought on by any number of things: emotional stress, overwork, tension…"

John rose, walked across the room, and stood looking out the window. The hour had grown late, and the street was silent. No voices, no sounds of carriages or cars rumbling along the cobblestones. The fog had lifted, and the night sky was lit with stars.

He'd asked the doctor if there was anything he could have done, but standing there in the silence of night he realized he already knew the answer. It had been there all along, but he'd failed to accept it. The truth was he could have offered help instead of criticism. He had any number of contacts in the manufacturing field. In a single afternoon, he could have made telephone calls and secured a second supplier. Instead, he'd stormed off.

She'd called out asking him to stay, but he hadn't even looked back. *Anger*.

He'd accused her of loving the business more than him, but that was not true. *Jealousy*.

She'd had a successful business in Philadelphia and walked away from it to be with him. She'd given up everything for him. He'd given up nothing.

Tears filled his eyes, and a mantle of shame settled on his shoulders as he recalled the bitterness of his words.

Regret.

What would happen now? In Templeton's moment of grief she'd called for May Ling, not him. She'd held May Ling's hand and asked her to stay.

John needed to talk with her, explain how sorry he was, make amends for his shameless behavior. He turned and started up the stairs, his steps heavy, weighted with sorrow and regret. At the second-floor landing, he stopped and listened. He heard Templeton moan and alongside of that cry was May Ling's voice, her words tender and comforting.

For several minutes, he remained there, listening to the anguish that would forever be carved into his soul. When his sorrow grew greater than hers, he turned and retreated back down the stairs.

That night, John did not sleep. He kneeled at the foot of the stairs and prayed for God to spare Templeton and their child. Then he paced the living room, thinking of how to undo the damage he'd done.

Never again, he vowed; never again would he turn his back on her when a better man would have offered help. If she wanted to have a dress business, then he would do all in his power to help her. She had given up everything for him; he would now give her a far greater measure in return.

WHEN THE BLUSH OF MORNING lit the sky, he heard her scream and knew it was over. The promise of a child was gone. In time they would start over. Hopefully it would be as the doctor said, and they would one day have a family.

Templeton

MAY LING HAS KNOWN MY secret from the start, and she's kept it to herself. She never spoke of it, not even to me. I thought perhaps she had forgotten, but obviously such was not the case. Like Mama, she knows far more than she says. Mama used to tell me it's better for a woman to know more and say less until her words become necessary. I can now see the wisdom of that thought.

May Ling knows more than anyone realizes. I suspect she's heard John and me arguing over the amount of time I spend at work. That's why she said what she did. It's true that I sat by the window waiting for him to return home, but I didn't fall on the stairs. Had she not said that, John would have most certainly blamed my work for the loss of our baby. Why would he not? I blame myself.

He was right when he said I should have turned down Mr. Bellingham's order. At the moment I thought it was the most important thing in the world; now I realize it was the least important.

When John accused me of putting the business before him, I argued that it wasn't true, but on those long nights when I waited for him to come home, I came to the realization that it was. I wanted a fashion empire the way a child wants a shiny new toy. It's a moment of glory, a temporary fascination, a glittering star to grab hold of and claim as your own.

After losing our child and almost losing my husband, I see things a lot differently. If you ever wonder what's the most important thing in your life, measure the love of family against anything else, then ask yourself which of those you can't live without. I assure you it won't be the shiny bright toy that's caught your eye.

I will forever carry the guilt of losing that baby. It's a part of me now, a scar that will never change. John claims the blame is partly his, but I know better and that too is a sorrow that has settled in my heart.

Someday, after enough time has passed, we'll again try to have a baby. I pray it'll happen and that the love of a child can replace this terrible grief I carry around with me. In all this world, there is no burden heavier than guilt. This I swear to you.

Changing Times

AFTER THAT NIGHT, SOMETHING IN their relationship changed. It was a subtle shift. John was more attentive than ever, but it was as if they moved around one another with great caution, measuring their words, avoiding even the tiniest hint of controversy.

Those first few evenings, while she was still bedridden, he came and sat at the edge of her bed, careful not to jerk or jostle her. His touch was as tender as one might use with a newborn babe, and when he spoke his words were gentle and consoling. He begged for her forgiveness and insisted the fault was his and his alone.

"Instead of criticizing you for working such long hours, I should have been more understanding," he said. "I should have offered to help. There were a thousand things I could have done, but I did none of them and now I live with the shame of that. Were it not for my thoughtlessness…"

As his words trailed off he looked away, shoulders stooped, head lowered.

Templeton took his hand in hers. "It's not your fault, John. You had no way of knowing. I'm the one to blame. I was overtired and not feeling well. I should have sensed something was wrong and asked for your help."

Her words danced along the edge of truth, but she couldn't bring herself to say it. The night of the miscarriage she had given birth to a lie, and she would have to live with it forever. Spoken now, the truth would destroy his love for her and tear apart their marriage. She couldn't let that happen.

Whatever blame John felt over the loss of their baby, Templeton felt tenfold. He apologized over and over again, and with each apology the guilt lodged inside her chest grew larger and heavier. She'd known about the pregnancy but believed she could do it all. It wasn't John who had failed her; she'd failed herself.

A thousand times over she wished she had turned away from Mr. Bellingham's offer. She even considered backing out of the deal. Doing so now would most likely mean she'd never get another order from the Emporium, but that seemed of little consequence. When she told John that she was going to send a note to Bellingham to inform him the dresses could not be delivered in the allotted time frame, he said such a move would be foolhardy.

"You've worked too hard to build this business. It would be a waste to let it slip away because of a single setback."

Templeton didn't see the miscarriage as a setback. She saw it as a tragedy, a heart-breaking loss of the child she'd already begun to love. A child she'd imagined as a fair-haired version of Isabelle.

"I've come to realize that I can't do everything," she said glumly. "Given my choice, I'd rather have a family."

"You don't have to choose," John reasoned. "With a bit of help, you *can* have both." He went on to say he had business contacts who could find the suppliers she needed.

"All you have to do is concentrate on getting better. I'll take care of everything else for you."

With a fragile-looking smile, she said it was more kindness than she deserved.

He leaned in, his eyes fixed on hers, his mouth a hair's breadth away.

"It's not just a kindness. I love you too much to see you unhappy. The work you do is part of who you are, part of why I love you. You're not like other women, Templeton, and I knew that from the start. I was wrong to think you'd change. I realize that now, and I'll do whatever I have to do to make this marriage work. From now on your dreams will be my dreams, and together we'll make them happen."

His kiss was soft as feather, but in it there was an iron-clad promise.

Tears welled in her eyes as the guilt rose in her throat and rendered her speechless. The lie she'd allowed him to believe was like a knife stuck in her heart, and each word of understanding or kindness he spoke thrust the blade deeper.

The truth was something Templeton hid from everyone, even her mama. After waiting a full week before writing home, she gave her mama the same whitewashed version John had heard—that there'd been none of the usual signs of pregnancy. On a tear-stained page she said she'd mistakenly spent her energy on chasing after a career and not stopped to take notice of what was happening.

You were right, Mama, she wrote. *My greatest happiness will be when I hold our first child in my arms.* An ink blob blurred the next few lines. She ended the paragraph saying *if* she was ever again blessed with the opportunity of having a child.

THAT FIRST WEEK DENISE STOPPED by to visit twice, and both times she brought Isabelle along. While the women chatted in the sitting room, John settled Isabelle at the butler's table with cookies and milk. When Templeton heard the sound of their laughter coming from the kitchen, she grew wistful.

"See how much he enjoys having a child around?" she said, then became teary-eyed as another wave of regret swept over her.

"Losing this baby is not your fault," Denise said. "It is God who decides whether or not a child is to be born into the world. It would be wise to accept His will and forgive yourself."

Although Denise's advice was well-intentioned, Templeton pushed it aside. She knew the miscarriage wasn't God's doing. She was the one who had decided the business was a higher priority than anything or anyone else, and now she had to pay the price. The thing that hurt most was that John would also pay for her mistake.

On the second visit, when Denise turned to talking about the business, John joined them. He listened as she wrinkled her brow and told about a delay in the delivery of trim fabric and a problem with the manufacturing company.

"I delivered the lace we had on hand just as you asked," she said, "but that foreman, Charlie, is a most unpleasant fellow. I certainly do not welcome the thought of ever seeing him again."

Templeton groaned. "Charlie hates dealing with a woman, but he's unpleasant with everyone. You won't have to go there again. I'll handle it."

Leaning into the conversation, John asked, "Unpleasant how?"

Denise gave Templeton a knowing glance, then looked back to John.

"I stopped at the factory on my way home from the shop yesterday, and when I asked how things were going he yelled at me for ten minutes."

"About what?" John asked.

"Only seven finishers came to work, and he said Templeton promised him nine. I apologized and said we'd try to get more tomorrow, but he was not happy with that."

"Neither of you ladies should have to deal with the factory," John said. "You need a project manager, someone to oversee day-to-day production and take care of problems."

Denise smiled. "Such a person sounds wonderful to me, but this business is mostly Templeton's. I am only a very small part. She should make the decision."

John looked across with a raised eyebrow. "What do you think, sweetheart? If we hired someone to assist both of you, do the running around, check the production schedules, follow up on deliveries, that would make things easier, wouldn't it?"

Templeton shrugged unenthusiastically. "Sure, it would be helpful, but what reputable person would want a job with such an uncertain future?"

"Why uncertain?"

Templeton leaned back into the sofa pillows, turned toward the window, and gazed up at the darkening sky. Several heartbeats thumped by before she spoke.

"I feel as though I've lost my love of design," she said. "I never realized the business would demand so much of me. I'm thinking it might be best for me to forget about designing and think only of raising a family."

John came and sat beside her on the sofa. He placed his hand on her cheek and gently turned her face to his.

"You've not lost your love of design, sweetheart. It's in here." He touched her heart. "It's a gift you were born with and will forever have. Having such a talent doesn't take away a woman's ability to be a good mother, it only enhances it."

In a voice smaller than a whisper, Templeton said, "But after all that's happened…"

"That's the past," he replied. "Let's forget the past and think about the future."

THREE WEEKS PASSED BEFORE TEMPLETON returned to work, and by then John had secured two manufacturing factories willing to produce the dresses on time and at a reasonable cost. He had also lined up three finishing houses and hired George Wilson.

George was a newcomer to San Francisco, a man with no experience in retail but a solid understanding of fabrics. He had an easy smile, quick wit, and uncanny ability for ferreting out a solution to almost any problem. A Kentuckian by birth, he'd grown up working in the cotton mills starting as a sweeper and rising to become a manager. When John asked what brought him to San Francisco, he said it was the loss of a wife to influenza and a finger to the machines. He held up his left hand, and, sure enough, the index finger was little more than a stub.

"I figured it was time for a fresh start," he said and grinned. He offered to work the first week for free to prove his worth, and John took him up on the offer.

As it turned out, George was as good as his word. Before two months had gone by, he had a production board hanging on the back wall of the fabric shop and every day he'd be there to update one thing or another. Without even looking at the board, George could say which factory had produced how many dresses and what color they were working on. He'd also set up a new workflow for the finishers, which meant seven women could now turn out the same number of garments as the nine Charlie originally claimed to need.

On slow days when there was little for him to do but twiddle his thumbs, George would stop by and have lunch with Templeton.

At first she found him a nuisance, an interruption of her afternoon even though she'd been doing nothing. But after the fourth visit, she began to look forward to his arrival. There was a certain excitement in hearing of how they'd switched the finishing stations around or delivered a bolt of crepe de chine two weeks earlier than expected.

In early February, he brought two of the first samples.

"I thought you'd like to see these before I deliver them to Millie Kent."

"Millie?" Templeton repeated and laughed. "You call the Emporium's women's wear manager Millie?"

He flashed that sly Kentucky grin of his.

"Not to her face," he said and laughed along with Templeton.

That afternoon instead of having lunch at the house, they went out. Feeling in a rather celebratory mood, she indulged in a glass of wine and returned home with a rosy blush coloring her cheeks.

That night she told John he'd done well to hire George.

"He's an extremely likeable fellow, and with him around to handle the production I've decided to do a winter collection."

John gave a nod and smiled. "I'm glad. Getting back to work will be good for you."

ONCE GEORGE WAS ON BOARD, everything seemed to run smoothly. On days when there was little else to do, he'd take over the fabric shop so that Denise could spend time with Isabelle. Templeton did indeed return to her drawing board. At first she just sat there doodling lace accents on a shirtwaist or sketching a tea dress with the unencumbered lines of a female figure rather than the pigeon-shape of a corseted woman. But before long, she started working on a winter collection: skirts that buttoned on and off a changeable shirtwaist, jackets that turned a wool jumper into a suit. Mix-and-match pieces that added versatility to a woman's wardrobe.

The day she sketched out a six-piece ensemble that could be worn a dozen different ways, she was still at the drawing board when John returned home from work.

Appearing at the door of her studio, he said, "Isn't it rather late to be working?"

She looked up and laughed. "I guess I lost track of time. I've come up with a new concept for interchangeable wardrobe pieces that I think

Bellingham is going to love." She dropped her charcoal stick into a jar, pushed back from the drawing board, and stood.

"Give me a few minutes to freshen up and change, then we'll go out to dinner."

What John said several weeks earlier had proven itself true. Templeton had not lost her love of design. It was still there but no longer outranked her desire to be a wife and mother.

In February, when the wind blew with a vengeance and the rain came at a slant, there was little else to do so she spent endless hours in her studio. During the bleakest days, she pulled the calendar tracking her monthlies from beneath a stack of rough sketches and studied it again. On the night she believed herself to be at the peak of fertility, she planned a quiet evening at home. When John came in, she had a bottle of wine waiting. That evening they dined by candlelight, then put a record on the Victrola and danced, his arm firm around her waist, her head resting against his shoulder.

Later, they mounted the stairs, climbed into bed, and made love as ardently as they had on their honeymoon. Afterward, when the moon was high in the sky and sleep was slow in coming, she lay there listening to the sounds of his breath and hoping that this was the night they'd made a baby.

As it turned out they hadn't; not that night nor any of the countless nights that followed.

After months of one disappointment following another, she remembered her mama's old adage that a watched pot never boils and tossed the calendar into the trash can. Turning back to the drawing board, she took a charcoal stick and began roughing out ideas for a cape that could go from day to evening.

Templeton began to work feverishly, starting the moment John left the house, often without breakfast or lunch. She believed if she could push the fear of not having a baby from her mind it would happen as it had the first time, naturally and without planning. Finishing one design, she immediately started on another, and before the month was out she had the entire winter collection.

Tacking the sketches to the wall, she stepped back to study them. They were good. The colors blended perfectly, sometimes contrasting, sometimes complementing one another. No question, these designs were the best she'd ever done. Earlier on Bellingham had hinted at the possibility of a collection that would be exclusive to the Emporium, but he'd qualified the thought saying, "Of course, it all depends on how well this line sells."

That was the question that stayed with her day and night. Would customers buy into this different way of purchasing dresses?

A WEEK BEFORE THE FASHION show, the Emporium's ads ran in all three newspapers: the *Chronicle*, the *Call*, and the *Examiner*. The following Thursday, the *Chronicle* had a full-page layout with photographs of five different dresses, an open invitation to the fashion show, and a lengthy interview with Bellingham, who again hinted at the possibility of an even more impressive winter collection.

On Saturday, Templeton was awake before dawn. The day before she'd had lunch with George, and they'd gone over every last detail. Nothing, absolutely nothing, could go wrong. She was almost positive of it.

Almost.

The word danced across her mind as she mentally retraced every phase of the program. No matter how many times she went through it, she could find nothing wrong. The merchandise had been delivered on time. They had held the price point despite a few last-minute changes, and the dresses were an exact match to the original designs.

All she could do now was wait and hope for the best.

THEY ARRIVED AT THE STORE together—Templeton, John, Denise, and George. It was two hours before the show was to start, but the store was already crowded. Not just women, but families lined up waiting for a lunch table at the Bandstand, wandering through the aisles of the gourmet food section. By two o'clock, there was no longer standing room in the ladies' wear department. Every seat was taken.

Templeton stood off to the side, her back pressed to the wall.

Bellingham was first to appear on stage. He introduced himself and spent a good ten minutes talking about how the Emporium prided itself in being a leader in both the fashion and food industry. As he rattled on Templeton felt beads of perspiration rising up on her forehead, and she was starting to feel a bit woozy.

Fanning her hand in front of her face, she leaned into John and whispered, "It's terribly warm in here, don't you think?"

He nodded. "Given the size of this crowd, I think we could slip away without being noticed if you need a breath of air."

She was tempted to say yes, but just then Bellingham introduced Mildred Kent.

As the first three models stepped onto the stage Mildred spoke in a loud clear voice, telling the audience that the models were wearing the same basic dress, but it had been customized to accommodate each of their preferences.

"Make no mistake, ladies," she said, "these dresses are the equivalent of custom-made. They are tailored to fit and finished in your selection of color and trim." She raised her arm and signaled the model to turn around. "The back detail on this afternoon tea dress includes mother-of-pearl buttons along with peau de soie trim."

After the last model crossed the stage, Mildred told the ladies to see one of the salesgirls if they wished to arrange a fitting. A rousing round of applause rose from the audience.

Templeton breathed a sigh of relief. She no longer felt the need of someone to assure her the collection would be a success; she'd watched it happen. Looking up at John, she smiled. He'd believed in her even when she'd stopped believing in herself.

THE EMPORIUM HIT A RECORD high for sales that Saturday, and the following week Templeton signed a contract guaranteeing the store exclusive rights to her fall collection. She'd asked Bellingham if he wanted to review the designs before giving her the contract, but he shook his head.

"I know all I need to know," he said. "You can work it out with Miss Kent."

Two days later she met with Mildred Kent and brought George along. Whether it was the way George joked with Mildred or the uniqueness of fashions that could be mixed and matched a dozen different ways, Templeton couldn't say, but Mildred Kent bought the entire collection. Every last piece. Even a bolero Templeton herself had been iffy about.

Templeton

THIS HAS BEEN A DIFFICULT winter to say the least. After I lost the baby, I thought for certain my heart would break. May Ling said that sweet little baby was half the size of a tadpole but already formed with tiny arms and legs. I didn't look at it that night; I couldn't. But since then I've thought about it a million times and shed an ocean full of tears.

Losing a child you've carried inside of you does something to a woman. It changes you in ways you never thought possible. You think less about yourself and more about being a wife and mother.

Knowing why I'd lost the baby took away any desire I had to work or, heaven forbid, have my own design business. If it weren't for John's encouragement, I probably would have never again set foot in the studio. Now I thank heaven I did.

By the end of July, all of the patterns will be laid out and the fabrics ordered. Then George can take it from there. He's dependable and everyone likes working with him, especially Denise, so I doubt my being gone for a month will present a problem.

Anyway, I think if I had to choose between staying here for the business and this trip, I'd choose the trip. It's been a year since I last saw Mama, and I miss her something fierce. I miss everyone: Daddy, Benjamin, Clara.

It's lovely here in San Francisco, but it's not Philadelphia. I miss my friends and my family and Mama's Sunday dinners with all the nieces and nephews running around. I used to think those dinners were impossibly chaotic; now I'm looking forward to the craziness of family.

Hopefully, John and I will start a family before too much longer, but it makes me sad to think the baby will never really get to know his or her cousins. Sure, we'll visit, but visiting isn't the same as living nearby. That's one thing I can say for certain.

John made reservations this morning for us to have a sleeping cabin on the train, and the thought of another trip like our honeymoon makes me tingle with delight. This past year has been difficult for him also, so maybe this trip will be good for both of us—bring back some sweet memories and maybe even make something magical happen.

I don't want to jinx anything by talking about it, but that's what I'm hoping for.

The Summer of 1904

THE TRIP BACK TO PHILADELPHIA somehow seemed longer to Templeton. Shortly after the train pulled out of the Union Station Depot in Columbus, Ohio, she gave a lingering sigh and asked when they'd be arriving in Philadelphia.

"It's still tomorrow afternoon," John said and laughed. "We should be at the station about four-thirty, barring any unforeseen problems."

"Unforeseen problems?"

"Trains get delayed from time to time, but the Intercontinental Express is pretty reliable."

"Oh, okay." She picked up the August issue of the *Ladies Home Journal* and leafed through the pages for what felt like the tenth time. "It seems as if this train is slower than it used to be, don't you think?"

John looked up from the newspaper and shook his head. "According to the timetable, this trip is three hours shorter than when we came home to San Francisco last summer."

Templeton had never really thought of San Francisco as home; Philadelphia was home.

She gave another weary-sounding sigh, then leaned back and watched the scenery go by. It was an endless stretch of corn fields and dairy farms with an occasional grist mill or a town that was little more than a wide spot in the road.

ON THURSDAY MORNING, TEMPLETON WOKE filled with the excitement of again seeing her family. When they went to the dining car for a late breakfast, she picked apart a hot roll and had to force down a glass of orange juice.

"You should eat something more," John said. "It's going to be a long day."

Templeton nibbled one corner of the roll. "I'm not one bit worried about being hungry. I'll bet Mama will have a great dinner waiting for us. Maybe a roast like she makes on Sunday."

When John asked if she'd enjoyed the trip in the sleeping cabin, she gave a quick nod, then went right back to saying the minute they stepped off the train, she was going to grab her mama and hug her.

"When I left home I didn't realize I'd miss Mama as much as I have, so we've got a lot of catching up to do."

For the remainder of the day, the minutes stretched into hours and moved as slowly as a snail crossing the garden. When the train finally pulled into the Philadelphia station, Templeton's smile broke open and stretched the full width of her face. Before the train had come to a full stop, she had her gloves on and was peering from the window in search of a familiar face.

"Do you see Mama yet?"

"Not yet," John answered. "They might be sitting inside the station."

Templeton shook her head. "Uh-uh. If they're as anxious to see me as I am to see them, they'll be standing on the platform waving like crazy."

As the train screeched to a stop, she straightened her hat and followed John down the aisle. He stepped down first then turned and held out his hand. Looking over his shoulder to scan the crowd of faces, she lost her footing, stumbled, and fell into his arms.

"Sorry. I was looking for Mama."

John steadied her on her feet. "They're probably inside. The platform is noisy and crowded. You wouldn't want your mama standing out here with all this hubbub, would you?"

Still scanning the crowd, she mumbled, "No, I suppose not."

THE INSIDE OF THE STATION was almost as crowded as the platform. Groups of people stood elbow to elbow, waving, calling out greetings, embracing returnees, kissing goodbye. Following John toward an empty bench, Templeton searched the sea of faces.

"It's odd that Mama and Daddy aren't here. I hope nothing is wrong."

John signaled a porter and handed him the claim check.

"Wait here and stop worrying," he said hurriedly. "I'll grab our luggage and if they're not here by then, we'll take a carriage to the house."

He disappeared back into the crowd and Templeton sat there, her chin dropped down on her chest and a disappointed-looking pout puckering her lips.

For a while the room crackled with the sound of hellos and goodbyes, but there was no sign of her parents. Little by little, the benches emptied. When John returned with the porter pushing a cart filled with their luggage, she was still sitting alone.

"No sign of them yet, huh?"

She shook her head. "This is not like Mama. I have a terrible feeling…"

"I doubt there's anything to worry about. They're probably just delayed." He turned to the porter. "We'll need to hire a carriage."

As he followed the porter toward the main exit, Templeton rose and trailed along. They had already begun to load the luggage onto the carriage when she spotted her daddy hurrying toward them. Red-faced and out of breath, Albert breathed hard.

"Sorry to be late." He tugged Templeton into his arms and kissed her cheek. "Glad to have you home, sweetheart."

"Where's Mama?"

Instead of answering her right away, he shook John's hand and cuffed him on the shoulder. "Good to see you."

"Where's Mama?" Templeton repeated.

"She wanted to come but couldn't. She's got Clara's girls and the baby."

A look of annoyance pinched Templeton's brows. "Why today? She knew we'd be on the four-thirty—"

"Yes, and she feels bad about not being here, but Clara had a doctor's appointment and Bernard couldn't take off work to stay home with the kids."

"What's wrong with Clara? Is she sick?"

"No, she's not sick, but I'm not supposed to say anything more. Clara wants to give you the good news herself."

Templeton's shoulders drooped. "She's having another baby, isn't she?" A hint of jealousy was threaded through her words.

Albert didn't say yes or no, but his grin said it for him. "Don't you dare let her know I said anything, because she's looking forward to telling you yourself."

Templeton gave an almost imperceptible nod.

"I'm happy for Clara," she said, but she didn't sound happy at all.

THE CARRIAGE HAD BARELY COME to a stop before the door swung open and Clara came running down the walkway. She flung her arms around Templeton and hugged her as if they'd been apart for ten years rather than just one.

"It's been forever!" She looked at Templeton for a second. "Daddy told you, didn't he?"

"Told me what?" Templeton replied innocently.

Clara tilted her head as if trying to decide whether or not to believe her sister, then gave way to a grin.

"It's true," she said. "We're having another baby, but I wanted to be the one to tell you. I knew you'd be happy for us."

Templeton folded Clara into her arms.

"I am happy for you," she whispered. "But I'm also a little bit jealous."

"Pshaw." Clara laughed. "Your life is ten times more exciting than mine."

Templeton forced a smile. "Working with the Emporium has been great, but it's not the same as having a family."

Clara pulled Templeton close and hugged her again.

"Mama told me what happened," she said softly. "I know how disappointed you were, but don't lose hope. One miscarriage doesn't mean you'll—"

Templeton broke free of Clara's embrace when she saw her mama standing on the front porch.

"Mama!" she shouted happily and went running up the walkway.

WHEN THEY SAT DOWN TO dinner that evening, there was no Sunday roast. Eleanor apologized saying she'd planned to have one, but with the children underfoot she'd lost track of time.

"Benjamin and his family will be coming over the day after tomorrow. I'll fix something special then. Maybe a beef roast with carrots and the little potatoes you like?"

"Mama," Templeton replied sadly, "the day after tomorrow is Sunday. You almost always make a roast on Sunday anyway."

"Yes, I guess I do," Eleanor said and chuckled. "Well, then, this one will have to be all the more special because you and John are here."

"Thanks, Mama," Templeton replied and stuffed a bite of chicken into her mouth.

That night she and John slept in the same room she'd occupied for most of her life. It felt familiar and yet different in an odd sort of way. The chenille bedspread was new but almost everything else was the same. After they turned off the lamp, the room was dark except for a sliver of moonlight that fell across the floor. John kissed her goodnight then turned on his side.

Speaking to his back, she said, "I was disappointed Mama didn't have a roast tonight."

He turned to face her. "Why? I thought the chicken was really good."

"It was, but Mama always makes a roast when it's a special occasion. Always. Tonight she didn't because she was so caught up in Clara having another baby. I should think us traveling all the way from California would be a special occasion, but apparently Mama didn't."

A cloud drifted past the moon, and the tiny shaft of light disappeared. He moved closer and pulled her into his arms.

"What's on the table is not the measure of your mama's love, Templeton. Take a look at her eyes; that's where you'll see the truth of what she's feeling."

"Well, do you think Mama was genuinely glad to see us?"

"I *know* she was glad to see us. Overjoyed."

His reassurance made her feel a little bit better, but there was still a niggling thought bouncing around inside her head. She'd missed her family far more than they'd missed her.

IN THE DAYS THAT FOLLOWED John went about his business meeting with bankers, cementing current relationships, and making new ones. He and Albert left the house shortly after breakfast and were usually gone until evening. On mornings such as that, Templeton and her mama lingered at the table having a second and sometimes third cup of coffee. After the dishes were cleared away, they'd sit side by side on the porch swing and push back and forth talking.

"Are you happy out there?" Eleanor asked.

Templeton nodded. "Mostly. John is very good to me, and our house is lovely. I have a design studio that's twice the size of our living room, but I miss everybody. Especially you and Daddy."

Eleanor scooted closer and took Templeton's hand in hers. "We miss you too, honey."

"Do you, Mama? Really?"

Eleanor laughed. "Of course I do. I miss you, your daddy misses you, the whole family does. Benjamin, Clara, why, her girls about drove me crazy asking when you'd get here. Why in the world would you think we didn't?"

The swing swayed back and forth several times before Templeton shrugged and said, "It just seems like everybody's moved on with living their life and forgotten I was ever here."

Eleanor wrapped her arm around her daughter's shoulders and pulled her close. "We have moved on with our life, honey, but not because we've forgotten you. We had no choice. You were in love with John and determined to go to San Francisco."

She reached across and brushed back a curl that had fallen onto Templeton's forehead.

"We were heartbroken when you left, but a person doesn't stop living because they're heartbroken. Somehow, some way, they push through and move from one day to the next doing the same as they've always done, but inside here"—she touched her hand to her heart—

"that's where I'm still holding onto you just as tightly as I did the day you were born."

They'd planned to visit Wannamaker's that afternoon, but they didn't. Instead they remained in the swing as Templeton told her mama the truth about the miscarriage.

"I pretty much knew I was having a baby," she said. "I should have stopped working, but I didn't. I thought that was my big chance and I had to make the most of it. Now I'm so sorry, Mama, so very, very sorry…"

When she began to sob, Eleanor pulled her closer.

"The miscarriage wasn't necessarily because you were working. Carrying a new life doesn't mean you stop living yours."

"You don't understand what it's like, Mama—"

"I understand more than you think. When you left here, I lost my baby and felt as broken-hearted as you do right now. But I couldn't let myself fall apart, because your daddy needed me. Clara and the girls needed me; so did Benjamin and his family. Because of them, I had to move from day to day and give my heart time to heal."

"That's different, Mama, you still had Clara and—"

Eleanor snugged her daughter a bit closer. "And I'll bet before long you and John have that family you're hoping for; then you'll be too busy to visit."

Templeton laughed. "I'll never be too busy to visit, Mama. Never."

THEIR THREE WEEKS IN PHILADELPHIA flew by. While John was off meeting with bankers, Templeton visited with her nieces and nephews, called on friends she hadn't seen in over a year, and even stopped in to chat with Lucille Bransfield, the women's wear buyer at Wanamaker.

When Templeton turned to leave, Lucille hugged her warmly. "If you ever decide to expand the business, Wanamaker's would definitely be interested in carrying the new line."

Although Templeton had promised her parents that each summer she'd stay on for another three weeks after John returned to California, she now had to tell them she couldn't. She explained how this was the launch of an exclusive collection with the Emporium, and she had to be there in September to approve the production samples.

"This year it's just impossible for me to stay," she said. "But next year I'll more than make up for it. I swear I will. Once the production schedule is set up and running smoothly, I'll be able to take more time off. Next summer we'll do all the things we didn't get to this year."

"Next summer seems so far away," Eleanor said and gave a fragile smile.

"It does to me too," Templeton replied and kissed her mama's cheek.

She promised that the very day they arrived back in San Francisco, she'd start designing the 1905 spring collection.

"Once that's done, I'll get to work on the winter collection and be done by June. With the winter season ready ahead of time, I'll be able to stay the full six weeks, perhaps even longer."

It was a promise Templeton intended to keep.

The Price of Success

IN 1905 TEMPLETON'S BUSINESS GREW by leaps and bounds. The winter collection was an overwhelming success, and Bellingham immediately suggested they expand the spring collection. At first he spoke of including more elaborate dinner gowns, which, with the added layers of lace and beading, already presented production problems. Then the first week of January he called another meeting.

Sitting behind his massive desk with a curl of cigar smoke rising above him, he announced that the Emporium wanted Templeton to add a line of children's dresses to the spring collection.

"I believe that by adding a premier line of children's dresses to our already successful women's wear collection, we will position the Emporium as San Francisco's preeminent department store for families."

"I'd love to do it," Templeton replied, "but that timeline is not feasible. The factories are already working on our women's wear collection, and they're booked solid. I don't see how I could finish the designs and—"

"Perhaps you didn't understand me." He pushed back his chair and stood, towering over both Templeton and Mildred Kent. "I intend to have a collection of children's dresses on the floor of the Emporium this spring, regardless of what it takes to make that happen."

"I can make time to do the designs, but when it comes to manu-facturing…"

The rest of her thought vanished when Bellingham glared at her.

"Miss Morehouse, debuting a children's dress collection would make you the featured designer here at the Emporium. Your brand would practically be synonymous with the Emporium name. Now, if you feel you can't handle it…"

That thought dangled in front of Templeton, tempting her as never before. It was the dream she'd chased for so many years. Her desire for motherhood picked at her for a few seconds, reminding her of what happened a year earlier, but in the end the fiery nature of the little girl who wanted to be a designer above all else won out.

"I'll make it happen, sir," she said. "Rest assured, I'll make it happen."

Bellingham looked at Mildred with that same unyielding glare. "Miss Kent, do you have any qualms about adding children's dresses?"

"Not at all sir," she answered. "However, I'd suggest we handle this as we did the women's wear collection. By starting with a few basic dresses and a selection of alternative trims, we could test the market, see what sells and what doesn't; then we focus on the more successful designs and perhaps include them in our fall fashion show."

Bellingham fingered his beard then gave a nod.

"Not a bad idea," he said. "That would minimize our risk, and we'd still be first on the market."

IN THE DAYS THAT FOLLOWED, Templeton, George, Denise, and Mildred Kent hammered out a program to have nine versions of three basic children's dresses in the store by mid-June. It was a breakneck schedule that barely left time for breathing, never mind starting on the winter collection as Templeton had planned to do.

Toward the end of March, she wrote her mama a letter saying it was doubtful she'd get to stay on for three extra weeks when they came to Philadelphia that summer.

Nothing seems to be happening the way I'd thought, she wrote. *There's been no baby and no free time. John and I seldom have an evening to ourselves, and if it weren't for George I don't know what I'd do.*

It seemed obvious that Mildred Kent felt the same way about George, because every time she had the tiniest little problem, she'd call him in for another meeting. Three times she suggested he make it at noon, saying they could then discuss things over lunch. While George was busy placating Mildred, Templeton was the one who had to run back and forth to the factory and Charlie became increasingly impossible to deal with.

On a day when two of the sewing machine operators ran out of trim fabric and had to stop working, he was in a mood to match no other. When Templeton arrived to check on what had gone wrong, he almost chased her out of the shop.

"Haphazard women have no place in business!" he screamed. Then he threatened to stop production of the entire job if George wasn't there to deal with the problem the next day.

In February, when the wind howled and the rain peppered the ground, it seemed as if each day brought a new crisis. A trim the wrong color, a seamstress who hadn't shown up for work, a machine with a bobbin that tangled the threads. Before Templeton could finish the master pattern layout for the children's dresses, she received a call saying that the fabric she'd selected for one of the dresses was no longer available. It was back to the drawing board. When they switched the ivory cotton voile to a stark white, she had to redo the pattern pieces to incorporate a colored underskirt.

The hectic pace continued throughout March and into April with one problem following the other. The fabric for the children's dresses didn't arrive until the ninth of May, and after almost four months of trying to hold things together Templeton was beginning to wonder if having a career was really worth it.

Caught up in the endless barrage of problematic ribbon trims, mismatched eyelet ruffles, and scheduling errors, her plans of having a baby got pushed aside. Not because she didn't care; she did. Very much. But the business had somehow turned into a hungry monster that consumed every minute of her time. Regardless of how early she started or how late she worked, there was always a list of things left undone. And it didn't help that Bellingham was always there with reminders of how this was the opportunity of a lifetime.

"Do you realize most designers would give their eye teeth for a chance such as this?" he'd ask offhandedly. It hit home and strengthened her resolve.

Inside Templeton's heart, a war waged. At times her desire to have a baby threatened to rise up and overcome the drive that pushed her from one day to the next, but then she'd hear Bellingham's words echoing through her brain and push on. She went from month to month checking the calendar, planning for the days when she'd be most likely to conceive, then arriving home so exhausted that she could do nothing but fall into bed. Instead of making love every night as she'd planned, it would happen once or twice. When her period arrived right on time, she again felt shattered.

After the letter she received saying Clara had given birth to another baby girl, she was despondent for two days.

"Four," she sobbed. "Why should Clara have four beautiful children when I've yet to have one?"

John tried to comfort her saying it would happen in time, but she was inconsolable.

"It's this damned business," she wailed. "It's taken over my life."

Twice he suggested that she lay it on the line with Bellingham, quit kowtowing to his every whim, and tell him that she didn't want the Emporium's business.

"But I do want it," she'd echoed remorsefully. Then she'd repeated Bellingham's words. "Don't you understand this is the opportunity of a lifetime?"

In June, the month Templeton had thought she would finish her designs and patterns for the forthcoming winter collection, she was doing a last-minute repair to the collar of a dress that would be worn in the fashion show. When the models paraded across the stage the following Saturday, Bellingham was standing beside her. He beamed each time the audience erupted in a burst of applause.

"Aren't you pleased with the changes we've made?" he asked.

She gave a slight nod. Last November she'd been thrilled at the reception the winter designs received, but this summer she found it hard to get excited over anything other than the fact the collection was finished.

Seconds after Mildred Kent stepped onto the stage and told the audience the salesgirls were now ready to take orders for both the women's and children's dresses, Bellingham turned to Templeton and asked when he could expect to see the designs for next November's show.

"I wasn't planning to do new sketches," she said. "Since last year's program of mix-and-match pieces was so successful, I thought we could simply reuse that basic concept. I'll update the collection with new fabrics, more vibrant colors, some—"

"No, no, no." Bellingham's beard bristled as he spoke. "The Emporium has a reputation to uphold! Customers expect a certain level of quality at our store. When they attend our fashion show, they expect to see something *new*, something exciting. They most certainly do not come to see a do-over of last year's styles."

"But it's mid-June now, I can't possibly—"

"You can and you will," he said emphatically. "You've got six weeks, but I expect to see new sketches by the end of July."

"We'll be away in July. I won't be back until mid-August. There's no way I can—"

He raised his hand, palm out. "I am not interested in hearing excuses. You have a job to do. Either you're going to do it, or I get someone else."

"But you told me that if I came through on the spring line, I'd be the Emporium's resident designer for—"

"And you will be, as long as you continue to produce the type of goods our customers have a right to expect."

Templeton argued that with different trims and bolder colors the winter collection would appear new, but Bellingham refused to listen.

Despite the success of the show, that night she went home feeling lower than she'd ever felt in her entire life. It seemed as though the life she had was nothing like the one she'd planned. When she arrived home, May Ling was coming through the hallway. Templeton passed her by with little more than a nod, then hurried up the stairs and fell across the bed. She wept as though her heart was broken, which in fact it was.

WHEN JOHN CAME IN A short while later, he asked if Templeton was home.

May Ling gave a solemn nod. "Missy not good. She close door, no talk."

"What's wrong? Is she sick? Did something happen at the show?"

May Ling shrugged. "She no say."

John turned and bounded up the staircase.

"Templeton," he called out as he burst through the bedroom door.

She was lying across the bed, face down, still in the suit she'd worn that morning. He squatted beside the bed, his face inches from hers. Brushing back a cluster of curls that had fallen across her cheek, he lifted her chin and kissed her forehead.

His touch was soft and gentle, his voice filled with concern. "What's wrong?"

"Everything," she said and sniffed back a sob.

He sat beside her and massaged the back of her neck. "I doubt that it's everything. You're still here, I'm still here, we still have each other. Maybe if we talk about—"

"What good will it do to talk?" she moaned. "Talking changes nothing. We've been married almost two years, and I still don't have a baby. Now, if I don't drop everything and do a new collection for the Emporium, I won't have a business either."

John drew back with a look of confusion. "What happened? Was today's show not a success?"

"The show was fine, but it wasn't enough to satisfy Bellingham. He wants more."

"More of what?"

"Sketches, designs. I was going to re-work the mix-and-match pieces from last year's winter collection, but he said that's not good enough. He got really snippy and told me the Emporium's customers expect something new, and if I can't do it he'll get another designer."

"So let him," John said angrily. "The Emporium is not your life. It's a damned department store. You don't need Bellingham or the store. You can be successful on your own, or you can stop working altogether. I've put up with all this nonsense because I thought it made you happy and if it's not then—"

"Being a designer does make me happy. At least for now. Once we have a family I'll have a reason to stay home, but until then I don't."

"For heaven's sake, Templeton, have a little patience. Give it time. You conceived once, and there's no reason to think you won't again. Until then, you could just relax and enjoy life."

Her eyes again grew misty. "But I wouldn't enjoy life. I'd sit around here day after day thinking about how I was a failure at being a mother *and* a designer."

"You haven't failed anything. Yours was one of the most successful showings the Emporium ever had. There's no need for you to cave to Bellingham. Leave the Emporium, and start designing for the City of Paris or I. Magnin."

"Once word gets out that I failed to deliver a collection while I was under contract to the Emporium, no department store is going to want me. Especially not the City of Paris."

John gave a lumbering sigh and shook his head. "You're not happy staying there and you don't want to leave, so what do you see as the answer?"

Templeton gave a half-hearted shrug. "Postpone the trip to Philadelphia, I guess. Then do the sketches as quickly as possible and go in the fall or maybe at Christmastime."

"I'm okay with that, if it's what you want to do."

"It's not what I want to do; it's what I have to do," she said ruefully.

And that's how it happened.

Two days later she wrote to her mother saying they would not be coming in July as she'd thought.

We're not cancelling the trip, just postponing it, she wrote.

She promised they'd come later in the year after the winter designs were approved and the patterns finished.

At that point the production can move ahead without me, she said, *then we can stay a bit longer, perhaps even have Thanksgiving with the family.*

Before she signed the letter, a tear splatted on the paper and smudged the sentence saying how much she was looking forward to seeing Clara's new baby. After blotting it away, she folded the letter into the envelope and sent it off.

TEMPLETON DELIVERED THE SKETCHES ON time, and all went well. But after the sketches there was finalization of the designs, then fabric swatches to be selected, cloth to be ordered, trims to be coordinated, pattern layout to be determined, patterns to be cut. Working with Charlie had become so difficult that she ultimately had to find a new manufacturing company and, after that, skilled finishers.

The summer turned to fall, and her mama sent pictures of Clara's new baby who was now sitting up in the carriage and laughing. Betsy, a toddler the year she and John were married, looked big enough to be starting school. The kids were all bundled in heavy sweaters, yet there in San Francisco the afternoons were still warm enough to go without so much as a shawl.

When Eleanor wrote that the oak in the front yard was already turning color, Templeton grew more homesick than ever and vowed to have the designs for the spring collection ready by early December so they could spend Christmas in Philadelphia. The problem was that when she sat at the drawing table trying to imagine the floaty dresses of spring, the only picture that came to mind was that of her nieces bundled in sweaters. Then she'd drift off to remembering the smell of her mama's pumpkin pie or chestnuts roasting in the oven.

A week before Christmas, she and John set a small Christmas tree on the table by the front window and decorated it with silver balls and tinsel. Templeton had thought having the tree would make her feel better, but it didn't. Instead it brought to mind the big tree that was probably standing in her mama's parlor. On Christmas Day she stood at the window wishing for even a single snowflake, but there again she was disappointed. The afternoon was balmy enough for nothing more than a lightweight jacket.

The despondency that haunted Templeton over the Christmas holiday ultimately fueled a new level of determination, and before January had come to a close she'd cranked out enough drawings for the entire spring collection. She pinned the drawings to the wall, dusted the charcoal from her hands, and stepped back to admire them.

They were good. Truly good. Bellingham was almost guaranteed to approve. She looked at the calendar and started mapping out a plan: a week for fabric selection and approvals, another for ordering cloth and setting up the production schedule, two weeks for pattern layout and cutting. Then she could be off.

That evening she told John he could go ahead and book a compartment on the train.

"We'll go in March," she said confidently.

He raised an eyebrow. "You're sure? You wouldn't rather I wait until you've shown Bellingham the collection?"

"I'm positive," she replied. "He'll like it. I know he will."

AS IT TURNED OUT, SHE was right. Bellingham loved the collection, and Mildred Kent said it was the best yet. The cloth was ordered, the trims specified, the patterns cut, and the remainder of the production was then turned over to George.

"We're leaving for Philadelphia on March tenth," Templeton told him. "If there's a question about fabric you can work with Denise, and if it's a timing issue work with Mildred. I'm certain you'll do just fine without me."

George gave a nod and grinned. "Don't worry about me. Just go and have a good time."

"I'm not the least bit worried," she said. And truthfully speaking, she wasn't.

Templeton

RIGHT NOW, I AM HAPPIER than I have been in ages. Tomorrow we leave for Philadelphia, and I'm thrilled at the thought of seeing everyone again. Mama promised she and Daddy will be at the train to meet us, and I'm pretty sure she'll keep that promise. The truth is, I think she's missed me almost as much as I've missed her. I say almost because it is utterly impossible for anyone to miss anyone as much as I've missed Mama these past eighteen months.

For the first time since I've been working with the Emporium, I am completely caught up and even ahead of schedule on almost everything. The factory will start working on the spring collection while I'm away, and George will handle everything. I don't have to do anything else until May 10th. That's when we'll have the production samples ready for approval.

This means I can stay in Philadelphia for another four weeks after John returns to San Francisco. It's a very long time for us to be apart, and for sure I'll end up missing him as much as I'm missing Mama right now, but it will be worth it to spend time with Mama and the family. When I married John and moved out here, I had no idea that I'd get as homesick as I've been. Yes, I knew it was 3,000 miles, but I didn't realize how terribly far that actually was.

Don't misunderstand, it's not that I regret marrying John; given the choice, I'd do it all over again. He's the best husband in the world. Most men would insist their wife not work and stay home so dinner is ready on the dot of six, but not John. He encourages me, says if working as a designer is what makes me happy then he's all for it.

Last year everything that could go wrong did, and there were days when I myself wondered if I really wanted to keep designing, but this year it's totally different. I'm happy with the work I'm doing and now that John and I can spend more time together, I'm thinking it won't be long before there's a baby on the way.

1905 may have been a terrible year, but that's all behind me. 1906 is going to be fabulous; that's something I can say for certain.

The Homecoming

THE MORNING THE TRAIN PULLED out of Union Station, a weight lifted from Templeton's shoulders. The knot that had troubled the back of her neck was suddenly gone, as were her worries that something would go wrong. Before the city had disappeared from view, she was humming "Yankee Doodle Dandy" and jiggling her foot as if she were ready to dance.

That afternoon John had the porter bring a bottle of wine and sandwiches, and rather than going to the dining car, they remained in the compartment. They made love, then talked and laughed as they hadn't in a very long time. The next evening when they had dinner in the dining car, her cheeks were aglow. After her second glass of champagne, she told John this trip was every bit as pleasurable as the one they'd taken for their honeymoon.

While their last trip had seemed unbearably slow, this one flew by. When the train arrived in Philadelphia, Templeton could hardly believe they were already there. She peered from the window, caught sight of her mama and daddy standing on the platform, and knew this visit was going to be everything she'd anticipated.

Before the week was out, Templeton had settled in as if she'd never left Philadelphia. In the morning she and Eleanor lingered over coffee. Then she spent the afternoon visiting friends, shopping at Wanamaker's, or strolling down East Market Street to browse the window displays at Strawbridge & Clothier.

On their first shopping expedition, Templeton bought a Brownie camera and snapped a picture of her mama standing in front of the ice cream shop. From that day forward, she carried the camera with her everywhere she went. She took pictures of everyone and everything she wanted to remember, including a day when the sky was drizzling and Eleanor fussed that her hair wasn't right. Templeton snapped the picture anyway.

"I want to remember things just the way they are," she said, then told how she planned to pin the pictures to the wall in her studio. "That way, if we get to talk on the telephone, I'll have you right there in front of me."

Twice they had dinner at Clara's and once at Benjamin's, but most evenings were spent at home. Albert and John sat in the parlor discussing business or politics while Templeton and her mama remained in the kitchen catching up on all the stories they'd been waiting to tell.

In what seemed like little more than the blink of an eye, the first three weeks were gone. That evening as John was packing his bag for the trip home, Templeton grew teary.

"I'm going to miss you something fierce," she said.

He smiled then slid his finger beneath her chin and tilted her face to his. "I'll miss you too, but I think the next four weeks will be here and gone before you know it. You'll be so busy I doubt you'll even have time to miss me."

"Sure, I'll be busy but that doesn't mean—"

He silenced her with a kiss. "There are no buts. You deserve this time with your family. Enjoy it. Just don't forget you've got a husband and a home in San Francisco."

That night, after her parents had gone to bed, Templeton and John went for a stroll and ended up in the park where he'd first asked her to marry him. As they sat beside the lake and reminisced about that night, he asked, "Do you ever regret saying yes?"

She turned to him wide-eyed. "Heavens, no. How could you even ask such a thing?"

He gave a one-shouldered shrug. "You're different when you're here with your family. Happier than I've seen you in a long time, and I can't help but wonder if it's because—"

She touched her finger to his lips. "Not another word. Yes, I'm happy to see my family, and I do wish they weren't so far away, but loving you is the greatest happiness I've ever known. I wouldn't trade that for anything in the world."

"Good, because I'm not up for trade," he said with a warm laugh. Wrapping his arm around her shoulders, he pulled her closer. "I know how much you like it here in Philadelphia, so I've been trying to build up my East Coast liaisons. This trip I met a lot of new investment financiers, and I expect to be doing business with several of them. If it happens, maybe next year we can both stay for the summer."

JOHN LEFT THE NEXT MORNING. Templeton accompanied him to the station and at the last minute snapped a picture as he was boarding the train. She planned to take a second one when he waved to her from the window, but seconds after he climbed aboard the train pulled out. As she stood there watching it disappear down the track, a huge emptiness settled in her chest. Four weeks was a terribly long time for them to be apart.

As she left the station, she began to wonder if staying on like this had been a foolhardy move. There were a dozen reasons why she should have left with John and only a handful of reasons for staying. Yes, she enjoyed spending time with her mama, but now that they'd already shared most of the stories they had to tell, there was considerably less to talk about. Besides, having three cups of coffee in the morning was playing havoc with her stomach. Over the past two days, she'd begun to feel a bit nauseous.

A driver standing at the side of the curb asked if she wanted to hire a carriage.

"No thanks," she said and kept walking.

Lost in thought, she moved so slowly that at times you could almost believe she'd stopped. By the time she made it back to the house, Eleanor was near frantic.

"Where on earth have you been?" she asked.

"Been?" Templeton said. "I haven't been anywhere. I saw John off at the train station and then came home."

"That was over four hours ago! I was about to send your daddy out to look for you."

"There was no need. I just wanted to walk."

Albert looked up from his newspaper and glowered at Templeton. "The station's over two miles away. Didn't you think to hire a carriage or take the trolley?"

Templeton blinked and turned to him with a bewildered expression. "Take the trolley where, Daddy?"

Albert rolled his eyes and went back to his newspaper.

THAT NIGHT TEMPLETON RETIRED EARLIER than usual. She was bone weary and thought sleep would come the moment she closed her eyes, but it didn't. The room was dark with only a tiny splinter of moonlight peeking through the curtain, and in the stillness of night she heard sounds that now seemed unfamiliar.

She missed John more than she'd thought possible. She'd slept in this same bed for most of her life, but without him beside her it seemed lumpier and less comfortable. At first she was too warm, but after she folded the blanket back her shoulders were chilled. She kept thinking of him, wondering where the train was now; most likely it had crossed over into Ohio and was now speeding toward Indiana. With every minute that ticked by, he was another mile farther away.

Trying to push the sorrow of that thought from her mind, she turned to wondering about the business. Had the bolts of fabric arrived? Had a piece of a pattern suddenly gone missing? Did Mildred Kent have an issue that needed her attention?

Those thoughts were there and gone in an instant. George would have telephoned if there was a problem. He hadn't called, so it seemed obvious that everything was moving along exactly as planned.

When the moon moved across the sky, the room grew darker still. She snuggled deeper into the bed, pulling the blanket up to her chin. Tomorrow she would visit Clara, and they would take the girls to the park. The girls tugging her this way and that, calling out for Auntie Templeton and begging for ice cream would certainly take her mind off of John. Yes, a visit with Clara and the girls was precisely what she needed; then she'd be able to relax and enjoy the remainder of her visit.

Turning on her side, Templeton closed her eyes, but just as she started to drift off the whistle of a train sounded in the distance and she gave way to the tears.

IN THE WEEKS THAT FOLLOWED, Templeton made plans for every day: lunch with her friends, Lydia and Josephine, visits with Benjamin's family, shopping trips to Wanamaker's, even a lunch date with her daddy, which was a first. When she arrived at his office, he smiled and said he was surprised to see her without her mama.

"I thought it would be nice for just the two of us to spend time together," she said. As they left the office, she latched onto his arm the same way she did with John.

Albert patted her hand and smiled. "It is nice; very nice."

Most mornings Templeton spent at home with her mama. Long after Albert had left for the office, the two of them remained at the breakfast table chatting about one thing and another. Twice Templeton complained that the coffee was upsetting her stomach.

"It tastes different," she said, wrinkling her nose.

"It's the same as always," Eleanor maintained. "There's a touch of chicory in the coffee because that's how your daddy likes it, but I've been making it the same way since before you were born." She went on to say perhaps Templeton was coming down with a stomach bug.

After that Eleanor began brewing a pot of chamomile tea each morning.

"Try this," she said, setting the tea on the table. "It might be easier on your stomach."

For two days, Templeton felt fine but then on the third day she threw up her entire breakfast.

"I don't feel one bit well," she said. "I think I'll cancel my plans to go bicycling with Durene today."

Eleanor nodded. "It won't hurt to take it easy for a day or two. With all the visiting and running around you're doing, you've probably exhausted yourself."

Although Templeton didn't argue the point, she doubted such was the case. Back in San Francisco she'd often been on the run from dawn 'til dark, and not once did it cause her to have an upset stomach. Missing

John; that's what was to blame for the way she was feeling. She'd been fine right up until the day he left; then she'd started having sleepless nights and an aversion to certain foods.

It was the same way for three days in a row. In the morning she'd be sick as a dog, and by afternoon ready to go shopping or visit with friends.

"I just don't understand it," she said. "Is it possible there's some of that chicory in the tea?"

Eleanor shook her head. "Nothing but chamomile." She hesitated a moment then suggested Templeton spend the day at home. "It's a beautiful day, warm enough for us to sit on the porch and crochet."

Templeton laughed. "Crochet? I don't know how to crochet."

"I'll teach you. I'm working on a blanket that I'm anxious to finish. You can help."

Eleanor took two baskets from the top shelf of the pantry and carried them to the porch. The first basket was filled with skeins of wool in pastel colors: pinks, blues, pale yellow, ivory. The second basket held stacks of granny squares in those same colors. Scooting her chair closer to Templeton, she took a skein of ivory-colored wool and a crochet hook and began.

"I got this pattern from the Butterick magazine," she said and pulled her hook through a doubled-over piece of yarn. Working slowly enough for Templeton to follow along, she formed the yarn into a circle then set it aside. "That's the center of the square. Once that's done, you change colors and move on to the next row. It's the same stitch, repeated over and over again, easy as pie."

With the sun warm on their shoulders they worked side by side all afternoon, but it wasn't until Eleanor began to join the squares together that Templeton noticed something.

"Mama, this looks like a baby blanket. Is that what we're making?"

Eleanor nodded. "I started it a while back, then set it aside. Now I need to get it finished."

Templeton gave a heavily weighted sigh. "Don't tell me Clara is having another—"

"It's not for Clara."

"Then who?"

Eleanor gave a sly smile. "You."

Templeton shook her head vigorously. "Not me, Mama. I'm not—"

"Are you absolutely sure?"

"Well, of course, I am. Don't you think I'd know…"

Her words trailed off as she thought back, trying to recall exactly when it was she'd had her last monthly. Before they left San Francisco; she was certain of that. In the rush of getting everything finalized for the trip, she hadn't thought to check her calendar.

How long had it been? Days? Weeks? Tears filled her eyes, then overflowed and ran down her cheeks.

"Dear God, after all this time, do you think it's possible that—"

Eleanor gave a nod. "More than possible. I always enjoyed the sweet tobacco-like smell of roasted chicory, but when I was carrying you I couldn't stand to be near it." She laughed. "For the whole nine months, your daddy had to do without the chicory in his coffee and he didn't like it one bit."

As they sat and talked, the thought that she was carrying a child settled in Templeton's heart, took root, and began to blossom. It was like the early crocuses, peeking out from beneath the frozen ground, tender and shy at first, then growing bolder and more hopeful. She wanted desperately to run to the telephone, call John, and tell him that after all those months of trying it had finally happened, but there was a whisper of doubt still clinging to her mind. What if she was wrong?

For the remainder of that day, Templeton could think of nothing else. She pictured herself growing big and round, the upstairs studio turned into a nursery, a rocking chair beside the window, the baby at her breast. She could easily imagine the wide grin on John's face when he learned that he would at long last be a father, and the thrill of sharing such news was what ultimately made her decide to wait and tell him when she arrived home in San Francisco. By then she'd be two months along and would know for certain.

That evening Albert complained that the after-dinner coffee was weak and flavorless.

"There's no chicory in it," Eleanor said. "And I'm afraid there won't be until after Templeton leaves."

"Dagnabbit," he blustered. "This is my house, and if I want—"

Eleanor reached across and covered his hand with hers. "Relax, Albert. I believe our baby is having a baby. The chicory bothers her the same as it did me."

His face softened. "Well, I'll be…"

"I'm not one hundred percent sure yet," Templeton added, "so if you talk to John, don't say anything. I want to wait and tell him in person."

"Understood." The corner of Albert's mouth tilted upward with amusement. "Well, I guess I can do with weak coffee for a while."

"It's already April 12th Daddy, so it'll only be for another 8 days. I leave here a week from Friday, and I've already got my train reservation."

THAT LAST WEEK, TEMPLETON CURTAILED her socializing and spent countless hours sitting on the front porch with her mama. They finished the baby blanket and wrapped it in muslin for the trip home. The swing became the place where Templeton told her mama about the fears, hopes, and dreams she had for the baby. Eleanor listened and, doing as mamas have done since the start of time, assured her that such worries were normal.

"With being on the train for four days, you'll have to exercise caution," she said. "Try to relax, remain seated, and don't go from car to car when the train is moving."

"I plan to stay in the compartment the whole time," Templeton replied. "It's smaller than the one John and I shared, but there's plenty of room to stretch out and put my feet up. I'll ring for the porter to bring my food, so I won't even have to go to the dining car."

When she'd first spoken of staying on, John had insisted she have the compartment for the return trip. She'd argued that she was perfectly capable of traveling in a coach as he did, but he wouldn't hear of it.

"How capable you are is not the issue," he'd said. "It's simply not safe for a woman to be traveling alone."

Now that she'd be carrying such a precious bundle, she was glad he'd prevailed.

By Tuesday, most of Templeton's luggage was packed and ready to go. The only exception was the small train case that she'd carry into the compartment. She was as excited about returning home as she'd been coming here.

That night as she lay in bed thinking about the trip, she realized that after being in Philadelphia for almost seven weeks, she now saw San Francisco as home. A soft chuckle rose from her throat. She'd foolishly wasted three years pining for home when she'd been there all along. Home wasn't a city or state. It was where her life was, where her husband was waiting, where her business was, where she'd soon be raising a family.

With a blanket of contentment warming her, she turned on her side and fell fast asleep.

While the City Slept

WHEN JOHN WENT TO BED Tuesday night, he was feeling on top of the world. He'd spent the evening with the president of Pacific Iron Works, the construction engineer, and the architect who was designing their new building. Although it had taken almost six hours, they'd hammered out a contract to fund the financing of the new factory. This deal was by far the largest John had ever worked on, and it meant that he and Templeton would now be able to afford that house on Nob Hill.

Once the terms of the mortgage on the property were settled, he'd gone to dinner with the Pacific Iron group and Harold Meyers, the consulting engineer. Afterward Harold had insisted they celebrate with a brandy. The first one led to a second, then a third and fourth before Harold was ready to call it a night. Earlier that evening John had planned to telephone Templeton and tell her the good news, but by the time he got back to the house it was late and he was feeling that last brandy.

THREE WEEKS EARLIER, JOHN HAD returned to San Francisco with a cooperative of new financiers, thanks to Albert Whittier. One of the partners in Albert's firm had a brother who was a key player in the Philadelphia Stock Exchange. That introduction ultimately led to a dozen more, all of them men with a measure of capital to invest and an interest in San Francisco's booming economy.

"Opportunities like this won't last forever," John had said. "The investors who buy in early are the ones who stand to make the greatest gains." He went on to explain how new construction projects could be seen from one end of the city to the other. "In addition to the houses, there are multi-storied office buildings and factories."

Most of the men were willing to risk fairly moderate amounts—five or ten thousand—which is what led him to suggest they set up a cooperative that would enable them to finance a few major construction projects.

Stephen Meissner was the exception. He had a far bigger bankroll than any of the others and was willing to add fifty thousand to the cooperative if John had something of interest.

"We've got plenty of small business and housing investment opportunities right here in Philadelphia," he said. "I'm looking for something big, more substantial."

John said he had a contact at Pacific Iron Works and knew for certain they had plans for another factory. At that point, Meissner leaned into the conversation and started to show interest.

After a brief overview of the way the Pacific Iron deal would be structured, John told the group, "If you're looking for long-term stability, this investment is rock solid."

"It sounds interesting," Meissner said, "but how do we know for sure you can get it?"

"I've done some machinery financing for Pacific, and my man is on the inside."

Meissner raised an eyebrow. "So you say, but does your guy have enough weight to influence a deal like this?"

"I can almost guarantee he does."

"Then show us that guarantee, and we'll do the financing." He went on to say his offer was good until May 1st. If John could produce a contract by then, the cooperative would be in for the full amount. If the contract wasn't signed by then, the offer would be withdrawn.

Since then John had worked night and day on getting every last detail nailed down. Tonight he'd finalized the deal.

WEARY FROM THE HOURS OF negotiations and woozy from the brandy, John climbed under the coverlet and was sound asleep in seconds. He didn't hear the thundering roar that rolled across the city, but when a cascade of bricks rained down on him he woke with an agonizing scream. Forcing his eyes open, he watched Templeton's dressing table slide across the room and slam into the wall. It broke apart, the mirror shattering into a million tiny shards of glass.

Earthquake.

The house shuddered and shook for another few moments then stopped and left an eerie silence behind. Nothing was as it was before. The room was pitched forward, the foot of the bed angled toward the window, the blanket chest half in and half out of the doorway. Seconds later the silence was shattered by the sound of something in the upstairs studio crashing to the floor. The house groaned and threatened to shift again.

John had to move. He had to get out before the building collapsed. Digging his elbows into the mattress, he tried to push himself into a sitting position, but when he leaned on his right arm, an excruciating pain shot across his shoulder. He could now see that the chimney had collapsed, and his legs were buried beneath a pile of plaster and bricks. Without enough upper body strength to drag himself from beneath the rubble, he had to find a way to get the weight off of his legs if he wanted to get out.

He lifted the first brick and dropped it to the floor. It was something a child should have been able to do, yet this tiny bit of movement felt like a Herculean task. Every movement was like a baseball bat slamming into his shoulder. Before he could clear away even a handful of bricks, the house began to tremble again.

Unable to move and fearing he would die here, a sense of dread settled in John's chest and he fell back thinking of Templeton. There would be no last goodbye, no promise that he would continue to watch over her from a heavenly realm, no guidance as to where the insurance policies were or how she could hold onto his business. As all the things he'd forgotten to tell her flashed through his mind, the house gave a violent shudder and lurched forward. Made of carved oak and too heavy for a man to lift, the blanket chest slid back across the floor and knocked the mattress off of the bedframe. The bed tumbled over, and John went with it.

When he fell, he came down hard against the floor and the pain of it caused him to black out. He again opened his eyes and saw he'd been freed from the bricks. Grabbing hold of the broken bed post, he used it as a crutch and tried to pull himself to his feet. He almost made it, but the moment he put pressure on his right leg it buckled. A blinding pain brought tears to his eyes.

Unable to walk, the best he could do was stand on his left leg and thrust himself toward the door, grabbing onto pieces of broken or overturned furniture as he went.

The center hall was less than eight feet away, but by the time John made it a slick of sweat covered his face and his heart hammered against his chest. Believing he could maneuver himself down the stairs if he grabbed hold of the banister, he lunged forward and stretched out his arm. His fingertips grazed the rail, and he fell to the floor.

The pain following the fall was so horrific that he lay there, unable to move anything, unable to even think about moving anything. How long he was there, John couldn't say. Minutes, maybe longer, but for now the house had ceased its moving. This was a small window of opportunity, a moment of reprieve before the aftershocks started. Snaking across the landing on his belly, he grabbed onto the banister and inched his way over to the stairs.

With his right leg now swollen and throbbing, it was impossible to put even the slightest bit of weight on it. There was little he could do but drag it and hope the railing would hold. Standing on his left leg and using the banister to support his weight, he tried jumping from one step to the next. He'd barely made it down four steps when the railing started to give way.

He dropped back onto the step and sat there long enough to catch his breath, then started scooting down the stairs on his backside. Each time he moved from one step to the next, a thrust of pain ricocheted up his spine and down the throbbing leg.

Halfway down, he heard sounds in the street—people talking, a child crying, someone hollering for a wagon. He called out for help, but no one came. His voice was smothered under the cries of anguish coming from outside.

His arm trembled, his shoulder ached, his leg throbbed, but he pushed on, moving from one step to the next, stopping just long enough to let the pain subside then moving again. If he could make it out the door, he'd wait for help to come. On the street he'd be safer. If he could get to the street, he wouldn't have to worry about the house collapsing on top of him.

If he could call for help... If he could make it to the street...

When he finally reached the bottom of the stairs, John's back was raw and bloody from scraping against the wooden steps, but he started feeling hopeful. The living room seemed reasonably intact, and he could see the door. After crawling the short distance to where he could grab hold of an overstuffed chair, he pulled himself up. Lurching from one piece of furniture to the next, he crossed the room, grabbed the door handle, and pulled.

Nothing happened. He pulled at it again and again. As the pain pulsed across his shoulder and his leg throbbed, he yanked and tugged at the door. It refused to budge. He noticed the tilt of the ceiling and knew the entire house had shifted. He was trapped inside the house and would most likely die here.

"No," he screamed. "No, no, no. It's not supposed to happen this way..."

His legs and his hope gave way at the same time. He slid to the floor and covered his face with an arm knowing this time he had lost.

In Philadelphia

TEMPLETON WOKE WITH A START. The sky was still pitch black and the house silent as a graveyard. The last vestige of a dream was lingering on the edge of her mind, but she couldn't remember the dream in its entirety. She was supposed to warn somebody of something, but who and what she couldn't say. She knew only that she'd been frightened and felt her heart racing; that much she was certain of.

She climbed from the bed, pushed aside the window curtain, and stood looking up into the night sky. An uneasiness that she hadn't felt before settled in her chest. She missed John something fierce and was anxious to get home; home to San Francisco. Four weeks was too long for them to be apart. Especially now.

She held her hand to her stomach hoping to feel a tiny movement, a sign there was a life growing inside of her. There was nothing but the fuzzy edge of nausea that had been with her the past few weeks. She touched her breast. There she did feel a difference. They were fuller, heavier, and tender. As she stood thinking about the baby that would come before Christmas, thoughts of the nightmare were eventually forgotten.

THAT MORNING ALBERT HAD BREAKFAST, read his newspaper, then left the house at 8:30. He took the trolley into town and settled at his

151

desk as he always did. There was absolutely nothing extraordinary about the day until Ernest Maxwell stuck his head in the door looking like he'd seen a ghost.

"Good God!" Ernest exclaimed. "Have you heard the news?"

Albert glanced up from the pile of documents he'd been studying. "I've read this morning's paper, but I didn't see anything—"

"It just happened less than an hour ago! A huge earthquake hit San Francisco. They're saying half the city has been—"

"Who's saying?"

"Pete, my brother-in-law. He got it off the ticker tape. They claim hundreds have been killed, half the city destroyed, and…"

Albert glanced at this watch. Nine o'clock. If it was nine here, it was only six out there. He grabbed a notebook from the desk drawer, flipped through the pages, and reached for the telephone. Telling the operator he wanted to place a call to San Francisco, he gave her John's home number. He sat listening to the click, click, click, willing the call to go through, praying to hear John's voice on the other end of the line.

Ernest lowered himself into the chair in front of Albert's desk, saying how this quake was supposedly the worst the city had ever seen.

"It's a good thing your daughter is still here in Philadelphia."

"She's here, but her husband has already returned to San Francisco."

Ernest shook his head sympathetically. "That's not good; not good at all."

The operator was back. "The call didn't go through. Are you sure of the number?"

"Try this one instead." Albert gave her John's office number and again waited.

After another series of clicks and a muffled conversation, the operator was back on the line.

"Sorry, sir, but it appears San Francisco has a switching problem. None of our calls are going through. Perhaps if you try later—"

Albert hung up the receiver and sat there, dumbfounded.

"Want me to call Pete and see if he knows anything more?" Ernest asked.

Albert nodded. "Ask how extensive the damage actually is and what area of town took the brunt of it."

As Ernest disappeared out the door, Albert scrubbed his forehead and started wondering what he was going to tell Templeton. He closed the file he'd been working on, slid it to the back of his desk, then hurried down the hall to Ernest's office.

For the better part of an hour, the two men sat together listening to the scraps of news Pete had to pass along. When the anxiety swelled in Albert's chest, he stood and paced from one side of the office to the other. Things went from bad to worse when Pete said the ticker tape was now reporting numerous fires throughout the city. That's when Albert decided to walk down to the Exchange building to see if he could find out something more. He stood around for two hours listening to every new communique: a fire here, another fire there, the water main broken, the fire spreading across Market Street. The entire city in a state of emergency.

When it became obvious that there would be no good news, Albert started for home. The sorrow in his chest was heavier than anything he'd ever known. Templeton would be devastated, but he had to tell her before it became a headline splashed across the front page of the *Evening Telegraph*.

He arrived home just after two, his expression a grim prediction of what was to come. Seeing Eleanor alone in the kitchen, he asked, "Where's Templeton?"

"Upstairs napping. She didn't sleep well last night. Anxious about the trip, I imagine."

He kissed her cheek, then with a heavily weighted sigh lowered himself into the chair. "Good. It might be easier if we talk first and then you can—"

"Talk about what, Albert? Is something wrong?"

He nodded and told her of what had happened and how he'd found out about it.

"According to the ticker tape, this one was big; really big. Destroyed one whole section of the city, snapped the water main, left hundreds dead—"

Eleanor clutched her chest. "Did you call John? Is he okay?"

Albert gave a weary shrug. "I called, but the wires are down. Nothing is going through."

"That's crazy. San Francisco is a big city, surely there's some way to get through."

"I've tried everything. Even went over to the Exchange building hoping to find something more than what Pete said, but it was just more of the same. Damage, fires, the city in shambles…"

When Eleanor's eyes grew watery, he stood and gathered her into his arms. "I don't want to do it, but we've got to tell Templeton before she sees it in the newspaper or hears it from someone else."

Eleanor dropped her head on his shoulder as tears came to her eyes. "She's already lost one baby. I hope to God this doesn't cause her to lose this one."

TEMPLETON CAME DOWNSTAIRS A SHORT while later. Glancing at her father, she smiled.

"I thought I heard your voice, Daddy. What are you doing home so early?" Noticing that he and her mama wore the same woebegone expression, she asked, "Is something wrong?"

Eleanor took her by the hand and tugged her down onto the sofa. "There's been an earthquake in San Francisco, and your daddy thought you should know about it."

Templeton's face went white. "Is John—"

"As far as we know he's okay," Albert said. "The phone lines are down, and I haven't been able to get through—"

"Then you can't possibly know he's okay!" Her voice was shrill and panic-ridden.

Eleanor tightened her grip on Templeton's hand. "Don't worry. Your daddy is trying to find out more, but until he does you've got to stay calm."

"How can you expect me to stay calm with John out there in San Francisco and God-knows-what happening?"

"I know you're worried, but I'm certain he'll call just as soon as the telephone lines are back up and running. Until then there's nothing any of us can do."

Templeton looked at her mama with a grim expression. "There *is* something I can do, Mama. I can go home and try to find my husband."

"That's as foolish a notion as I've ever heard," Albert said. "It takes four days just to get there, and by then John will most likely have called."

"And if I waste four days sitting around and he still hasn't called, what then?"

"We'll cross that bridge when we come to it," Eleanor said. "Until then your job is to take care of that baby you're carrying. If John were here, that's what he'd say."

Although every fiber of her being screamed out *Do something*, Templeton knew what her mama said was true. For over two years they'd been trying to have a baby, and now that it was finally happening she was forced to make a choice too horrible for words. Did she go in search of John, or stay here and safeguard this baby? Knowing there was no good answer, Templeton folded herself over and burst into tears.

THAT EVENING THE *TELEGRAPH* RELAYED the story, just as Albert had feared. It told of the earth opening up and swallowing houses whole, of horses dead in the street, of fires spreading through the Mission District, people standing in the street too frightened to return to their homes, and devastation everywhere. Templeton scoured the article looking for any mention of Jones Street, but there was none. When she read how the City Hall building was in shambles, she felt her blood run cold.

"City Hall is gone," she moaned. "City Hall! It wasn't some flimsy little wooden shack. City Hall was made of steel, stone, and bricks."

Her daddy wrapped his arm around her shoulders. "Templeton, it says parts of the city were destroyed; parts, not the entire city. Let's not assume the worst. John might be okay but unable to call because the telephone wires are down."

"Maybe," Templeton said.

She wanted to believe what her daddy said was true. With all her heart she wanted to, but a sense of dread had settled over her and refused to let go. For every positive point her mama or daddy made, she responded with another disaster, each more horrifying than the other.

"The Valencia Hotel collapsed," she said. "Fell to the ground, crushing everyone inside."

"But John had no reason to be at that hotel," Eleanor argued.

"Maybe not, but George lived in the area. He could have been there."

When she wasn't worrying about John, Templeton worried about

Denise and Isabelle or Mildred Kent or poor old Mrs. Abernathy who lived at the far end of the street. It was as if fear had seeped through her skin and settled in her bones.

ON THURSDAY MORNING, TEMPLETON WAS waiting at the door when the paper boy tossed the *Record* onto the front porch. She snatched it up and stood looking at the front page. "Hundreds dead in San Francisco," the headline read. "Mayor Schmitz calls for federal troops."

Her face lost all trace of color as a wave of nausea swelled and rose into her throat.

She'd hoped to learn that the damage was under control, that the city was returning to normal, but it had grown worse. Far worse. The fires had taken the Emporium, jumped Market Street, and spread. The hospital was gone, and the injured were being treated at Mechanics Pavilion.

"Mechanics Pavilion," she exclaimed. "Where they have circuses and cattle shows…"

Eleanor came up behind her. "Please, Templeton, you've got to sit down and calm yourself." She took the newspaper from her daughter's hand and laid it aside. "I know you don't have much of an appetite, but try to eat something. The baby needs nourishment, even if you don't."

Templeton turned, tears streaming down her cheeks, and lip quivering. "Thousands injured, Mama. Thousands. What if one of them is John or Denise or George? What if they're hungry? Who's going to feed them?"

When Eleanor opened her arms, Templeton fell into them and cried as never before. She cried for John, afraid he was injured and in need of help. She cried for the baby who might never know its daddy, the friends she'd made, the people who counted on her, the house she'd not thought of as home. No matter what anyone said, the tears continued.

"Can't you do something, Albert?" Eleanor asked.

He pressed his fingertips to his brows with a worrisome grimace. "Do what?"

Albert, who usually had the answer to almost anything, now felt stymied. That afternoon he went into the office and began calling every contact he could come up with: business associates, friends, friends of friends. He asked everyone the same question: Did they know anyone in San Francisco, or had they found a way to get through? It was almost four when he spoke to Ed Southe who said his cousin, Henry, lived in Oakland.

"It's just across the bay," Ed said. "I can't say whether or not he'd be able to help you, but he's got a telephone at the office. You could call."

When Albert spoke to Henry, all he got was more bad news. The city was evacuating a number of those who had been injured, ferrying them from San Francisco across to Oakland. Golden Gate Park had become a campground with people sleeping in tents. The fires still burned, and the mayor had now declared martial law. People were warned to stay off the streets, and looters were being shot on sight.

"My daughter's husband is there," Albert said. "She wants to go in search of him."

"A woman alone in a city that's run amuck? That's suicide. Don't even think of it."

When he hung up the telephone, Albert sat there for a long while, his head cradled in his hands, his thoughts scrambling around for what he might tell Templeton.

Not the truth. Anything but the truth.

Pushing back from his desk, Albert started for home, his heart heavy and his thoughts a jumble of emotions. The best he could hope for was that the evening edition of the *Enquirer* did not tell the same story as Henry.

WHEN ALBERT ARRIVED HOME, THE evening edition of the Enquirer was opened up and spread across the dining room table. Eleanor and Templeton sat side by side, one looking as almost desolate as the other.

Eleanor spoke first. "It's bad, Albert. Really bad. The fires are everywhere."

"Everywhere," Templeton echoed. "Even Mechanics Pavilion. The building burned to the ground, and they moved people who were sick and dying to tents in Golden Gate Park. Tents, Daddy, tents! What if John is one of those people? I have got to try and find him."

Eleanor pressed her hand to her forehead. "Are you trying to lose this baby, Templeton? Given the state San Francisco is in, you don't know if you'll have a house to live in or a place to stay! You've got to wait. John will call, I'm certain—"

"Mama, do you think if the situation were reversed, John would wait for me to call? He wouldn't! He'd jump on the first train to come looking for me."

"He's a man! You're a woman, a pregnant woman at that!" Eleanor turned to Albert. "You're her father, do something!"

Albert told of his call to Henry.

"I spoke to a man in Oakland today, and he says the city is not safe for a woman to be walking around alone. There's very little food, no clean water, no place to stay. You may not like what your mama says, Templeton, but she's right. You can't go."

"John made a reservation for me on the Intercontinental Express. He expects me to be on that train," she sniffed. "If he's alive and able to walk, he'll be there at the station, waiting."

Albert shook his head. "No trains are going into San Francisco. They're being used to evacuate people. There are refugees, thousands of them, just trying to get away from the city. If you start to miscarry, there will be no one to help you. The city is already ferrying patients over to the hospital in Oakland. San Francisco's hospital is gone, and the doctors who are still there have their hands full trying to care for the people who were injured. Chances are John is okay and will call when the telephone lines are up, but if he has been hurt, Oakland is where he'll be."

"Then I'll go to Oakland and find him."

Albert's shoulders drooped as he again shook his head. "No. You stay here with your mama. I'll go. I'll find John, and hopefully I can bring him back here."

"Oh, Daddy…" Templeton flung her arms around her father, pressed her face to his chest, and sobbed even louder than before.

The petrified look that clung to Templeton's face had now settled on Eleanor's as well.

"Albert, at your age, I don't think that's such a good idea."

Looking over his daughter's shoulder, Albert dipped his head and gave a whisper thin smile. "It'll be okay, Eleanor. I promise, it'll be okay."

Albert

ELEANOR IS EXTREMELY WORRIED ABOUT me. She doesn't come right out and say it, but I can see it in her face. When people are married as long as we've been, you don't need words to know what each other is feeling. You just know.

I understand why she's worried. I have apprehensions about the trip too. She's right when she says I'm not a young man anymore. I've got a bad back and don't move as fast as I once did, but I'm still a father. That's why I'm going. If I don't, Templeton will. That I can say for certain. Seeing the look of determination in her eyes, I knew there would be no dissuading her. That girl is as headstrong and willful as they come, and once she makes up her mind to do something, absolutely nothing is going to stop her.

Given the state of affairs out there, I have no idea what I'm in for. The newspaper stories alone should be enough to convince a person to stay away, but, as I said, I don't have a choice—it's either me or Templeton. No self-respecting father in the world would let his baby girl venture off to a place like that.

It's not safe to be on the streets of San Francisco right now, so I'll be bringing a gun with me. Hopefully I won't need it, but it's better to have it and not need it than it be the other way around. If I'm lucky I'll be able to find John in Oakland; then we can turn around and come back. But if I have to go to San Francisco, I will.

The thing I'm most frightened of is that I won't find him. What then? I doubt I'd have courage enough to face Templeton and tell her I'd failed. Eleanor always knows what to say or do to comfort someone. She has a way about her that I don't have. Ask me to slay a dragon for one of my kids and I'm ready to do it, but when it comes to having the right words to soothe hurt feelings or a broken heart I'm at a total loss.

I'm not much of a praying man, but right now I'm praying I can find my son-in-law and bring him back here without one of us getting killed.

The Message

TEMPLETON SPENT ANOTHER SLEEPLESS NIGHT worrying about both John and her father. While the stars were still scattered across the sky, she climbed from the bed and began drawing maps showing where the house was and the roundabout ways her daddy could get to Jones Street. Had she not read that Market Street was now in ashes, she would have told him that from the ferry building he could go straight down Market and turn right on Jones. Now it would not be quite so simple.

She mapped out five different routes, streets that wound around, crawled over to Montgomery or Battery, then turned east or west and crossed over to Jones. She'd thought of mapping out where he could find John's office, but that seemed futile. According to the *Enquirer*, the Call building had been gutted by fire. John's office was two doors down in a building half the size of the Call and nowhere near as sturdy.

She was working on yet another map when she remembered something her daddy had said. Hopefully, he'd bring John back here. Hopefully? Why hopefully? She thought back to the days before they were married and remembered how her daddy had pushed John to move his business to Philadelphia. John had claimed such a thing was not possible; he was a San Francisco man. *It's where my business is, where I've built my life*, he'd said. *It's where I belong.*

With the city in ruins, surely he'd feel differently now. Wouldn't he? She thought back to a year earlier when he'd financed a factory in Chinatown. They'd demolished a block of run-down shanties and built a good-sized factory, a factory John bragged about.

This is just the start, he'd said. *San Francisco is a city growing by leaps and bounds. A lot of these old buildings will be coming down and new ones going up. When that happens, I'll be here with the financing.*

But that was before the earthquake, before it became a city too dangerous for a woman to walk alone. Before she knew she was carrying their child. Back then, the city had a hospital with doctors and grocers who delivered fresh produce to her doorstep. There were places like the Palace Hotel where couples could sip champagne and dance, the air sweet with the scent of fresh-cut flowers, not weighed down by soot and cinders.

Everything was different now. And with a baby on the way, John would have to see the wisdom of living in Philadelphia. At least until after the baby was born and perhaps toddling around. They could stay here for a year or two and then, when it was safe to return, go back to San Francisco. Nowadays most businesses had a telephone. He could do business over the telephone, couldn't he? Here in Philadelphia, there were plenty of bankers for him to work with, a doctor to oversee their baby's delivery, and family to help out through the early months as she learned how to be a mama.

Only...John didn't know about the baby.

Last time she'd hidden her pregnancy. Said nothing about the baby until it was too late. He'd held her in his arms and said, *If only I'd known.*

Had he known, things might have turned out differently. He would have reached out, taken some of the burden from her shoulders, hired George sooner, seen to it that she drank milk so the baby would grow healthy and strong, and got the rest she needed. If only she had told him. That thought picked at her mind like a vulture at a dead carcass.

She had to make John understand what was at stake. He had to know why she needed him to come back to Philadelphia. She'd tell her daddy to explain that she was pregnant and couldn't risk...

Before the thought had time to settle in her mind, she brushed it away. She didn't want someone else to tell him. She wanted to be the one to do it. After two years of hoping for a child and having nothing but an endless string of disappointments, she had to tell him herself.

She closed her eyes and could almost see the smile that would light his face. He would take her in his arms and tell her he knew that sooner or later it would happen. Afterward they'd talk of baby names and how they'd turn the third-floor rooms into a nursery. With all they'd been through, didn't they deserve that glorious moment of celebration?

Her daddy said the streets were unsafe for a woman alone, but what if she went with him? With him beside her, she wouldn't be alone. The longer she thought about it, the more it made sense. Believing she had found the perfect solution, she climbed into the bed and fell back against the pillows.

THE NEXT MORNING AT THE breakfast table Templeton told them of her plan, but Eleanor started shaking her head before she was halfway through the explanation.

"Absolutely not," she said. "Traveling such a distance this early in your pregnancy is foolhardy and—"

"Mama, traveling in a compartment is like sitting in your own living room."

"There is no compartment," Albert said. "There's no express train either. The only accommodations I could get going to Oakland was a coach seat, and I'll have to change trains twice." He went on to explain that the trip would take six days rather than four, and once they arrived in Oakland there was the added challenge of getting a ferry over to San Francisco.

"Your mama's right," he finished. "A trip like that would not be good for you or the baby."

The tiny bit of hope that had carried Templeton through the night disappeared, and a look of sadness settled on her face.

"John needs to know about the baby," she said glumly, "and I wanted to be the one to tell him."

Eleanor took Templeton's hand in hers. "You can still be the one to tell him, sweetheart. Write a letter and tell him about the baby in your own words. Say all the things you'd say if you were with him. When your daddy gives him the letter, it'll be almost as if you're there."

"But I won't have the joy of seeing the expression on his face when he hears—"

"That's true, but are you willing to risk losing this baby for a single moment of joy?"

Templeton lowered her eyes and shook her head. "No, Mama, I'm not."

THAT AFTERNOON TEMPLETON WROTE HER letter. She told John that it had been a heartbreaking decision for her not to come in search of him herself, and she hoped he would understand the urgency of her daddy's visit.

My darling, we've waited so long for this to happen, she said, *and now that it finally has, I'm determined to do everything within my power to make certain our child comes into this world healthy and strong.*

I pray you're safe and well, that you haven't been injured in the terrible tragedy that has befallen San Francisco, and that you'll return to Philadelphia with my father. I need you here with me. We'll stay for a while, a year perhaps. Once the baby is born and the city has regained its sense of normalcy, we'll return to San Francisco. I know it's our home, and I wish for nothing more than to be there with you, my darling husband.

She went on to express concern for May Ling, George, Denise, and Isabelle and say she was also praying for their safety.

I worry about these dear friends and ask that you provide them comfort if you can do so. Newspaper reports say the Emporium is now gone, but that doesn't trouble my heart as does the safety of our friends. It seems as though the things I once saw as the focus of my life have now proven themselves unimportant. Buildings that are gone in one day can in time be rebuilt, but when we lose someone we love that loss is forever.

She wiped away the tear that threatened to smudge the ink on the pale blue paper, folded the letter, and slid it into an envelope.

ON SATURDAY MORNING BOTH ELEANOR and Templeton accompanied Albert to the train station. They walked out to the platform with him and, with equally sad expressions, watched as he climbed aboard. For a brief moment his face was visible through the window. All too soon he was gone.

As the train chugged away, Eleanor whispered, "Be safe, Albert dear. Be safe."

Only Templeton heard her.

Arm in arm they left the station, each of them leaning heavily on the other.

Eleanor

THE MOST DIFFICULT JOB IN the world is that of being a parent. The minute your baby is born, your life changes. There's no rule book that says for the rest of your life you'll have to forget about yourself and only make decisions that are best for your child, yet you do it. You do it because that child is your responsibility. I know that's what Albert was thinking about when he said he'd go to San Francisco.

Templeton might be a grown woman, but she's still our baby. She came along when Albert and I thought we were through having children. Benjamin and Clara were half-grown at the time, and I wasn't too happy about having another baby. When Templeton got old enough to prove herself as willful as Albert's great-uncle, I said to him, What in the world are we going to do with a child like her?

Now I look back and laugh, because we both find ourselves wondering what we'd have done without her. She's always been a challenge, but she's kept us young and alive. You can't be around her for a day before you find yourself caught up in whatever she's doing.

Albert claims he doesn't have a favorite child, but I can say for a fact he does. It's Templeton. He pretends that her willfulness is an annoyance he's forced to contend with, but the truth is he's proud of her. Although he'd certainly not admit it, her determination is a lot like his.

I didn't ask him to go after John. He decided that all by himself, which is precisely the kind of thing Templeton would do. He saw the newspaper reports the same as we had, and he was well aware of how dangerous it is out there, but once he'd said he'd go there was no way I could stop him.

Six days of sitting on a train is enough to kill a young man, never mind someone in their sixties. Albert's too old to be doing something like that. The truth is I'm worried sick about him, and I know Templeton is just as worried about John. I can't say if her daddy going out there is right or wrong. I suppose time will tell. For now, the only thing we can do is pray they both come back alive.

An Uncertain Journey

AFTER PHILADELPHIA DISAPPEARED FROM VIEW, Albert leaned back in the seat thinking of how he'd go about finding John. He pulled the list Templeton had given him from his pocket and studied it. There were eight names on the list—the people she was concerned about—and John's name was at the top. She'd drawn maps of where he might look for each of them, but after reading the newspaper reports he doubted the maps were anywhere near accurate.

Although he'd told Templeton to be patient, that John would most likely call once the telephone lines were back up, he feared that wasn't the case. John was highly resourceful; it was one of the things Albert admired about him. If he were able to leave town, he would have. He could have taken the ferry over to Oakland and called from there. According to the *Enquirer*, Oakland had suffered some damage but had most of their services back by the day after the quake.

Albert ran down the list of names again. Denise Laurent lived on Jones Street, a block down from John's house. He pulled a pen from his pocket and circled Denise's name. If he couldn't locate John, she might be able to shed some light on what happened. George Wilson was another story. He lived on the south side of Market on Howard Street, but where on Howard Templeton wasn't sure. She also wasn't sure of May Ling's address, only that it was somewhere on Dupont Street.

When the conductor went through the car yelling they'd soon be arriving in Harrisburg, Albert folded the list and slid it back into his pocket. They pulled into the station, and he got off, hurried into the depot, bought a copy of *Collier's Weekly* and the afternoon edition of the *Star-Independent*, then got back on the train. That afternoon he read the newspapers cover to cover, ate the sandwiches Eleanor packed, and chatted with a fellow traveler who was only going as far as Pittsburgh.

One day was the same as the next, long and tiring. His knees grew stiff, his back ached, and he found it pretty much impossible to sleep. On the few occasions when he did doze off, he was inevitably awakened by the screech of a whistle or a sudden stop that jolted him out of his seat. At every station, new people got on and others got off. As they clambered through the aisle with bags and satchels, Albert seized the opportunity to step down from the train, hurry into the depot, buy a newspaper and a snack he could carry back, then climb aboard and return to his seat.

Regardless of the town or state, the front page of the newspaper always had headlines about San Francisco. "Fire Chief Now Dead." "Thousands Homeless! Militia Enforces Curfew." "City Prays for Rain." On Sunday as the train rumbled across Ohio, he read how the fire that had ravaged a major portion of the city was no longer a threat.

"On Saturday morning the fire simply stopped in the center of a block filled with wood frame houses," the reporter wrote. There was no explanation for how or why, only the encouraging news that the fire had at long last been extinguished.

On the third day, when they finally pulled into Davenport, he had to switch trains. He'd originally felt the four-hour layover was a waste of time, but after three days of sitting in the same rock-hard seat he welcomed the chance to stretch his legs. He bought a postcard at the depot and mailed it to Eleanor. *So far, so good.* he wrote. *Will arrive in Oakland on Thursday.* After he'd mailed the postcard, he found a nearby restaurant and had a bourbon and a steak dinner.

In Salt Lake City he changed trains again and arrived on Thursday afternoon as expected. As soon as they chugged into the station, Albert was struck by the crowds. He was one of the few getting off the train, but there were hordes of people pushing to get on. It was no better outside the station. The streets of Oakland were almost as crowded as the depot, and when Albert asked a passerby where he might get a room for the night the man looked at him as if he'd gone daft.

"Room?" the man said. "Why, there ain't a room to be had anywhere in town. We're full up with refugees from across the bay."

Albert explained that he'd come from Philadelphia to look for his son-in-law and was unfamiliar with the city.

"I understand some of the injured and homeless have been evacuated over here and—" Before he could get to asking about the hospital, the man guffawed.

"Some?" he echoed with an air of incredulity. "Half the people living in San Francisco is over here. Some that got here after the rooming houses and hotels were filled up are sleeping at First Church over on Fourteenth Street."

Figuring he had to start somewhere, Albert asked for directions to the church.

The guy motioned to the wide street across from where they were standing. "Follow that down ten blocks or so, then turn west on Brighton. Ask for Margaret. She's keeping a list of those who have come and gone."

Albert thanked the man and started off. He was encouraged by the thought of someone keeping track of the arrivals. Maybe, if he got lucky, he'd find John or one of the others on Templeton's list.

The newspaper reports claimed Oakland had been spared the damage of the quake, but along the street there were piles of rubble everywhere. A mound of bricks, a porch railing, a downed tree, a broken window. The bag he carried had seemed light at first, but it grew heavier and heavier as he pushed forward. The man indicated it was ten blocks, but Albert had begun to believe it was more like twenty or thirty. He was dead tired and his back ached, a constant throbbing that banged against his spine with every step. When he turned onto Brighton and saw the steeple in the distance, he was ready to fall in with those sleeping in the church.

The church was filled with refugees, people clad in all manner of clothing. Here and there he could spy an empty pew, but most of them were filled. An old man with a gray beard leaned against a cushion; another was rolled over on his back sound asleep. Off to the side a woman sat with a baby at her breast. Two rows back he saw a child sucking on her thumb.

Albert walked down the center aisle, searching the faces, seeing anguish in many of them, and somehow knowing he was not going to find John. Not this day and not in this place. At the far end of the aisle he asked for Margaret, and the woman pointed toward the back.

The corridor led to a large kitchen. When Albert walked in, the man at the stove stopped stirring and looked over. "Supper's not until seven."

"I'm not here for supper," Albert replied. "I'm looking for Margaret."

"I'm Margaret," a woman said. She sat at a table in the far corner of the room.

Albert walked back and dropped down into the chair opposite her. "I'm looking for my son-in-law and hoping you can help me." He gave her John's name and waited while she searched through a handwritten ledger.

"I've a John Morton who's gone to stay with a cousin in Cincinnati, could that be him?"

Albert shook his head. "It's Morehouse, and his family is in London. We're his only family here in America."

Margaret continued to search but found nothing more.

One by one they went through the names on Templeton's list. Mildred Kent was the last name. She'd added it almost as an afterthought, saying that it was the woman she'd worked with at the Emporium. Nine pages in, Margaret found a Mildred Kent. She'd arrived at the church last Friday, was there for one night, then went to stay with her sister there in Oakland. Margaret gave him an address over on Poplar Street.

"Poplar is only a mile or so west of here," she said.

Weary as he was, one mile might just as well have been ten. He pocketed the address and continued to run through questions about where the evacuees were taken. He could check on Mildred Kent tomorrow. John was the one he needed to find.

"The Trades Council has a message board set up in their building; look there," Margaret said. "If he's a union man, they'll have him on their list."

"He's not union, at least not that I know of."

She continued on, naming a dozen other places for Albert to check: hotels, boarding houses, Providence Hospital, other churches, a field hospital manned by a handful of doctors who had left San Francisco. She wrote each one down and handed him the list.

His last question was about the Western Union office.

"Is it up and running?" he asked.

"I haven't heard anything about the one in San Francisco, but Oakland is."

"That's what I figured," he said and added that address to his list.

WITH NOWHERE ELSE TO GO and too weary to move on, Albert spent the night at the church. He ate biscuits and a bowl of ragout alongside the others, then slept on an empty pew with a cushion only marginally softer than the wooden bench.

When he woke, his neck was stiff and his back throbbing. Pulling himself to a sitting position, he remained there for a few minutes then stood and fished the list of addresses from his pocket. The Western Union office would be his first stop.

That morning he sent a telegram to Eleanor asking if they'd heard anything from John.

Not sure where I'll be tonight, he wrote. *Reply to Western Union, Oakland.*

Once that was done, he continued his search for John, first checking Providence Hospital, then moving on to the scattering of emergency hospitals set up days earlier. He asked around, talked to anyone who would talk to him, and checked every message board in sight. Nowhere was there a mention of John Morehouse or any of the other names on Templeton's list.

The day was unseasonably warm, and by early afternoon Albert was soaked through with perspiration and near exhaustion. With an aching back and an urgent need for good news, he returned to the Western Union office.

"Any messages for Whittier?" he asked.

The girl shuffled through the bin, then handed him a yellow envelope.

No word yet, the message read.

Albert rubbed his hand across the back of his neck, stuffed the telegram in his pocket, and left. Having already checked the hospitals and medical camps, he figured Mildred Kent might be his best bet.

From the Western Union office, the walk to Poplar Street was close to two miles. It was a street lined with huge oaks and fairly small houses. The number Margaret had given him for Mildred's sister, 272, was a wooden two-story with a broken window on the left side and a load of bricks scattered across the front porch blocking the front door.

Standing on the walkway, Albert called out, "Hello in there! Anybody home?" When there was no answer, he hollered a second time.

A few minutes later a woman with an apron tied around her waist came from the back yard.

"Sorry," she said. "I didn't hear you."

"Afternoon, ma'am." Albert doffed his hat and introduced himself. "I'm looking for Miss Mildred Kent. Margaret Wythe over at First Church suggested I'd find her here."

The woman smiled. "You certainly can. I'm Grace Buckley, Millie's sister. Are you a friend of hers?"

Albert shook his head. "Not exactly a friend," he said, then told how he'd come from Philadelphia in search of John. "You sister's name was on the list of people my daughter wanted me to inquire about."

"You came all the way from Philadelphia?" she said in amazement. "It's a wonder you're not exhausted!"

"I am but I've got a job to do, and I've got to stick to it. So far, I'm not making much headway, and I thought maybe Miss Kent could—"

She turned and motioned for him to follow her. "Come on in. I'll get you a lemonade and fetch Millie. You look like a little bit of rest would do you good."

Trailing along behind her, Albert said, "Indeed it would."

Grace was a woman much like her name. She gave an easy smile, led him through the kitchen into a parlor, and motioned to an overstuffed club chair and told him to sit. She looked nothing like Eleanor and yet in a way reminded him of her. When Grace scurried off for the lemonade, Albert lowered himself into the chair and gave an almost pleasurable groan. Sitting in that chair with its soft cushions and fat arms reminded him of home.

When Grace returned with her sister and the lemonade, he was sound asleep.

Albert woke when he heard voices, and it took him a minute to recall where he was. Feeling a bit embarrassed, he followed the sound back to the kitchen and saw Grace with a woman who, if looks were any indicator, had to be her sister. The only way he could tell one from the other was that Grace was still wearing the apron she'd worn earlier.

"I apologize for falling asleep like that," he said sheepishly. "It's been a long week."

Both women laughed.

"It's been a long week for everyone," Grace said and handed him the glass of lemonade she had waiting.

Mildred Kent introduced herself, and the three of them moved back to the parlor and talked for a long while. Mildred settled on the sofa alongside her sister then told how she'd been thrown out of bed by the first jolt and barely escaped being crushed by the wall that came down moments later.

"I ran into the street wearing only my nightdress, happy to be alive."

She went on to say that after wandering around the street for most of the day, an army relief worker directed her and a group of others to Golden Gate Park.

"We had to walk quite a way to get there, and the walk was made longer by the fact that we had to circle around a number of streets that were on fire. By the time we got there, the army had set up a food tent and some smaller ones for people to sleep in." She gazed off into space for a moment and shook her head. "You never believe something like this can happen until it happens to you."

When Albert asked about John, she said she'd not seen or heard anything of him.

"I saw George Wilson at the park; at least I think I did. He was in the food line a fair distance away from me. I called to him, but with such a crowd I doubt he heard me and there was no way for me to get through to him."

"Do you think John may have been with George and you didn't notice him?"

She shrugged. "I guess it's possible. I used to meet with George three or four times a week, and I barely recognized him. I've only seen John a few times, so he may have been there and I didn't notice."

AFTER A SECOND GLASS OF lemonade Grace invited Albert to stay for dinner, which he did gladly. Although it was a simple dish of stewed chicken and vegetables, Albert ate heartily and said he'd never tasted a more enjoyable meal in all his life. As they lingered over coffee, Mildred continued to tell of the devastation in San Francisco.

"What about Jones Street?" Albert asked. "Are those houses still standing?"

She thought for a moment then said she couldn't be sure.

"Some might be," she said. "It was all so terrible, I find it hard to remember."

In time the hour grew late, and Albert rose to leave. Mildred suggested he stay the night.

"You won't find a room in town, and with Grace's husband away I can bunk in with her."

Albert didn't hesitate to accept. If Eleanor were here, she would have asked if Mildred were sure it was not an inconvenience, and that thought had crossed his mind, but after six days on the train and a night of sleeping on a wooden pew he wasn't willing to risk it.

That night he was asleep before his head hit the pillow.

THE FOLLOWING MORNING HE ROSE early, had breakfast with the sisters, then took his leave. As they said their goodbyes in the back yard, Mildred asked if Templeton knew the Emporium was gone.

"The fire took it that first day."

Albert nodded. "She read about it in the newspaper."

"The front's still standing, but the inside is gone. It'll be a long time before any of us are working there again." She paused a moment then added, "If ever."

Catching the glint of sadness that clung to her words, Albert said, "Surely in time they'll rebuild it."

"Maybe; maybe not." She reached out and took his hand in hers. "Give Templeton my love, and tell her I said it was an honor to have worked with her."

"I'll do that," Albert replied. When she disappeared into the house, he headed back to the Western Union office.

Templeton

TODAY WHEN THE WESTERN UNION boy said he had a telegram for Templeton Morehouse, I almost died of fright. I thought for sure something terrible had happened to John, but that wasn't it at all. The telegram was from Daddy. He said Mildred was safe and sound at her sister's house in Oakland, and she'd seen George at the Golden Gate refugee camp.

Now Daddy's taking the ferry over to San Francisco to look for John. I'd be lying if I said I wasn't worried sick about them both. Knowing Mildred was able to get to Oakland only makes me that much more worried. I keep thinking if she could get there, why couldn't John? I won't even consider the possibility that he could be injured or, God forbid, dead! When that thought pops into my mind, I push it away and tell myself it's because he's busy taking care of Denise and Isabelle or poor Mrs. Abernathy who can barely walk without that cane of hers. I have to keep believing that, because if I don't I'll go insane.

I thought being back here in Philadelphia I'd be busy as a bee, visiting Clara to play with those adorable nieces of mine, spending time with Benjamin's family, seeing friends, and catching up on all the things I'd missed. The first few weeks I did that, but once John left it just wasn't the same. Instead of enjoying myself, I kept thinking about him and counting the days until I returned home to San Francisco. Then when I found out about the earthquake, I felt like the bottom of my world had caved in.

Imagining him out there in the midst of all that devastation has torn the heart out of me. I haven't left the house since then. I just sit here day after day hoping the mailman will bring a letter saying he's okay or that he'll come strolling up the walkway himself. A hundred times a day I ask God, "Please don't let my baby be born without a daddy."

Mama keeps telling me not to worry. She says this day-in, day-out fretting isn't good for the baby. I don't doubt she's right, but when I look at her face she looks every bit as worried as I am. Trust me, it's a lot easier to say not to worry than it is to do it.

The Search Continues

WITH A GOOD NIGHT'S SLEEP and a hearty breakfast in his stomach, Albert was ready to tackle the day. Striking out at the medical care facilities had left him less hopeful of finding answers in Oakland, and he'd begun to believe if John were here he would have found a way to send word by now.

He pulled Margaret's list from his pocket and made note of the next place he needed to check out. First he'd stop by the Trades Council building; then he'd head off to San Francisco.

Leaving the Western Union office, he went west on Clinton then turned onto Eleventh.

In the lobby of the building, a fellow who looked barely old enough to shave sat at the information desk. Albert gave him John's name and waited as he flipped through page after page of listings.

"He's not registered," he finally said.

"What if he were injured when he arrived?"

"He wouldn't come here. He'd have gone to Providence or the medical camp on Ninth."

Albert shook his head. "He's not there, I've checked both places. Any other hospitals?"

"Not in Oakland. But a lot of people are being treated in Frisco."

"I thought that hospital was down."

"It is, but the army's opened up the Presidio and they've got a field hospital set up at Golden Gate. If he's not at Providence, he's probably still over there."

Feeling a greater than ever sense of urgency to move on, Albert thanked the lad and left the building. He folded Margaret's list, stuck it in his pocket, and headed for the waterfront.

As he walked, he thought about how he'd handle the search. Mildred had also mentioned Golden Gate Park, so that seemed the place to start. He'd ask about John at the field hospital, then try to find George Wilson. He felt for the packet in his pocket; Templeton's letter and the maps she'd drawn. He'd studied them on the train but didn't recall seeing any indication of Golden Gate Park or the Presidio. He now wished he'd asked for directions or had Mildred give a description of George.

Nearing the dock, he noticed how crowded it was. Boxes and crates stacked everywhere, men pushing or pulling overloaded carts, others hoisting cartons onto their shoulders or barking orders to move one thing or another. Off to the side there was a handful of people standing in a loosely formed line. Albert approached a young man in the back and asked, "Is this the line for the San Francisco ferry?"

The young man gave a polite nod. "You must not be from around here."

"I'm not," Albert replied. "I came out to look for my son-in law."

"Same here, only I'm in search of my parents." He stuck out his hand. "Leonard Braun. Folks call me Leo."

"Albert Whittier. Philadelphia."

"A northeasterner, huh? Me too. I'm from New York."

"Is this your first time in California?" Albert asked.

"No, I was born and raised here in San Francisco."

"Oh. Well, then, you know how to get to Golden Gate Park and the Presidio, right?"

"Blindfolded," Leo said with bittersweet smile. "That's where I'm headed."

"Mind if I join you?" Albert asked.

"Not at all. Having someone along might help take my mind off of what's happened."

The bellowing of a boat horn interrupted their conversation, and as Albert looked up the ferry was pulling into the slip. When the gangplank was lowered, a crowd of evacuees poured onto the dock. Every man, woman, and child wore that same sad-eyed look. It was as if the weight of their experience had seeped through their skin and become a part of them.

As people got off and cargo was loaded on, Albert and the young man continued to talk. Leo told of how he'd gone to New York because of a terrific job offer.

"That was three years ago," he said, "and I haven't been back since. With Mom and Dad getting older, I should've made time to visit, but I didn't. Now I'm regretting it."

"Our daughter moved out here three years ago, probably about the same time you left. She married a San Francisco man, and they've been fairly good about coming back to visit. She just learned that they're expecting a baby, so she's back in Philadelphia." Albert went on to explain how John had returned to San Francisco and she'd stayed on for another four weeks. "She was set to start back two days after the earthquake; thank God she didn't."

Leo nodded.

A short while later the line began to move. Once everyone was aboard, the ferry eased back out of the slip, turned, and began its journey across the bay.

As they continued to talk, Albert told of his two days in Oakland, explained what he'd learned so far, then showed him the maps Templeton had drawn.

Seeing the drawing that led to Templeton's house, Leo's eyes widened. "Jones Street? They live on Jones?"

The way he said it unnerved Albert. He nodded. "What's wrong with Jones?"

"It's east of Van Ness, the same as my folks."

"Your parents live on Jones?"

"No, Hyde, two blocks over. But both streets are east of Van Ness." Leo pulled a long deep breath before he continued. "That's where the fires did the most damage. From Van Ness back to Powell; most of that's gone."

"Gone?" A feeling of apprehension grabbed hold of Albert's chest, and his heart raced.

Leo seemed to sense he'd said too much. "Some buildings might still be standing, but the fire took a lot of them." He lowered his eyes and looked down into the choppy water of the bay. "That's why I'm so worried about my parents. They're older and..."

"How'd you find out about—"

"The newspaper. The *Times* said on Thursday the fire crossed Montgomery and moved westward. It had already taken most of Tyler and Leavenworth, and they believed a fire break was the only way to stop it. Van Ness is wider than most of the streets, so they dynamited everything on the east side of the street, hoping the fire wouldn't jump the break."

Albert recalled reading about it on the train, but since the article hadn't mentioned Jones Street he'd not realized the significance.

"What about the people?" he asked. "Were they able to get out in time?"

"I think so. The worst of the quake didn't hit that area the way it did south of Market. There was some damage—cracked walls, chimneys down, stuff like that—but the fires that started on the south side didn't spread across Market until the next day. People had enough time to grab what they could and leave. I'm hopeful that's what my parents did."

Albert gave a nod of acknowledgment and said nothing more. His heart was in his throat. He remembered the empty-eyed look of sorrow he'd seen on Mildred's face and knew it would be equally as bad for Templeton.

The two men stood looking out over the water, silent as the ferry moved into the slip. Leo pointed to the clock in the tower that rose above the ferry building.

"It stopped at five-twelve," he said. "When the quake hit."

As soon as they started down the gangplank they saw the piles of rubble scattered about, but they didn't grasp the full magnitude of it until they left the ferry building. On Market Street, there was destruction for as far as the eye could see. What the earthquake had not taken, the flames had destroyed. It had been seven days since the fires were brought to a halt, but the air was still peppered with flying cinders and the stench of smoke.

"I knew it would be bad," Leo said, "but I didn't expect this." Before they reached Montgomery, his eyes grew teary.

Albert had read countless newspaper articles describing the damage, but he too had not imagined it would be as devastating as what they saw before them.

Market Street, the wide shopping thoroughfare Templeton had spoken of so lovingly, was in ruins. Block after block was filled with crushed stone, twisted iron, and rubble. Here and there Albert could see the shell of a structure still standing or the framework of a tall building, now naked and scarred, silhouetted against the gray sky.

As they trudged westward toward Golden Gate Park, an endless stream of refugees moved eastward toward the ferry. A few hauled bags or carts filled with the belongings they'd been able to save. Many had nothing but the clothes on their back. Armed troops were visible everywhere, and the scattering of cars on the street carried soldiers or flew Red Cross flags. Military teams were already at work clearing debris from the street but the task seemed almost insurmountable, the type that would take ten thousand men ten thousand days to complete.

Doggedly moving one foot in front of the other, Leo told of the city as it once was. He nodded toward a piece of wall surrounded by smoldering mounds of brick and marble.

"That was the Palace Hotel, a beauty if ever I've seen one. Every bit as grand as anything we've got in New York." Two blocks down, he pointed out the Call building, a sixteen-story skyscraper, now a skeleton with only the tower intact.

Continuing along Market, he described the Mechanics Pavilion that had gone up in smoke then motioned to the shell of the City Hall building that sat just beyond and spoke of the fine columns that once graced the front of it.

Many of the streets to the right of them were unrecognizable. One looked the same as the next with only pieces of broken brick and piles of ash to mark where a house once stood. The lone exception was Van Ness. There was no mistaking it. Everything along the eastern side of the street had been flattened while the stately mansions directly opposite had little or no damage.

The walk was long and made more difficult by ripples and cracks in the sidewalk. When they turned right at Buchannan, Leo must have noticed the weariness in Albert's step. He reached across and grabbed onto the handle of Albert's bag.

"Let me carry this for a while," he said and smiled.

Another time Albert might have held onto the bag, proven himself strong enough to keep pace with his younger companion, but he felt bone-tired. He allowed Leo to take the bag, then nodded and thanked him.

"When you find your parents, you can tell them I said they raised a fine young man. A man they can easily be proud of."

Leo smiled. "I'm sure Mom will appreciate hearing that."

A short while later, they made a left and started westward on Fulton. The damage in this area was nowhere near what they'd passed through. Chimneys were down, bricks scattered across lawns, sidewalks cracked and porches tilted, but the houses were standing.

They walked for over an hour before the park came into view, and by the time they reached the east entrance Albert was ready to drop.

A short way past the crumbled columns at the park entrance, they stopped and surveyed what lay before them: an endless sea of tents stretched straight ahead with more rows than Albert could count. Off to the side sat a table with volunteers offering coffee, cups of water, and snacks. Workers with white aprons tied around their waist hustled back and forth. Red Cross nurses and soldiers moved everywhere.

The sight of it was daunting.

"Let's rest a minute before we get started," Albert said.

"I'm okay for now," Leo replied. "Wait here, and I'll see if I can find an information desk or someone to help us out."

Albert moved to a shady spot beneath a large oak, dropped down in the grass, and leaned his back against the tree. He closed his eyes for a moment and dozed off. When he woke, it was to the sound of Leo's voice.

"Albert? I checked the hospital tent and the camp registration, and neither my parents nor John are listed," he said. "But that doesn't mean they're not here. The woman I spoke with said a lot of the people who arrived that first day or two weren't registered." He handed Albert a tin cup of coffee and a biscuit. "That's the best I could get for now. They'll be serving supper in about an hour."

"This is plenty." Albert eagerly downed a gulp of coffee and could almost swear there was a bit of chicory in it. "Did they offer any suggestions about how to find people?"

Leo shook his head. "Not really. She did say to leave a note on the message board. Apparently, that's how a lot of people are finding one another. When you're up to it, we'll walk over and leave messages for your son-in-law and my parents."

Albert chugged the last of his coffee and pushed himself to his feet. "I'm ready now."

THE MESSAGE BOARD WAS A wooden park sign that people had taken over. It was covered with notes, saying things like "Elaine Sapp is alive and well," "the Storm family can be found in the tent with a blue ribbon pinned to the flap," or "Edgar Farley is looking for his sister Jeanne." There was nothing about John or Leonard's parents, Louise and Joseph Braun.

After he'd read through all the messages and come up empty, Albert pulled a business card from his pocket. On the back of it he wrote: *John Morehouse, TM home with her mama, I'm to bring you back. Albert.*

He'd wanted to write something more, spell out Templeton's name and make it clear that he meant back to Philadelphia, but he could barely fit what he did write on the card. As it was, he'd had to squeeze the letters in Morehouse together until they were almost illegible. As Leo was posting a note to his parents, Albert remembered what Mildred had said about seeing George here at the camp. If George were here, there was the possibility he'd seen John.

Taking another card from his pocket, he posted a second note. On the face of this card he scribbled *Looking for George Wilson.* Below his message was the line "Albert J. Whittier, Attorney at Law."

Once they'd finished posting their messages, Leo suggested they join the line-up for supper.

"After we eat, I'll try to find us someplace to sleep. Tomorrow we'll check the messages, then start for the Presidio."

Albert nodded. In another time and place, he would have laughed at the thought of camping out with a man he'd met just hours ago but not here in this tent city. It was their only refuge from the burned-out buildings and devastation behind them. Here, a man forgot such inhibitions and thought only of survival, of doing what he'd come to do, and then returning home. A few weeks earlier he'd complained when Eleanor served him a slice of beef that he'd insisted was dry and overcooked.

Now he'd gobble it down with relish and praise it as a truly enjoyable meal.

LATER ON, AFTER THEY'D WAITED in the food line, dined at a long table with strangers, and checked the message board, they returned to the information desk and were given blankets and a tent assignment.

The tent was tiny with little more than walking space between the two cots, but Albert was glad to have it. His back ached, and his legs felt as though he'd walked the full distance in lead boots. As he lay there waiting for sleep to come, he thought of home. Sheets fresh in from the wash line and Eleanor beside him, soft and warm, the scent of rose water on her nightdress, her hair loose of its pins and combs. Oh, how he wished to be home.

He pushed back the thought and started to turn on his side. When the narrow cot creaked and wobbled as if it might collapse, he fell back and remained where he was. He couldn't afford to pamper his aches and pains; there'd be time enough to think about those once he and John were on the train headed home. Right now he had to focus every bit of energy he had on finding John. There would be no rest, no giving in, until he did.

The thought that troubled him earlier returned. If John were here and able to walk, he would have headed to the ferry as so many of the other refugees had. If this, if that; a thousand ifs and not one answer.

In the distance a dog howled, and Albert felt a stab of pain shoot across his back.

Templeton

THIS MORNING I WOKE UP with a jolt that gave me the scare of my life. I had to sit there waiting for my heart to stop pounding and my breath to return before I came to the realization that what I'd gone through wasn't real. It was a nightmare but one so horrible I hope to never again experience anything like it. In my entire life I have never been that frightened. Even after I'd gotten out of bed and splashed water on my face, I couldn't shake the feeling that it was real.

I was standing on the street looking up at a building so huge that the top of it disappeared into the clouds. The small buildings surrounding it were all on fire, but that building wasn't. When the clouds drifted away, I looked up and saw the top of that building burning like a giant candle stuck in the middle of a blackened cake. A few floors down from the flames, John's face was in the window.

I hollered for him to get out of there, but he just kept looking at me. Save him, I screamed, somebody save him. I heard a baby start to cry; then I saw Daddy climbing up the side of the building. He was almost to the top when the bricks he'd been climbing on broke apart, and he started to fall. It seemed like he kept falling and falling, and the whole while I could feel myself screaming... That's when I woke up.

The terror of that dream has been with me this whole day long. I keep thinking it's a warning, a sign of something, but for the life of me

I can't figure out what. First of all, there's no building that tall in San Francisco. The Call is the biggest building I know of, and that's half the size of the one in my dream. And secondly, they had the fires out over a week ago. Every rational bone in my body says there's nothing to worry about, but I keep right on worrying.

I wasn't going to tell Mama, but then tonight I did. I told her I was afraid it was a sign of something bad, but she said that dreams are nothing more than your worries of the day coming back to haunt you at night. I wanted to believe her, but truthfully she looked a little teary-eyed when she said it.

Neither of us had a stomach for supper, but right before we got ready to go to bed Mama made us each a cup of chamomile tea and added a nip of brandy to both cups. She claims it will help us to sleep better.

I'm hoping she's right.

The Interloper

THE GOLDEN GATE PARK REFUGEE camp was as diverse a mix as San Francisco itself. Rich man, poor man, beggar man, con man, all were there, housed in the same small tents, sleeping on the same narrow cots.

Charlie Muller, once the foreman of the Acorn factory, now simply one of the thousands of homeless, was as bossy and authoritative as ever. He told children where they should or shouldn't play, berated anyone who failed to keep their tent area tidy, and took it upon himself to check the message board every morning. He'd pull down the messages for those in his tent row and deliver them personally.

On Sunday morning, Charlie was at the message board shortly after sunrise. Gertrude Hepplewhite seemed certain her nephew would come looking for her. The nephew's message was what he was looking for when he spotted a card that read *Looking for George Wilson*. George was not in the second row, but Charlie had seen him here at the camp and figured he couldn't be all that hard to find.

He'd happened upon George a week earlier. They'd chatted for a few minutes, then George hurried off. He'd had a woman and a kid with him, and he'd seemed overly anxious to get going. The woman looked vaguely familiar, but at the time Charlie had been unable to place her.

Now some hotshot lawyer from Philadelphia was looking for George. The thought of what could be involved intrigued Charlie, and he wanted to know more. He pulled the card down and stuck it in his pocket. After breakfast, he'd find George, deliver the message, and get the lowdown. If he played his cards right, maybe there'd be something in it for him.

WHEN ALBERT WOKE, HE WAS feeling worse than ever. His back ached, his head throbbed, and his right knee felt as if it would give way any minute. He gave a groan as he pushed himself up from the cot.

"Are you okay?" Leo asked.

Albert nodded. "Just a bit stiff this morning. I'll be fine once we get going."

Leo raised an eyebrow. "You don't look good. It's over three miles to the Presidio. You think you'll be able to make it?"

"I might be a bit slower than you, but I'll make it."

The expression on Leo's face didn't change. "Let's get something to eat and check the message board, then see how you're feeling."

Albert agreed, and they started for the food tent. His determination pushed him forward, but it didn't stop him from dragging his right foot. As they moved through the row of tents and over to the grassy area that had become a pathway to the food tent, Leo slowed his step to match Albert's pace.

"Seems to me you're favoring that right leg," he said.

"Just stiff. I'll be fine once I've had my coffee."

"Probably, but I hear they've got a regular hospital set up in the medical tent. They might be able to give you something to ease that stiffness."

"I'll think about it."

"My dad has a bad back too. Walking here from the ferry would have done him in."

"I'm feeling it, but I'll be fine."

"I'm sure," Leo said with a nod. "I'm just saying, if you were my dad, I'd insist on you seeing a doctor."

When they arrived at the food tent, the line was long and stretched out to what looked like a mile. Leo suggested Albert grab a seat at the table while he got the food, and Albert didn't argue. As he waited, Albert turned to the man sitting alongside of him.

"I'm looking for a John Morehouse. You know anyone here by that name?"

The guy thought for a moment then shook his head.

"Anybody here know a John Morehouse?" he hollered down to his companions. After several headshakes, he turned back to Albert. "Don't reckon any of my group's seen him."

"What about Braun? Louise and Joseph Braun, anybody seen either of them?"

More headshakes.

"Thanks anyway," Albert said, then scooted over to make room for Leo who was carrying back two plates of food.

After Albert polished off a full plate of grits, sausage, and biscuits and downed two cups of coffee, they started toward the message board.

More notes had been added to what was there yesterday. Written in a woman's hand, a scrap of paper said Linda Levack had been moved to the Presidio. A torn corner of cardboard said Ed Willoughby could be found in the back row, third tent from the left. The note to John was still there as was Leo's note regarding his parents. The card for George Wilson was gone. Some people had posted responses to a request, but George Wilson had not.

Albert scrubbed his chin and turned to Leo with a puzzled expression. "What do you think this means?"

"He's probably here at the park; maybe gone to look for you."

That somehow didn't seem right to Albert. Others had left messages saying where they were, where someone could find them. Why would George simply take the card down and make off with it?

"You think it's possible someone else took it?"

Leo shrugged. "Anything's possible, but why would someone carry off a note not intended for them?"

Albert had no answer for that.

They went back and forth for a while. Although Albert insisted he had no need of a doctor, he was willing to consider the plan for Leo to go to the Presidio alone. With a pain running from his spine down to his right foot, the truth was he'd be struggling to make a mile, never mind three.

"The problem is you don't know what John looks like," he said to Leo. "It's possible you could pass him by and not even know it."

"I'm certain the Presidio's set-up is better than what they've got here," Leo said. "That's an army base; they'll be much more organized. I'll look for Mom and Dad and check if they've got any record of your son-in-law. If he's there, I'll let him know you're over here looking for him."

Although he'd known Leo for only one day, the thought of being without him seemed somehow frightening. Leo was young and strong. He knew his way around. He was the crutch Albert could lean on.

"Are you sure you'll be back?" he asked nervously. "Even if you find your parents?"

Leo nodded. "I'll be back, even if I find my parents."

Albert watched the young man walk away and turned back to the message board. Reaching into his pocket, he pulled out the last card he carried. On the face of it he wrote another message. *George Wilson, I am in the fifth row back, 2 tents in from right.*

He pinned the note to the board then returned to the tent.

CHARLIE HAD ALL BUT FORGOTTEN about the card he'd stuck in his pocket earlier until he passed by Gertrude Hepplewhite. She asked if there'd been a message from her nephew.

"Not yet," Charlie said. "I checked this morning."

"Would you be a dear and check again?" Gertrude asked. "I'm quite certain if you help Ronald locate me, he'll reward you handsomely."

Charlie found Gertrude Hepplewhite extremely annoying. She was old, fidgety, and always asking for something, but she came from money and that was enough to motivate him. He gave a nod.

"Sure thing, Mrs. Hepplewhite, I'll run over right now and check."

STANDING IN FRONT OF THE message board, he spotted the second card Albert posted.

"Well, now, look at what I've found here," he said and grinned.

Ten minutes later, he was at the tent asking for Albert Whittier.

"I'm Whittier," Albert said.

"You posted a note looking for George Wilson?"

"Yes, I did. Are you George?"

"I ain't George, but I just might know where to find him."

"Excellent. Is he here at the park?"

"Maybe. But with you being a lawyer, I gotta know why you're looking for him before I say where he might be."

Albert chuckled. "It's nothing like you think. I'm Templeton Morehouse's father. It's her husband, John, I'm actually looking for, but I thought George might know—"

"Templeton Morehouse," Charlie echoed. "Well, I'll be damned. She here at the camp?"

"No, back in Pennsylvania. You know Templeton?"

"Oh, yeah. I know her real well. I was the foreman at Acorn. My girls did all the sewing when she first started making those dresses of hers."

"Well, then, you probably know John. Have you seen him here at the camp?"

"Maybe, maybe not. Depends on what you're offering."

"Offering?" Albert said.

"Yeah, like a reward for finding him."

Albert's eyes narrowed.

"I wasn't offering any reward," he said, sliding into his courtroom voice, "and for you to demand one could be considered extortion."

"Hold on there, I ain't said I know for sure where he is. I'd be willing to take a look around if you're willing to pay for my time. Far as I can see, there ain't nothing illegal in that."

Charlie paused for half a second; when Albert didn't budge, he turned away.

"Okay then, I see you ain't interested, so I won't trouble you no more."

"Wait," Albert called out. "I might be interested after all."

Charlie ducked back inside. He'd been called on the carpet a number of times because of Templeton's complaints; then he'd been let go. They didn't say it was because she'd taken her business elsewhere, but Charlie could read between the lines.

He'd waited a long time to settle the score with Templeton Morehouse, and this was his opportunity.

"I'm thinking fifty bucks is a fair price," he said.

"Fifty dollars! A ticket to Philadelphia costs less than that!"

Charlie grinned. "Yeah, but your guy ain't in Philadelphia; he's here, ain't he?"

"I'll give you thirty."

"Nope. Fifty."

"That's highway robbery."

"Take it or leave it," Charlie said.

Albert sat silent for a few moments, then said, "Okay, but not just for looking. You have to find John Morehouse and bring him to me."

"Okay, but I want twenty-five up front and twenty-five when I deliver Morehouse."

"Nothing up front. Fifty when you come back with John."

They argued back and forth for several minutes, both men seemingly wary of the other. In the end, Albert agreed to give Charlie ten up front and the remainder when he returned with John. Taking his wallet from his traveling case, he pulled out a ten-dollar bill.

Charlie caught sight of the wallet stuffed with notes and knew he hadn't asked for half enough.

"I'm trusting that you're a man of your word and will be back with my son-in-law," Albert said as he handed the money to Charlie.

"Don't worry, I'll be back. You can be sure of it."

Charlie pocketed the money and walked off whistling.

AS A LAWYER, ALBERT WHITTIER had dealt with a lot of shady characters but none that struck him as more underhanded than Charlie Muller. He'd not had a good feeling about Charlie, but he'd pushed past it because his need to find John was greater than his distrust. The situation reminded him of Herb Cotter, a bookkeeper accused of embezzling money from his employer's account.

Cotter had claimed innocence, but Albert only half-heartedly believed him and mounted a defense that was less than stellar. Cotter was found guilty. Six months later, they discovered the man's business partner was responsible for the theft.

Albert had been wrong then; hopefully he was also wrong about Charlie Muller.

As the afternoon dragged by, Albert continued to think about it. At times he thought himself a fool for believing such a man but eventually decided he had no choice. If he'd not given Charlie the money and then failed to find John, he'd never forgive himself. It was a gamble he simply had to take.

With such a low level of trust in Charlie, Albert decided that he too would continue the search. That afternoon he walked back to the hospital tent and asked about both John and Leo's parents. The girl at the front table was a freckled-faced kid who looked like she should have been playing with dolls rather than working at a hospital tent. She flipped through several pages of a handwritten ledger, then shook her head.

"There's no Braun or Morehouse," she said. "But check back tomorrow. I think there's another listing for the earlier patients."

Albert thanked her and headed back to the main registration desk. It was the same there; no Morehouse, no Braun. That afternoon, he checked the message board twice. Still nothing from John nor from the Brauns. He wanted to believe that it was taking longer than originally thought because Leo had found his parents at the Presidio, and they were now on their way back to the park.

The thought that Leo wasn't coming back flitted through his mind, but he pushed it away. He knew the young man didn't owe him anything, but they'd become friends. It was a friendship Albert wanted to believe in.

When it grew late and the crowd at the food tent thinned, Albert went alone. Leo should have been back by now, but so far there'd been no sign of him. The events of the afternoon had left Albert without much of an appetite. He ate sparingly then wrapped a piece of bread, meat, and cheese in his handkerchief and carried it back to the tent. Leo would soon be returning, and after the long walk he was sure to be hungry.

Albert set the bundle of food on Leo's cot then climbed into his own. He left the door flap partly open for Leo and lay there watching the fog roll in and the sky grow dark. In time, a blanket of weariness settled over him and he drifted off.

SOUND ASLEEP, ALBERT DIDN'T HEAR the door flap being pulled back, but moments later he felt someone bump the cot and it wobbled. Still groggy, he lifted his head and saw a dark-clad figure rummaging through his travel case.

"Leo?"

The figure bolted up. Before Albert could say anything more, something smashed into the side of his head and he lost consciousness.

The Presidio

LEO ARRIVED AT THE PRESIDIO early in the afternoon. It was probably three miles from where he'd left the park and another mile from the gate back to where the hospital stood. The hospital had been first on his list. They had no record of either Louise or Joseph Braun and no record of John Morehouse.

He asked if there was a registration desk.

The young officer at the desk nodded toward the front of the building and said, "Follow that road down to where it forks, then bear left. There's an administration tent about fifty yards in. They've got a list of everyone staying here at the camp."

At the administration tent, the search under Mr. and Mrs. Joseph Braun turned up nothing.

"Nothing on Joseph," the attendant said, "but there's a Louise Braun in section nine."

Leo's heart sank. "That's my mom's name."

For as long as he could remember, his parents had been inseparable. There could be only one reason she'd be here without him. Leo felt numb as he listened to the soldier's directions to section nine. Thinking only of finding his mother, he started to leave then, remembering Albert, turned back.

"What about a John Morehouse?" he asked. "Anything on him?"

The solider searched the list then shook his head. "Sorry, nothing."

Leo left the tent, his head down and shoulders slumped, his heart heavy with the knowledge that he should have come to visit sooner. The three years had flown by and he'd written a few dozen letters, less than one a month. Instead of coming back to check on his parents, he'd stayed late at the office night after night. He was the golden boy being groomed for a top-level management spot, a huge achievement for someone his age they'd said.

At the time he'd thought it something to be proud of. Now he wasn't so sure. He couldn't help but wonder: if the clock were turned back, would he do things differently? A sadness he'd not known before settled in his heart, and he knew the answer would be yes.

The guilt of doing nothing weighed heavily on his shoulders; that's why he'd told Albert he'd be back. Albert wasn't his dad but he was somebody's dad, and Leo would do for him what he couldn't do for his own father.

When he reached section nine, Leo sought out tent 3B, cautiously lifted the corner of the flap, and called softly, "Mom?"

"Leonard," his mother squealed and came flying at him.

They both spoke at the same time, their words tumbling over one another. His were filled with apology and regret, hers with eagerness and excitement.

"I'm so sorry, I should have come sooner. I never dreamed this would happen—"

"Well, of course you didn't. Nobody did."

"I should have made time, written more letters, come for a visit once a year..."

"I won't disagree with that, but you're here now and that's all that matters."

"I feel sick about Dad—"

"Don't. He brought it on himself—"

"Mom!"

"Don't look at me that way, it's true. If I told him once, I told him fifty times to fix that banister. He knew it was loose and had no business—"

"Don't you even feel bad that he's gone?"

"Of course not. I'll join him in time. Right now, I've got—"

"Good Lord, Mom, don't even say such a thing! It's bad enough that I've lost Dad without you—"

"Your father's not lost. I know exactly where he is."

Leo gave a sigh of exasperation and shook his head. There were times when his mother could be such a know-it-all.

"Mom, I realize you have pretty specific ideas about all this, but the truth is nobody knows whether they're going to heaven or hell. It's imposs—"

"What are you talking about? Your father went to Oakland. The hospital here was full, and since he wasn't critical they sent him to Oakland. I told him as soon as I can find a way to get over there, I'll join him."

"Dad's not dead?"

"Of course not! He fell down the stairs and did God-knows-what to his back."

Leo laughed and wrapped his mother in a bear hug. "You can't imagine how glad I am to find you and know that Dad is okay. When they said you were here alone, I thought for sure…"

"I'm not alone. Mrs. Silver is with me. You remember Elizabeth Silver, don't you?"

Leo nodded. "Is she the only neighbor here?"

"No, there's a handful of us, but a lot of our friends left town."

As she told of the fires that swept through their neighborhood, she spoke slowly and had to stop from time to time. Her voice trembled, and tears filled her eyes as she described moving to the high ground of Russian Hill and looking back to see their home be swallowed up by the flames.

"You need to leave too, Mom. I want you and Dad to come back to New York with me. There's two bedrooms in my apartment and—"

She was already shaking her head. "I doubt your daddy will want to leave San Francisco. This is our home. It's where we—"

"I know," Leo said sympathetically. "But right now, you can't live here. The house is gone; your whole neighborhood is gone. The city needs time to breathe and rebuild itself. In time it will, Mom, and when it does you and Dad can come back. But until then, I'd like you to stay in New York with me."

He segued into telling her about the things New York had to offer:

Central Park with its winding pathways and gardens, the Times Square theaters, the pushcart vendors of Mulberry Street, the shops along Fifth Avenue, and how from his apartment window he could look out and see New Jersey.

"It sounds lovely, but it's not home."

"No, it's not. But you'll only be there for a visit. Then when the time is right…"

"I might be willing to consider it, but I doubt that your father will."

"If I can talk Dad into it, will you come?"

She laughed. "Considering how stubborn your father is, that's a pretty big if. But, yes, if he agrees to it, I will."

As they chatted, Leo told her about Albert.

"He's a lot like Dad, not as stubborn maybe, but I think he's come to depend on me. I promised him I'd come back and let him know if his son-in-law is here or not, and that's something I've got to do, Mom. I can go there tonight and come back for you tomorrow morning so we can catch the ferry over to Oakland."

"You're a good boy, Leo, and it's very sweet of you to watch out for this Albert, but all that running back and forth is ridiculous."

"Mom, I promised him…"

"Well, then, you'll go back, but I'll go with you. It's easier to get to the ferry from the park than it is from here anyway."

Leo shook his head. "No, Mom, it's too far for you to walk."

"I don't plan on walking."

"The trolleys are down, there's no way—"

Leaning forward, she spoke in a conspiratorial whisper. "I know someone who'll take us in a car."

"I doubt that's still true. The army has conscripted most vehicles for military use."

She gave a smug smile. "Exactly."

The young soldier Louise rounded up was a neighbor's son, but by the time she gathered her belongings and said goodbye to Elizabeth Silver it was almost dark. The sky was pitch black when they finally arrived at the east entrance of Golden Gate Park.

"It's late," Leo said. "I doubt anyone will be there to get you a tent assignment. Since Albert and I already have one, you can sleep on my cot and I'll make do with a blanket on the ground."

She turned to him with a look of shock. "Sleep alongside a man who's a total stranger?"

"It's okay, Mom. Albert's very much the gentleman, and I'll be there with you."

Leo led the way through the maze of tents, and as he neared the one he shared with Albert he heard movement inside.

"It looks like Albert's still awake. I can introduce you."

Reaching out, he pulled back the entrance flap and spotted Albert lying on the floor, the side of his head bloody.

"What the hell—"

A dark figure rose from the shadows, hurled the traveling case at Leo, then charged.

That's when all hell broke loose. Fists flew, and the two men fought. Louise Braun screamed loud enough to wake the entire camp, and suddenly heads began popping out of the nearby tents. Moments later they were surrounded by military police.

A couple of soldiers pulled the men apart and asked, "What's going on here?"

Louise spoke up. "That hoodlum attacked my son!"

One of the MPs eyed Charlie. "Aren't you barracked over in the second row? What are you doing over here?"

"Visiting a friend," Charlie said.

"Friend, my ass! He's a looter!" Leo pushed past the MP and helped Albert to his feet. "Are you okay?"

Looking glassy-eyed and dazed, Albert said, "What happened?"

"I got back and found this guy going through your travel case and you on the floor."

Albert blinked a few times then rubbed his eyes. "Charlie?"

"You know this guy?" the MP asked.

Albert nodded. "Yes, he said he'd find my son-in-law."

Little by little the story unfolded. Albert told how Charlie claimed to know where John was and would bring him back for fifty dollars. The big MP grabbed Charlie by the front of his shirt and practically lifted him off his feet.

"Do you actually know where this John is or not?"

Charlie shook his head. "Not yet. I was gonna look for him."

"If you hadn't found him yet, why'd you come back to this tent?"

"To get the rest of the money he owed me."

"He wasn't supposed to give you the rest until you found his son-in-law, right?" When Charlie gave a half-shrug, the MP began to pepper him with questions. "How'd you find out who he was looking for? This ain't your first time doing this, is it? You ever been arrested before?"

When no answers were forthcoming, the MP stuck his nose in Charlie's face. "We've got orders to shoot looters on the spot. You're lucky you're not dead." He shoved him toward the other two MPs. "Get this weasel out of here."

Albert stood there, holding his hand to his head. Blood crusted around his eyebrow, and the knot at his temple had started to turn blue.

As the MPs began to shoo people back to their tents, the big one turned to Albert. "Come on, buddy, let's get you over to the medical tent and have them take a look at you."

The last anyone saw of Charlie, two MPs had him in restraints and were leading him off.

Louise looked at her son. "If not for you, who knows what would have happened to that poor man. It's a good thing you kept your promise and came back."

"Yes, it is," Leo replied. "But with us leaving tomorrow—"

"We don't have to leave tomorrow. If you're worried about your friend, we can stay here a few days and you can help him find that son-in-law he's looking for."

"Thanks, Mom, but the problem is I wouldn't even know where to start looking."

"Sleep on it, dear. Problems look very different in the daylight."

That night Louise slept on her son's cot, and he slept on Albert's. Long after the night had grown silent and his mother had fallen into a deep sleep, Leo lay there thinking about how he could possibly go about finding John Morehouse. The pale pink of morning was edging the horizon when he finally gave up and closed his eyes.

WHEN ALBERT ARRIVED AT THE medical tent, they bandaged his head and had him stay for the night.

"Chances are you'll be fine," the nurse said, "but we'd like to make sure."

She led him to the makeshift men's ward. Beds were spaced a few feet apart and lined up one after another along both sides of the tent. The tent was quiet. Most of the men were asleep, and only a few nurses moved about silently. With the beds in the front section already filled, Albert was led to the back and given a bed and a headache powder. Before long, he was fast asleep.

Philadelphia

AFTER SHE'D RECEIVED A TELEGRAM from her daddy saying that he'd found Mildred and was now heading over to San Francisco in search of John, Templeton expected to hear some good news in a day or two. That first afternoon, she sat on the front porch embroidering a row of yellow flowers along the edge of a flannel baby blanket. Although she claimed not to be worried, her fingers were clumsy and fidgety. Twice she had to tear out a full row of stitches and start over again. The sky was dark by the time she finished three tiny little flowers that should've taken no more than an hour.

The following day dawned drizzly and damp, but she barely noticed.

"I'm going to sit outside so I can keep an eye out for the Western Union boy," she told her mama.

Eleanor frowned. "In this weather?"

Templeton gave a nod then grabbed a shawl and shrugged it around her shoulders.

"You sitting out here is not going to change anything. With your daddy in San Francisco, it's going to be difficult for him to contact us. It could easily be another three or four days before we hear from him."

Templeton looked up wide-eyed. "Why would it take that long?"

"The telephone and telegraph lines are down, and there's no telling how long it will take before they're up and running again." Eleanor touched her daughter's cheek. "Stop worrying, sweetheart. Just because we haven't heard from your daddy yet doesn't mean anything's wrong. It may be that he and John are finding it difficult to connect to one another."

Although Templeton acknowledged her mama's words, the worried look remained on her face, her brows pinched tight and a washboard of ridges on her forehead. "But Daddy has the maps I made. He knows where to look."

For almost two weeks, Templeton had pored over the newspaper reports of fire damage, homes and buildings gone, countless dead, and thousands homeless, but even as reporters told of the devastation her heart had held onto the hope that those she loved were safe. She told herself John had been one of the lucky ones, that Jones Street was one of the few blocks the flames had skipped over. She even tried to convince herself that John might already be on a train headed back to Philadelphia to fetch her and bring her home. Now those beliefs had begun to wane.

There was no telegram that day or the next. Two days turned into three, then four, and with every passing hour Templeton grew more nervous. Before noon she felt as though two days had come and gone, and by nightfall it seemed as if a week had passed. When the rain finally stopped, she returned to sitting outside. From time to time, she walked to the corner and looked along the side streets hoping to see a boy in the familiar Western Union cap pedaling toward her.

By the fifth day, she'd worked herself into such a state that she could think of nothing else. A dozen different scenarios ran through her mind, each one more terrible than the other. That afternoon as she stood at the end of the walkway looking for the Western Union boy, she felt a stab of pain that started in her back and then grabbed hold of her stomach.

Turning quickly, she started back toward the house. The cramps, the sharp ache across the small of her back, the pounding of her heart, all of it was the same as she'd experienced that fateful day three years earlier.

"No," she whispered in desperation. "Please, God, no—" Holding to the rail as she mounted the steps, she cried out, "Mama!"

Seconds later, Eleanor appeared in the doorway a dishtowel in her hands. "What in heaven's name are you hollering about—"

Templeton's face was beaded with perspiration and her eyes teary.

Her hands protectively cradled the belly bump that had begun to take shape. "The baby…"

Before she could say anything more, Eleanor wrapped an arm around her waist, walked her into the sitting room, had her lie on the davenport, and loosened the ties on her corset. With her palms open and fingers spread wide, she felt across and down Templeton's abdomen, then shook her head and frowned.

"Your stomach is in knots. You shouldn't be wearing this thing. I can feel your tension, and I think the baby can also. Worrying will not solve anything. You've got to relax."

"And just how am I supposed to do that, Mama? Yes, I'm worried, worried sick over John and Daddy. Now I'm worried about the baby also. How am I supposed to relax when they're all I can think about?"

"No, they're all you're *letting* yourself think about. You need to force that fear out of your head and start thinking of something pleasant."

Eleanor's voice had a tone that Templeton remembered from childhood. It was the sound of comfort and reason, of a wisdom that somehow made things better. Templeton drew in a long breath and willed her heart to slow.

"I'll try, Mama."

"You'll have to do better than try." Eleanor slid a pillow beneath her daughter's head. "I'm going to send for Doctor Cooper, but try to calm yourself until he gets here."

Templeton couldn't rid herself of the worry that if something happened to her daddy, it would be her fault. She was the one who'd sent him out there. What if he didn't come back? What if neither of them were never heard from again? The fleeting image of her and Eleanor living together as two lonely spinsters flickered through her mind, but she pushed it away and tried to picture a baby with John's dark hair and eyes. She'd seen the earlier images clearly, but the baby seemed far away and out of focus. It was not a living, breathing baby, only the dim shadow of one.

Her heart thudded hard against her chest, and a tear slid from her eye.

Try harder.

There was one thing that had never failed Templeton; it was still there, not first in her heart, but she would have to try it.

Slowly the image came to mind. She saw herself sitting at the drawing board, a charcoal stick in her hand, pastel chalks scattered about, a tablet nearby. Her hand moved slowly across the paper, and a smile began to curl her lips. Following the lines as they took shape on paper, she realized that these drawings were not of tea gowns or traveling suits. They were baby clothes. A tiny pink bonnet, a white christening gown, a bunting that wrapped itself around the dim baby shadow and breathed life into it. If she could see it, she could make it happen.

By the time Dr. Cooper arrived, her heart had slowed to a near normal rate, but her back still ached and her stomach was cramping.

"I don't want to lose this baby," she said, "but I'm frightened because this is the same way it happened three years ago, when I had the first miscarriage."

She was hoping he'd reassure her nothing was wrong, but he didn't. Instead he asked an endless string of questions. When did the pain start? Had she fallen? Ridden a horse? Undertaken any overly strenuous activity? As she answered question after question, he proceeded with his examination. He had a full beard, thick mustache, and heavy brows, which made it impossible for her to read his expression. Once he paused as if he'd found something of interest, then asked if she'd seen any change in bowel movements and continued on. After almost fifteen minutes of poking and prodding, he asked what she'd eaten today.

"I've not had much of an appetite," she replied. "This morning I managed a cup of tea."

"Nothing else?"

She shook her head. "Not today. But yesterday I had toast."

The doctor gave a grunt of dissatisfaction and frowned. "You have no spotting or other indications of a miscarriage, and since you have nothing in your stomach it's probably gas." He stood, dropped the stethoscope back into his bag, and turned to Eleanor. "It would seem as a mother yourself, you'd know a pregnant woman needs to eat."

"I've said that a dozen times, but she's stubborn as a mule and claims—"

Templeton cut in. "It isn't that I don't want to eat, I have no appetite and—"

His bushy eyebrows hooded his eyes, and it now became simple enough to read his expression. "I don't give a fig about whether or not you have an appetite. If you want your baby born healthy, you'll start eating."

After that Templeton had nothing more to say. He snapped his bag shut and suggested she get plenty of rest and eat four times a day. As Eleanor walked him out, she explained the situation with Templeton's husband and daddy both caught up in the San Francisco mess.

"I think it would help her appetite if you could prescribe something to calm her nerves."

"Mrs. Winslow's Soothing Syrup," he said. "A teaspoon in the morning and another before bedtime. That should calm her nerves and have her sleeping through the night."

Eleanor

I'M EVERY BIT AS WORRIED as Templeton is, but I can't afford to let her see it. She's a nervous wreck now and if she starts to suspect that I'm also worried, heaven only knows what can happen. I've no doubt Emmitt Cooper is a good doctor, but he's a man and can't possibly understand the fear in an expectant mother's heart after she's already had one miscarriage.

I can understand how Templeton feels, because it's happened to me twice. Once before Benjamin was born and again the year after. For a while there, I thought Benjamin would be the only child Albert and I ever had. Then I got pregnant for the fourth time. Trust me, I was on pins and needles the whole time I carried Clara, fearful of doing anything that might cause me to lose that second baby.

With Templeton, I didn't worry one iota because I figured it was the changes. Six months along she started moving around inside of me, and that's when I realized we were having another baby. Now my baby is having a baby, and I feel just as protective of this one as I did my own. Doctor Cooper said not to bother sending for him when it's nothing more than a bit of gas or indigestion, but I say better safe than sorry.

When you love someone, you can't help but worry. So, yes, I'm worried about Templeton, but I'm even more worried about Albert. It's almost two weeks since he left here, and my heart has been in my throat ever since he stepped onto that train. I was the one who told him to do something, so I'm partly to blame for him going but I didn't have much of a choice. I knew that if he didn't go, Templeton would. I think if I had it to do over again, I'd probably do the same.

Life is full of hard choices. You try to do what you think is best and pray that you've chosen wisely. Right now I'm praying for Albert, Templeton, and John, and I surely hope God is listening.

The Reunion

WHEN ALBERT OPENED HIS EYES the next morning, he was in the field hospital and Leo was standing at his bedside.

"Feeling better this morning?" Leo asked.

"I think so, but I don't actually remember what happened."

As Leo told how he came back and found Charlie going through the traveling case, the pieces began to fall into place.

"The thing I don't understand is why," Albert said. "He told me he knew Templeton and had worked with her, so why would he lie about knowing John and then try to steal money from me?"

Leo shrugged. "Why a guy like him does anything is a puzzle to me. When you get home, ask Templeton about him."

A weary look settled on Albert's face.

"Home," he echoed sadly. "Who knows how long it'll be before I get back? I've yet to find John, and I can't leave without him." He glanced up at Leo. "How'd you make out at the Presidio?"

"I was able to locate Mom. She came back to the park with me. Dad's at the hospital in Oakland. Nothing too bad, she said. He fell on the stairs and hurt his back."

"What about John?"

"I couldn't find anything on him. I know for sure he's not at the Presidio, not in the hospital, and not at the campground. But he's got

THE FAULT BETWEEN US

to be somewhere, so we're not going to stop looking."

"We?" Albert repeated.

Leo nodded. "After what happened last night, Mom and I decided to stay here for a while. We figured we can help you find John; then we'll go to Oakland together."

Albert's heart swelled. He wanted to say how much that meant to him, but to gush over such an action seemed unmanly.

"Thanks," he said and gave Leo a chuck on the shoulder. Seconds later the nurse happened by and said Albert could leave anytime he was ready.

"I'm ready now." He gingerly lowered his feet to the floor and stood.

On their way out, Albert scanned the long row of beds. Last night he'd been groggy, and in the darkness he hadn't seen anything more than shapeless figures covered with blankets. In the light of day, he could see faces. In the bed third from the end, he spied what looked like a familiar face. The eyes seemed the same, but the beard made it difficult to say for sure.

He quickened his step, and the closer he got the more certain he became. Two beds away, he called out, "John Morehouse?"

The bearded man turned toward the sound with a look of surprise. "Albert?"

Both men had changed since the last time they'd seen one another. Albert had a covering of grey stubble on his chin and the right side of his head bandaged. John, normally clean-shaven, now had his face all but hidden behind the heavy growth of the past two weeks.

John had a million questions. Was Templeton okay? Was she here in San Francisco? Did she know what happened?

Albert said she was still in Philadelphia and he'd come in her stead. He pulled the letter Templeton had written from his pocket, but before giving it to John he stopped and introduced Leo.

"Leo's a banker from New York. He came out here looking for his parents, but if it weren't for him I might not be alive."

"I think you're giving me more credit than I deserve," Leo said jokingly. He reached over and stuck out his hand. "Leonard Braun."

"Braun," John repeated. A puzzled look tugged at his brow. "The same Leonard Braun who heads up lending for Corn Exchange?"

"Afraid so," Leonard said.

"We spoke on the telephone last year. I was working on the financing for the Ironworks building and you—"

Leo smacked his forehead. "Of course, now I remember. I thought you were out of Philadelphia; that's why I didn't place the name."

They talked for a few minutes longer. Leo excused himself, saying he was going to check on his mother and would see Albert back at the tent. Once he was gone, Albert handed John the letter then stood silent.

As his eyes moved from one line to the next, John began to smile. After he'd finished reading, he sat there for a moment then looked up at Albert with a smile that stretched from one ear to the other.

"We're having a baby," he said.

Albert nodded. "That's why Templeton is hoping you'll come back with me. You can stay with us until the baby's born. Once you feel well enough and you want to go back to work, I'll get you set up at my office. You've already got contacts in Philadelphia; you can work from there. Then after—"

It seemed impossible for John's smile to grow wider, but it did as he repeated, "We're having a baby. After all this time, it finally happened."

Albert pulled a chair over and sat beside the bed as they talked. John told him of how his leg broke when the bricks from the chimney rained down on top of him and how he'd wrenched his shoulder trying to pull himself free of the debris.

"It was a miracle I made it down the stairs. If not for George, I would have been trapped inside when the fires came through."

"George Wilson?" Albert asked.

"Yes. He showed up an hour or so after the first shock. By then people were outside in the street. With the aftershocks coming one behind the other, everyone knew it wasn't safe to be inside the houses."

"Why didn't you get out like everyone else?"

"I couldn't. The earthquake shifted the building, and the door was jammed. At first I thought about climbing out the window, but it was a ten-foot drop to the street. I was calling out for help, but with everything going on no one heard me."

"How did George know to look for you?"

"He didn't, actually. He came to check on Denise and her little girl. She and George are pretty close friends. Denise lives opposite us, a few doors down. George knew I was back from Pennsylvania and here alone, so when he saw I wasn't in the street like everyone else he started asking around. When no one could remember seeing me come out, he started knocking on the door. That's when he heard me call for help."

Albert leaned in. "Good grief, I can't begin to imagine…"

John continued on telling how George broke through the garden door, then carried him down a flight of stairs and out the back.

"The city was in turmoil by then. There was no help to be had, no ambulance, no policeman, no fireman. Every available man was trying to hold back the fire south of Market. George used a neighbor's wheelbarrow to cart me over to the hospital, but by the time we got there the hospital was gone and Mechanic's Pavilion was on fire. The nurses were carrying patients out and loading them into whatever wagons they could get hold of. Some were brought here to the park and some to the Presidio."

"Did George come with you?"

John shook his head. "They only transported the patients. If you were able to stand, you had to find a way to get here on your own."

"Then how—"

"He and Denise walked. By the time they got to Eddy Street they could see the fire coming at them, so George picked up Isabelle and carried her the rest of the way."

"I guess they made it okay?"

John nodded. "Frightened but okay."

"Templeton wanted me to check on both of them. Are they here at the park?"

"They were but left three days ago. George has a sister in Kentucky. He took Denise and Isabelle with him, and they'll stay with his sister for a while. He was supposed to mail my letter once they got to Oakland. Do you know if Templeton has received it yet?"

Albert shrugged. "Saturday was the last I heard from home." He explained how he'd sent a telegram asking if they'd heard from John, and they'd responded to the Western Union office in Oakland. "It's possible there's another telegram waiting for me."

They talked for hours as Albert told him of his trip out, how he'd found Mildred Kent and then met Leo on the ferry line. He also told of his encounter with Charlie Muller.

"Charlie's wanted to get even with Templeton for a long time," John said. "Unfortunately, he saw you as his way to do it."

"Thank God Leo showed up when he did. If he hadn't, Charlie would have made off with every last nickel I had and since I'd seen his face I doubt he'd leave me alive."

After they'd told all the stories they had to tell, John asked, "What now? Are you going back to Philadelphia to let Templeton know I'm okay?"

"Not yet. I'll wait until you can hobble out of here and bring you home with me."

John chuckled. "I'm afraid it may be a while before I can walk that far. It's a good five miles to the ferry."

Albert leaned closer and shared what Louise Braun had told Leo.

"According to someone who's got a friend on the inside, they've cleared most of the debris from Market Street. Within the next two or three days, there will be a trolley running from the park clear over to the ferry building."

"You're kidding."

Albert shook his head and smiled.

IN THE DAYS THAT FOLLOWED, Albert spent countless hours at John's bedside. They spoke of past mistakes and future plans. Albert told how Eleanor had been pestering him to have a telephone installed at the house for nearly a year. He'd stubbornly insisted that while it was a business necessity, having one at the house served no purpose.

"You can bet your bottom dollar she'll get that telephone now," he said and laughed.

John spoke of how they had once planned to put a nursery and nanny's room on the third floor and how over the years Templeton's business had grown to the point where it consumed every inch of space.

"For a while she worried that we wouldn't have room enough for both a baby and the business. When she stopped worrying about it, I began to worry that she'd given up hope of us ever having a child." He straightened himself on the bed, then pulled a deep breath. "Now that we finally do have a baby on the way, there's no house to worry about. I guess life has an irony that we humans will never truly understand."

Later on, he asked if Templeton was terribly saddened by the loss of all her drawings.

Again, Albert shrugged. "If she is, she hasn't said so. The only thing she wanted me to bring back was you."

Once Albert arrived, John's ability to move around seemed to improve rapidly. Two days later, he was given crutches and told he could move into a tent if he wished to do so. The cot in the tent was nowhere near as comfortable as the hospital bed he'd been sleeping on, but the company more than made up for it.

Louise Braun had somehow secured a family tent that was big enough for all four of them, had a wooden crate table, and room to move about. She also came up with a deck of cards that no one could account for. When Leo asked how she'd come by them, she simply replied that it was in the poorest of taste to look a gift horse in the mouth.

As it turned out, she was an extremely adept poker player. Before their stay at the camp ended, Albert owed her seventy-six dollars and forty-five cents.

The Letter

FOR THE NEXT TWO DAYS, Eleanor tried to busy herself with cooking things Templeton might eat. She boiled egg custards, sprinkled triangles of toast with cinnamon and sugar, and made a blackberry pudding fit for a king. But even as she stood there folding the berries into the mix, she kept her eyes and ears open. When the delivery boy headed on a bicycle for Heidi Rose's house on the corner, she ran to the front porch thinking it might be the lad from Western Union. Like Templeton, she expected Albert would send another telegram. Hopefully he'd say he'd found John and they were on their way back to Philadelphia.

On Thursday morning she heard the postman's footsteps on the front walkway but thought nothing of it. He would holler through the screen door then leave the mail on the porch table. A few seconds later she heard his voice.

"Mail's here," he called out.

"Thank you, Jesse," she called back and kept stirring the pudding.

Once the pudding was done, she brewed a pot of chamomile tea and added a sugary topping to the cookies she'd pulled from the oven. That morning she carried the tray upstairs and sat beside the bed as they drank their tea together.

"No word yet?" Templeton asked.

Eleanor shook her head. "Not yet, but the telegraph lines are still down. I bet they're still in San Francisco. John might have had business to take care of before starting back."

"Well, Daddy could have at least taken the ferry over to Oakland and sent another telegram. They've got to know how worried we are about them."

"You would think so, but men are men and they don't consider things like that."

Trying to ease her daughter into a less troublesome subject matter, Eleanor asked if Templeton had given any thought to a name for the baby.

"Not yet," she said. "John needs to have a say in it." With little more than a breath in between, she went back to worrying about why they hadn't yet heard from John or her daddy.

The fears Templeton expressed were the same ones that troubled Eleanor's heart, but she kept them to herself and continued to suggest there was absolutely nothing to worry about.

Later on, when Templeton's eyes grew heavy and she leaned her head back into the pillow, Eleanor picked up the tray and headed downstairs.

It wasn't until after she'd washed the teapot and set the drying towel aside that she remembered the mail and carried it in from the porch. Shuffling through the envelopes, she spotted the brown envelope with a Red Cross insignia in the upper left-hand corner. For a moment she stood there with dread filling her heart. It was addressed to Templeton, so it had to be news about John, but what kind of news? And why hadn't she heard from Albert?

With each footfall feeling as though she were walking toward an execution, she carried the letter upstairs and peered into Templeton's room.

TEMPLETON WAS LYING BACK AGAINST the pillow with her face turned toward the window when Eleanor said, "Something came for you."

She bolted upright. "A telegram?"

"No, a letter." Eleanor pulled the brown envelope from her pocket and handed it to her.

Templeton recognized the handwriting immediately.

"It's from John!" she squealed and tore into the envelope.

There were three sheets of paper, the front and back of each page filled with words telling of what happened. It spoke of his injured leg, how he'd been trapped in the house until George rescued him, and then transported in a bread wagon to the hastily set-up medical facility at Golden Gate Park. On the second page it said George had come to Jones Street to check on Denise and Isabelle and came in search of him only after realizing that John was not in the crowd gathered outside.

I pray you've had the good sense to remain in Philadelphia, he wrote, *for there's nothing in San Francisco to come home to. We've lost the house and all that was in it, but we're among the lucky ones, for we have insurance enough to rebuild. I cannot give back all the many hours you spent working on the drawings in your studio, but I can give you that house on Nob Hill I promised you three years ago.*

My darling, I have not given up hope that one day we'll have a family, and when it happens I assure you we will have a safe home with plenty of room for a nursery.

Templeton stopped reading and looked up at her mama. "That's odd; he doesn't know about the baby. I would think that by now Daddy would have given him my letter."

Eleanor's face lost all color. "I would have thought so too. Is there a date on the letter?"

Templeton looked back at the first page and shook her head. "No. He says he's in a field hospital at Golden Gate Park but didn't say how long he'd been there."

"Did he mention seeing Albert?"

"Not yet," Templeton said; she went back to reading the letter.

Eleanor's face suddenly took on the same woeful look her daughter had been wearing. "Your daddy said he checked the hospitals and didn't find him."

"That was in Oakland, but Golden Gate Park is in San Francisco."

Thinking she might have missed something, Templeton turned back to the first page and read the letter aloud.

There was not a single mention of seeing Albert. John told how anyone who could leave San Francisco had already done so. Saying George was among the last of their friends to leave, John wrote that he had taken Denise and Isabelle to Kentucky where they would stay with his sister. He urged Templeton to remain in Philadelphia with her parents and ended the letter saying he would contact her as soon as possible.

Her first reaction had been pure unadulterated joy, but as she read the letter a second and then third time, a feeling of fear started to swell in her chest.

"Even if it took the letter five days to get here, he would have written it after Daddy arrived in San Francisco. Why would he not say something about it?"

"Maybe the mail's slower than we're thinking?"

"I guess it's possible but even so…" Templeton started to count up the days. "The last telegram from Daddy was on April 28th when he left Oakland. The ferry ride is short so even if he left in the late afternoon, he'd still get to San Francisco that same day."

"April 28th," Eleanor repeated. "That's eight days ago. You said Golden Gate Park was on your list of places for him to look. Doesn't it seem that—"

"Not necessarily. According to John's letter, there are no trolleys or cable cars, so if Daddy had to walk to all those places, it would take forever."

"Walk? With Albert's back the way it is? Why, that would kill him!"

Recognizing the fear in her mama's face, Templeton softened the thought. "Even if the trolleys are out, there'd be carriages for hire. Scads of them are always waiting right outside the ferry building. Daddy would have hired a carriage, don't you think?"

"I would certainly hope so," Eleanor replied, but her voice didn't sound the least bit hopeful. Nor did her expression change.

ELEANOR COULD SEE THE LETTER had lifted Templeton's spirits, but she had simply gone from worrying about her daughter to worrying about her husband. The thought of Albert hiking from one side of San Francisco to the other troubled her to no end. His office was less than a mile away, but the last time he walked home was well over ten years ago. If he couldn't handle that distance, how could he possibly survive the trek clear across a city where everything was unfamiliar and he'd struggle to find his way around?

Concerned that she might upset Templeton, Eleanor tried to hide the nervousness she'd felt when there was no mention of Albert in the letter. But after she'd listened to it three times and measured the weight of every word, she'd grown even more anxious. The truth was she ached to see Albert come walking through the door; to feel his weight in the bed beside her and hear the whoosh of weariness he gave right before he drifted off to sleep.

For weeks the newspapers had carried stories of suspected looters being shot in the street, people who'd disappeared without a trace and casualties who had yet to be identified. What if one of them were Albert? He was a man ill-equipped to deal with disasters. A man who spent most of his time sitting—at home, at the office, in a courtroom. He certainly wasn't used to walking long distances.

What if his back gave out and he collapsed somewhere along the way? A man lying on the sidewalk could easily be mistaken for a drunk and tossed in jail. What if he'd been mugged on the walk crosstown and never even made it to Golden Gate Park?

Templeton was saying something about a letter when Eleanor felt a strange flutter in her chest. At first it seemed little more than a flitting butterfly; then it grew stronger and felt like a large bird trying to break free of its cage. She pressed her hand to her chest and felt the hammering of her heart.

"Are you okay, Mama?" Templeton asked.

Eleanor gave a forced smile and nodded. "A touch of indigestion, that's all."

"Are you sure? You look awfully pale."

"Just tired and worried about your daddy."

Templeton hugged Eleanor, told her to try not to worry, then repeated all the things her mama had told her: communications were down, obviously there was no way for them to get in touch other than by mail, and under ordinary circumstances a letter took at least five or six days to travel from San Francisco to Philadelphia. Given the way things were now, it could easily take eight or ten days.

"For all we know, John may have written this letter before Daddy even left here."

"I suppose that's possible," Eleanor said, but she wasn't the least bit convinced.

THE APPREHENSION THAT SETTLED IN Eleanor's mind that afternoon remained with her, as did the discomfort in her chest. Twice she thought of sending for Doctor Cooper then decided against it. Emmitt Cooper was fine with broken bones and deadly influenzas, but he fell short of understanding when it involved matters of the heart.

That night she downed two spoons of the soothing syrup the doctor prescribed for Templeton and climbed into bed. For a long while she lay there trying to convince herself that tomorrow or the day after there would be another letter, one saying Albert had arrived safely and they would soon be starting home.

But what if there was no letter? What if they never had a chance to say one last goodbye?

When the pain in her chest grew worse, she climbed from the bed, padded downstairs, and sat at the desk in Albert's study. Taking several sheets of stationery from the drawer, she wrote of all the things she wanted to say to Albert. She told him of her love, of how proud she'd been to bear his children, and of how empty the bed seemed with him away.

We're not young lovers as we once were, but the love I now have for you is in many ways stronger, deeper, and more complete. You've become as much a part of me as I am of myself. Some say the pathway we travel in life is ordained the day we're born, and we have no choice in these matters. Still, I cannot help but wish I'd stopped you from undertaking such a dangerous trip. I know you did it for our daughter, and if our situations were reversed I likely would have done the same. Now I can only pray for your safe return and trust that God will watch over you while we're apart.

She signed it *Your ever loving wife,* wrote his name on the envelope, left it on the desk, and returned to bed.

Dawn was edging the horizon when Eleanor finally closed her eyes. As she did so, a sharp pain shot across her back.

San Francisco

ON SUNDAY, MAY 6TH, NINETEEN days after the earthquake, a single trolley resumed operation. It ran along Market Street, went east to the ferry building, then turned and reversed course. That same day, Albert and John left the refugee camp along with Leo and his mom. John was still on crutches and moved slowly, but at long last they were on their way home.

The ferry arrived in Oakland shortly before noon. As they were pulling into the dock, Leo announced that he was taking everyone to lunch at the Belvedere Hotel.

"Jack Moore, a friend of mine, owns the place," he said. "We can have lunch, check the train schedule, and hopefully get rooms."

"You go ahead," Albert said. "I'll meet you there. First I need to send a telegram."

Once they were clear of the dock, Leo found a hansom carriage for hire. Although the two-seat carriage was a squeeze for the three of them, it was low to the ground and easy enough for John to climb into. Albert waited until the cab pulled away; then he turned and started walking toward the Western Union office.

Eight days earlier, when he'd gone from the Western Union office to the ferry, the walk had seemed long and tiring and the anticipation of what lay ahead as heavy as a boulder strapped to his back. Now everything was different. His step was spryer, the future rosier, and he had nothing but good news to report.

During the time he'd spent in the refugee camp he'd not only thought about sending the telegram, he'd even pictured it in his mind. He'd start off with the two words he'd been waiting to say: "Good news."

The girl behind the counter was the same one who'd sent his last telegram.

"Remember me?" he said. "Albert Whittier. Any new telegrams for me this week?"

"Yes, sir. Three of them." She pulled the yellow envelopes from the basket on the back counter and handed them to him. "That top one came in just this morning; the others came earlier in the week."

He tore open the top envelope.

"Received John's letter. Mama very sick. Worried about you. Come home soon. Send word you're OK." It was signed Templeton Morehouse.

For a moment Albert was taken aback by the thought that Eleanor was sick, but then he remembered how Templeton had a penchant for drama and made even a hangnail sound life-threatening. The first two telegrams were similar to this, each with her customary note of drama— urgent that I hear from you, desperate to know if you've found John. All three were signed Templeton Morehouse.

Albert smiled. He had never really gotten used to calling her Morehouse. To him she was still their baby, still a Whittier.

He pocketed the telegrams then sent a reply that read exactly as he'd pictured it. "Good news. All well. With John in Oakland. Heading home soon. Will advise travel plans. Take care of Mama. Tell her I love her." He signed it Albert Whittier, hesitated a moment, then crossed out his name and wrote "Dad."

There was so much to tell—the stories of making his way across the country, sleeping in a church, finding Mildred, meeting Leo, the long walk across San Francisco, the refugee camp, his encounter with Charlie, stories that Eleanor would insist he tell over and over again. She'd claim he was a brave and dedicated father and he'd allow her to say it, although there were many times when he didn't feel brave, when he wished only to be home in his own bed, sleeping beside his wife.

The stories would have to wait a while to be told, but he'd remember them for the rest of his life. He'd tell Eleanor that he might not be alive were it not for the chance meeting with Leo Braun and claim it was fate that brought them together. He'd explain how finding John as he did was truly a miracle wrought by a hand far more powerful than his.

Yes, he'd tell her the truth of everything, but she'd hear it differently and in turn tell their neighbor Heidi Rose that he was a bonafide hero who had saved the day and rescued their daughter's husband. Heidi would in time tell Anne Wolters, and she would tell the other ladies that lived along Spruce Street. The stories would no doubt grow with each telling, but Albert would always know the truth in his heart. He'd been lucky, not brave, and blessed in meeting Leonard Braun.

As he hurried down Broadway, Albert heard a trolley rumbling down the street. He let it pass him by. He was stronger now, and the walk seemed far less intimidating. As he walked he thought of Eleanor and how right there at the train station, in front of all onlookers, he'd take her in his arms and kiss her in a way she'd long remember. The more he thought about it the faster he walked, and by the time he reached the Belvedere Hotel his cheeks were flushed and beads of perspiration lined his forehead.

TWO DAYS AFTER TEMPLETON RECEIVED the letter from John, she had to send for Doctor Cooper again. When he arrived at the house, he was wearing a scowl.

"Today is Saturday. I do not like making house calls on a Saturday, so please tell me that this is not another bit of silliness about your lack of appetite."

"No, it's about Mama. Last night she wasn't feeling well, and this morning she looked pale as a ghost. When I saw her looking like that, I made her get right back in the bed and asked Mrs. Rose to send for you."

She pulled the door back and motioned for him to follow her up the stairs. Eleanor was lying in bed, half-asleep. Templeton reached out and touched her shoulder.

"Mama, Doctor Cooper's here to see you."

Eleanor opened her eyes, blinked a few times, then closed them, gave a weary sigh, and leaned back into the pillow.

"I'm just tired," she said. "You shouldn't have bothered the doctor."

"Actually, she did the right thing." He opened his bag and pulled out his stethoscope. After listening to Eleanor's chest, he frowned and said her heartbeat was too slow. "Prior to this morning, were you feeling tired?"

Eleanor nodded.

"For how long? When was the first time you noticed it?"

"Yesterday evening. Before then I felt fine"

"And was there a reason for it? Were you involved in some overly strenuous activity? Excited about something? Emotionally overwrought?"

Although Eleanor shook her head, Templeton spoke up. "She doesn't want to worry me, so she won't say it, but I will. Yes, she was upset. Very upset. We both were when we got the letter and John didn't say a word about daddy being there."

"That was yesterday afternoon?" he asked.

"Yes. And afterward, when I asked if she was feeling okay, she said yes, but I don't think that was true, because even then she looked pale."

Doctor Cooper looked at Eleanor, his brows pinched together and a frown tugging at his face. "Is what she says correct?"

She gave a sheepish nod. "Mostly true. My daughter has lost one baby, and I didn't want my worries to be the reason for her losing another."

"Well, if you don't take care of yourself and get some rest, she'll have a lot more to be concerned about. Your heart is not functioning correctly. It's too slow, and that can lead to trouble if you continue to ignore it."

"I think that's just a fluke, because yesterday it seemed like it was beating too fast," Eleanor said defensively.

"You're right, it could be a fluke, but it could also be the precursor to apoplexy. Would you like to spend the rest of your life sitting in a chair, possibly unable to speak?"

"Of course not."

"Well, then, you'll do as I say and get the rest you need." He pulled a syringe of morphine from his bag. "I'm going to give you a shot so you can relax and get some sleep. Keep whatever you eat light, nothing too heavy. Do not skip meals and remain in bed."

He turned to Templeton. "Make certain she does not leave this bed. I'll be back tomorrow to check on her. In the meantime, you'll have to keep an eye on her. If she seems confused or unresponsive in any way, send for me immediately."

TEMPLETON SPENT THAT NIGHT IN the chair beside her mama's bed. She took Eleanor's hand in hers and watched as her mama slept. As the hours crept by, she thought of her childhood and the countless nights Eleanor had kept this same type of vigil over her. In the wee hours of the morning, when the sky was so dark that even the moon and stars were hidden, she prayed.

"Please, God," she said, "don't let me lose my mama. Please give me the strength to keep her and our baby safe until our family is back together again."

Twice it seemed as if Eleanor was about to wake up, but both times she mumbled a few words and dozed off again.

On Sunday morning, when the blackness of night faded to a deep blue and the sun showed itself as a speck of candlelight on the horizon, Templeton shrugged on a shawl and walked to the Western Union office. The only address she had for her daddy was the Western Union office in Oakland, so she sent the telegram there. On the walk home, she prayed that he would receive her message and understand the urgency of it.

AFTER LUNCH LEO AND HIS mom were off to the Oakland Hospital. John grabbed a comfy chair in the lobby, and Albert headed over to the train station.

"I'm looking for the first train going to Philadelphia then on to New York," he told the clerk at the ticket window.

The clerk looked at the schedule and turned back to Albert. "You want the first or the fastest?"

"What's the difference?"

"The first leaves tomorrow morning and gets into Philadelphia next Monday. That one's got three changes, Cincinnati—"

Having experienced just such a train on the way to San Francisco, Albert didn't wait for him to finish. "What about the fastest?"

"That's the Intercontinental Express. It leaves here Tuesday morning, gets into Philadelphia Friday afternoon, and New York Friday night."

The thought of being home before the week was out brought a smile to Albert's face. "Yes, that's the one I want. I'll need five sleeping car tickets."

The clerk scratched his ear. "Not sure I've got five of the Pullman berths; one or two maybe. I've got second-class seats in the passenger cars, if you're interested."

Remembering Templeton's stories of their trips back and forth, Albert asked, "What about compartments?"

"I got compartments, but they cost quite a bit more."

After figuring the cost for two compartments to be slightly below the six hundred dollars he'd brought with him, Albert gave a nod and pulled out the money he'd hidden in his vest pocket. Paying that much for the compartments meant he'd arrive home broke, but he'd arrive home and right now that was all he cared about.

BY THE TIME ALBERT RETURNED to the hotel, Leo had returned with his mom. They were sitting across from John when Albert approached them.

Leo glanced up. "Good news, Dad is going to be released from the hospital tomorrow."

"Perfect!" Albert gave a wide grin. "I've reserved us two compartments on Tuesday's Intercontinental Express. You'll be back in New York Friday evening."

Louise Braun clapped her hands. "Better than I could have done."

As they sat there going over the plan, an attractive brunette carried over a tray of coffee and small pastries. She set the tray on the cocktail table in front of them.

"We didn't order—"

The girl smiled. "I know. Jackie asked me to bring it over. He's getting two rooms set up for you." She looked at Leo. "You don't remember me, do you?"

He shook his head. "Afraid not."

"I'm Linda, Jackie's wife."

Leo jumped to his feet. "Good grief, how could I have forgotten?" He hugged her. "It's been, what, six or seven years?"

"Try nine. The last time I saw you was at our wedding."

Leo stepped aside and offered her his seat. "Please join us."

"I'd love to, but I can't. I'm manning the desk. Jackie just wanted me to let you know he's moving some people around and will have two rooms for you in an hour."

Leo thanked her. They chatted for a minute or so, and then she hurried off. The coffee was good, just as Albert liked it, strong and dark. He could almost swear it was flavored with a bit of chicory, which made him feel all the more nostalgic for home.

Later on, when the others settled in their rooms—the three men in one room, Louise Braun in the other—Albert excused himself and said he had another errand to run. Returning to the Western Union office, he sent Templeton a second telegram.

"Arriving on Intercontinental Express, 4:10 pm Friday. Meet us at the station. There's someone I want you and Mama to meet."

ON MONDAY JOSEPH BRAUN WAS released from the hospital and joined the group. He wore a back brace and moved about gingerly but seemed genuinely glad to be free of the hospital bed and nurses who he claimed shuffled him about like a sack of potatoes. That evening Jack and Linda Moore joined them for dinner in the Belvedere dining room, and everyone laughed as Leo and Jack reminisced over stories of their wild teenage shenanigans.

Louise gave an exaggerated sigh. "There were times when I thought for sure both of you would grow up to be nothing more than hooligans."

"I know what you mean," Albert replied nostalgically. "When Templeton was a child, I thought her ideas of becoming a designer were downright foolish, but just like Leo, she's turned out to be an amazing person." He hesitated a moment, stirred another spoonful of sugar into his coffee then added, "I think we can both be pretty proud of our children."

ON TUESDAY MORNING THEY BOARDED the Intercontinental Express, Albert, John, and Leo sharing one compartment, and the Brauns taking the other. As the train pulled away from the station, Albert noticed John swipe away a tear.

"You okay?" he asked.

John nodded. "Yes, but it's hard to see the city I love in such ruins.

I'm glad Templeton didn't return with me. I always want her to remember it the way it was."

"Don't you think they'll rebuild?" Leo asked.

"In time they will. But it'll never be the same as it was before."

"Nothing ever is," Albert said. "Earthquake or not, things change and they keep right on changing. The years roll by, one after the other. Old ways are lost, and new ones slip in. A carriage gets traded for an automobile, candles replaced by electric lights, a person in Philadelphia can talk to someone in California." He hesitated for a moment and shook his head. "At first you don't notice it; then one day you look around and start wondering what happened to the world you once knew."

"But these changes are for the better," Leo said. "They make life easier, travel faster…"

Albert nodded. "True. But to appreciate them, you've got to jump in and be part of the change, not just sit around and let it happen to you."

John sat silent for most of the conversation; now he spoke.

"You're right, Albert, and I plan to be part of the rebuilding of San Francisco. My business is financing construction, and there's going to be plenty of that needed once the rebuilding is underway. Working from Philadelphia, I can reach out and pull resources from the entire East Coast. I can and will be part of making San Francisco into a city greater than it once was."

"On behalf of Corn Exchange Bank, I wouldn't mind being in on some of that action," Leo added.

After they'd talked for a long while, the men grew silent, each lost in their own thoughts as the train sped eastward toward home.

Philadelphia

TEMPLETON FORGOT IT WAS SUNDAY. All morning she watched for the mailman, hoping there would be a second letter, one saying her dad was now with John, perhaps saying they'd soon be starting home. She'd purposely left the door ajar so she could hear Jesse when he called through the screen. Normally he was there by nine, but here it was almost eleven and there'd been no sign of him.

Shortly after she carried Eleanor's breakfast tray down, she heard footsteps: a clicking sound, not the usual clomp of Jesse's boots. She was at the door before Dr. Cooper had a chance to knock, but the eagerness in her face disappeared.

"Darn, I thought you were the mailman."

He looked at her with a strange expression. "The mailman? On a Sunday?"

Realizing she would have to wait another day for a letter, she gave a sorrowful shrug and said, "I forgot it was Sunday."

Pushing the screen door open, she invited the doctor in and led him upstairs. Eleanor was sitting up in the bed, her color pale but no longer the ghastly white of the previous day.

"Doctor Cooper," she said and smiled. "I feel terrible that you should spend your Sunday making a house call. Honestly, there was no need. I'm already feeling a bit better."

He raised a bushy eyebrow. "Since I'm the doctor, why not let me decide if you're better or not?" He opened his bag, took out the stethoscope, and held it to her chest. "Deep breath, please."

Templeton stood by watching nervously as Eleanor followed his instructions. A deep breath, then a cough, then another deep breath. Over a minute ticked by before he spoke again.

"Your lungs are clear, but I'm still not happy with your heartbeat. It's better but only marginally. I'm concerned that this could be indicative of something else."

"Like what?" Templeton asked.

He fingered his beard and gave an almost imperceptible shrug. "It's too soon to tell, but a weak heart can lead to any number of things." He turned back to Eleanor. "I want you to continue bed rest and a light diet, and I'll stop by on my way into the office tomorrow morning."

"It's foolish for you to go out of your way like this. If you feel there's a need to check me again, I can come to your office and—"

He began shaking his head before she'd finished. "I don't want you putting any undue stress on that heart. A few days of bed rest and a light diet; then we'll see where you are. I'm also going to prescribe Doctor Blaud's Pills. If you're anemic, a healthy dose of iron might help to strengthen your blood and get that heartbeat up."

As he followed Templeton back down the stairs, he spoke in a low voice. "Make sure your mama remains in bed. No stress or excitement. I'm concerned about that heart of hers."

Templeton nodded somberly.

That afternoon she sat beside her mama's bed reading from a well-worn copy of *Little Women*. Later on, after she'd carried Eleanor's dinner up on a tray and waited for her to drift off to sleep, Templeton tiptoed down the stairs and set about making an egg custard for the next day.

The sky had long since grown dark, but with so many concerns crowding her head she'd neglected to light a lamp in the front sitting room. When a knock sounded, it startled her. As she wondered who would come calling at that time of night, the knock sounded again. This time it was harder and more insistent. Were it not for the fear that the noise would wake her mama, Templeton would have ignored the caller.

"Does this fool not know the hour?" she grumbled as she wiped her hands on a dish towel and hurried through the darkened rooms.

With only a thin glimmer of moonlight lighting the porch, she could see a figure standing at the door. The person seemed too tall for a woman; it had to be a man. The doctor had come and gone, and she could think of no one else who was expected.

Speaking from behind the closed door she said, "It's too late for callers. What do you want?"

"I've got a telegram for Templeton Morehouse," he said. "Somebody's got to sign for it."

His voice was not that of a man. It was the high-pitched sound of a boy. Templeton unlatched the door, pulled it open, and signed his receipt. She took the yellow envelope from him, her hand trembling. Turning back inside, she switched on the lamp and dropped down on the settee.

Before she could bring herself to open it, she said a prayer that it was news of her daddy and that nothing bad had come of his trip. As the slid the telegram from the envelope, she vowed that if it were bad news she would not tell her mama. She would carry the weight of it until Eleanor was well and strong again.

The first two words caused her heart to swell. "Good news," it said, and Templeton breathed a sigh of relief. For a few moments she sat there, absorbing every word, reading it over and over again until she could recite the text from memory.

With her heart thumping against her chest and her eyes already growing watery, she climbed the stairs with the sheet of yellow paper clutched in her hand.

Stepping into her mama's room, she whispered, "Mama, are you still awake?"

"Yes," Eleanor answered softly. "I haven't been able to sleep, because I'm still worried about your daddy."

The tears that had been sitting on the rims of Templeton's eyes overflowed, and her voice trembled with emotion as she spoke.

"We can stop worrying now, Mama. They're both coming home."

Eleanor bolted up. "What? When? How do you…"

Templeton sat on the side of the bed and handed her mama the telegram. "I was afraid to give you this, because Doctor Cooper said for me not to let you get excited, and I just knew—"

"Excited is not the same as worrying," Eleanor said. "Why, news like this makes me feel as if I could get up and dance around the room!"

"Mama! Doctor Cooper said..."

Eleanor laughed gleefully. "Sorrow is what kills people; happiness is the cure."

Long into the night, Templeton and her mama sat talking about the homecoming and what arrangements would have to be made. There were any number of questions but no answers. In time they would learn the when and where of Albert and John's arrival, but for now they had to be content with simply knowing they would soon be on their way.

That night Templeton crawled into bed and slept alongside her mama as she had done when she was a little girl. In the wee hours of the morning, she turned on her side and felt the baby move for the first time. That's when she knew that this time her child would be born whole and healthy. The troubling events of the past were where they would forever be kept; in the past.

WHEN DOCTOR COOPER ARRIVED THE next morning, Eleanor answered the door.

"Mrs. Whittier," he said in a stern voice, "why on earth are you out of bed?"

"Because I feel fine, and I'm much too busy to waste time lying around."

"You might think you feel fine, but that doesn't mean your condition has changed. Sit down and let me have a look at you."

As he moved the stethoscope across her chest, a puzzled look settled on his face. "How many of those iron pills did you take?"

"None. Templeton was going to pick them up at the drugstore today."

"If you didn't take the iron pills, what did you take?"

"Nothing."

"No pills? No tonic?"

"Nothing," Eleanor said. "I added an extra spoonful of honey to my cream of wheat this morning but nothing more than that."

He furrowed his brow. "There's been a remarkable improvement in your heart rate. It's still on the low side but within what I'd consider a normal range." He scratched at his beard. "If you didn't take anything or do anything, I don't understand what brought this change about."

"It was the telegram," Templeton said.

"Telegram?"

She nodded. "We got the good news we'd been hoping for."

"Telegram, huh?" The doctor shook his head and laughed as Templeton had never seen him do before.

THE SECOND TELEGRAM CAME THAT morning, and they began making plans. What had yesterday seemed endless days of waiting had now been whittled down to just four. The hours were gone in the blink of an eye, and the days hurried off before they'd finished all there was to do.

The house was cleaned until there was not a speck of dust to be found, furniture was pushed aside and rooms rearranged, and the aroma of fresh-baked cookies wafted through the rooms. On Friday morning, the butcher delivered what he swore would be the finest roast they'd ever sunk a tooth into.

Later that afternoon after the roast was in the oven and the table set for dinner, the carriage Templeton had ordered arrived and carried her and her mama to the train station. She told the driver to wait. They hurried through the stationhouse and stood on the platform.

Templeton's heart thudded against her chest as she and her mama waited to see a plume of black smoke rising in the distance or hear the rumble of the train, and she was reminded of the first time she'd climbed aboard the Intercontinental Express. So much had happened since then. Her life was different now, more different than she'd ever imagined possible. She'd gone to California believing something magical would happen, but now she knew better. The magic was never because of where she was; it was because of who she was with.

The sound of a shrill whistle cut through her reverie as the big engine rounded the bend. Soot flew everywhere, but instead of stepping back to the shelter of the stationhouse, Templeton remained on the platform, moving even closer to the track. When the Intercontinental Express finally screeched to a stop, she ran alongside the train, looking up at the windows, searching for the familiar face of John or her daddy.

"Templeton," a voice called. "Templeton Morehouse?"

She turned and saw a young man waving to her, a handsome fellow with tousled brown hair but not someone she knew.

"I'm Templeton Morehouse," she answered.

"Leo Braun," he said as he walked toward her. "Your husband—"

A lightning bolt of fear shot through Templeton.

"No," she cried. "No, please don't tell me something has happened to John…"

The inside of her head started to spin, her knees turned to jelly, and just as she began to topple over, his arm shot out and grabbed hold of her elbow.

"Steady there. Nothing's wrong with John, he's just a bit slow because of the cast. Your dad's with him. We had a compartment, so we were up there in the first coach."

Looking over his shoulder, Templeton caught sight of her father waving one arm in the air and holding onto John with the other. Turning back to her mama she yelled, "They're here!" then broke into a run.

With John and Albert hooked together as they were, it was impossible to separate one from the other, so she spread her arms wide and wrapped both of them in a wildly enthusiastic hug. Eleanor was but a few steps behind. When Albert saw her, he allowed Templeton to slide in beside John to provide the necessary support. Then he took Eleanor in his arms and kissed her with a passion Templeton had never before witnessed.

"Daddy," she exclaimed, "where in the world did *that* come from?"

Eleanor blushed as everyone laughed.

After a whirlwind round of introductions to Leo and his parents, they said goodbye and got back onto the train. As Leo climbed aboard, he looked back and waved.

"I'll be in touch," he called out and disappeared into the coach.

"He's a nice guy," Templeton said, "but if he's from New York, how'd you meet him?"

"It's a long story," Albert replied. "A very long story."

THERE WAS NO BIG HOMECOMING celebration that night, just a quiet gathering of family around the table with the most delicious roast anyone had ever tasted. Albert told how he had met Leo as they stood waiting for the ferry and how a stroke of bad luck led to the good luck of finding John. He claimed there were a lot more stories to be told, but they could wait.

"For now I just want to enjoy being back home with my family," he said. John echoed the sentiment.

Shortly after the table was cleared, Albert said he couldn't wait to sleep in his own bed again. He and Eleanor disappeared upstairs.

John looked at the staircase, shook his head, and turned back to Templeton. "As much as I'd like to crawl into bed beside you, I doubt that I can make it up the stairs."

Templeton leaned in, kissed his cheek, and moved her lips close to his ear. "Then maybe you'll like the surprise I have for you."

She led him over to her daddy's study and pulled the door open. The large oak desk that once commanded the center of the room was gone as were the high-backed chair, the shelves of books, and the smoking stand. The room had been transformed into a cozy bedroom with plump pillows and a chintz coverlet. It would be another month or two before the cast came off of John's leg, and until then this was where they would sleep.

That night as they wrapped themselves in each other's arms, they found the bulky cast on John's leg was not nearly as troublesome as they'd thought it might be.

In the Days That Followed

A LOT HAPPENED IN THE Whittier household that summer. Eleanor got the telephone she'd wanted for so long, and her heartbeat settled into a rhythm that was as dependable as the sunrise.

Once the telephone was installed at the Whittier house, John began making business calls. Weeks before the cast came off his leg, he was back at work. At first he settled in a small office at Albert's firm, but before the month was out he'd outgrown the space and needed a clerk. He rented a three-room suite in the same building. There he had a reception area, a meeting room, and desks for two clerks. In that first three months, he tripled the amount of business he was doing.

After the earthquake, it was as though the entire country had decided to come to San Francisco's aid. In the earliest days, it became obvious that the city would not only be rebuilt but rebuilt on a grander-than-ever scale. Big investors wanted to be part of it, and John became the man to talk to.

He knew the city, knew which companies were rock solid, and could point investors to the most lucrative locations. He also had the right connections. Rumor on the street was that his connection to Leonard Braun was what ultimately led to the Corn Exchange Bank financing the rebuilding of The Emporium, two hotels, and nine Market Street office buildings. Once word of that got out, no investment banker refused a deal offered by Morehouse Financial.

EARLY ON TEMPLETON HAD BEEN on pins and needles waiting to feel the baby's movement, but as the summer wore on she began to wish the child would settle down and let her get some rest. When she complained that the baby never stopped moving, Eleanor laughed and said she felt the same way when she carried Templeton.

"You were so active, I thought for sure I was having twins."

"Well, then I guess this is retribution," Templeton said, laughing along with her mother.

That summer Templeton grew fuller and rounder, but the bigger she got the smaller the house began to seem. The downstairs bedroom that was at first cozy and intimate soon became cluttered with no place to put things away. Before long, sketch books were left here, there, and everywhere. Charcoal sticks were lost in the seat of a chair or behind a flower pot. Her new sewing machine was shoved into a corner of the kitchen, and she had to use her daddy's smoking stand as a makeshift drawing table.

In early July, Templeton began preparing for the baby's arrival. Eleanor climbed up into the attic and brought down the bassinette she had used for all three of her babies, and they scrubbed it top to bottom. Once it was sparkly clean, Templeton set about making a soft flannel lining to pad the inside.

That evening dinner was served in the kitchen because the dining room table was piled high with pieces of flannel and strips of cotton batting. Two days later an organdy ruffle was added to the bassinette, and it was finished. Since it was impossible to fit another thing into their overcrowded bedroom, it ended up in the hallway.

As Albert squeezed by, he shook his head. "Seems to me you're rushing things a bit. The baby's not due for another two months."

"I'd still rather be prepared."

Templeton had projected September, but that was little more than a guess. In those last few months before they left San Francisco, she'd been so focused on getting the spring collection into production and readying herself for the trip that she'd completely forgotten to track her monthlies.

"It was after Thanksgiving," she'd said. "Or possibly after Christmas."

Eleanor smiled knowingly. "Mark my words, a baby as active as this one will be here sooner than you think.

Settling herself in the kitchen chair, Templeton sighed. "It can't happen too soon for me. I've got a dozen new ideas for children's wear, but even if I had a real drawing table, I wouldn't be able to reach across my stomach to get to it."

Although Templeton now claimed that fashion design was not the most important thing in her life, it was not at all unusual to find her with a charcoal stick in her hand. As she and Eleanor lingered at the breakfast table, she'd start doodling on a sketch pad and before you knew it she'd drawn a little girl's pinafore or a toddler's sailor suit. When she wasn't dreaming up fashionable outfits for children, she was stitching a baby dress or writing letters.

That summer Templeton was able to connect with almost all of her friends and the people she'd worked with in San Francisco. All except May Ling. Chinatown had been flattened by the earthquake, and the few buildings left standing were destroyed by fire. Before the dust settled, there was talk of moving the Chinese to an area on the edge of town and using the existing location for high-end commercial development. With their homes and businesses now gone and the future seemingly questionable, many of the Chinese who had lived there for years left San Francisco. Some settled in Oakland; others moved on with no word of where they were going.

After Templeton was unable to locate May Ling John made further inquiries, but he too came up dry. It was as if she and her family had simply vanished from the face of the earth.

With Denise it was a different story. She and Templeton exchanged letters almost every week. She told of the trip to Kentucky and the small town where she now lived with George's sister. She spoke of a flower garden she'd planted and how in many ways the town reminded her of the village she'd left behind in France. Templeton could almost feel the happiness woven through Denise's words as she told of meeting new friends, Isabelle playing with the neighbor's children, and her growing affection for George.

Isabelle adores him, and I believe he has feelings for me, she wrote, *but I worry that to love again would be disloyal to Jacques.*

Templeton wrote back and said that giving Isabelle a man like George for a daddy should certainly take precedence over any guilt she might feel.

Finding love once is fortunate, but finding love a second time is a God-given gift. Treasure it.

Less than a month later, a wedding photo was tucked inside the envelope along with Denise's letter. In the picture, George and Denise stood together on the steps of a small white church. He held Isabelle in one arm and had the other wrapped around Denise's waist. Templeton slid the picture into a frame and set it on the windowsill in their bedroom. It made her feel good to see the three of them together as a family, and she couldn't remember a time she'd ever seen Denise looking as happy as she did in that picture.

IN EARLY AUGUST, ON A day that was neither too hot nor too muggy, Templeton was sitting on the back porch tatting a lace trim onto what would be the baby's christening gown when a cramp slammed into her back and shot through to her groin. Her back had been aching all morning, but it was nothing like this. She doubled over, waited for it to pass, then pushed herself up and waddled into the kitchen.

"Mama, I'm afraid the baby might be coming."

"Let's get you into bed and call Dr. Cooper."

Eleanor's first call was to Dr. Cooper who said he would be there within the hour. Her second call was to John's office.

"There's no need to rush," she said. "First babies can take a notorious amount of time to be born."

Elizabeth Anne Morehouse was an exception. She arrived moments after Dr. Cooper got there and came into the world howling at the top of her lungs. Her hair was the same fiery red Templeton's had been, but she had her daddy's beautiful brown eyes.

"Oh, dear," Eleanor said and laughed. "I have a feeling this one is going to be a handful."

TWO WEEKS LATER, ON A night when her parents had retired early, and Lizzy, as they now called her, had fallen asleep at Templeton's breast, John said, "It's time for us to think about leaving here."

The look of contentment she'd been wearing vanished. "It's too soon."

"No, it's not. We're practically crowding Albert and your mom out of their own house. It's not fair to them, and it's not fair to us."

"That's not true. Mama said they like having us around."

"Your parents are far too nice to ever make anyone feel unwelcome. They won't say anything, but I can see it happening."

"I don't see anything of the sort."

"You don't see it because you don't want to see it. Last night Lizzy was crying when your dad was reading the newspaper. I noticed how he'd rub his temples, then look at the newspaper for few seconds, then lift his head and rub his temples again. With her crying he couldn't concentrate and read his paper in peace. That's wrong, Templeton, very wrong."

Her eyes grew teary. "Daddy loves Lizzy; he'd never feel she was—"

Catching hold of her shoulder, he drew her closer. "Of course he loves her. You can love someone and still want some peace and quiet for yourself. Your parents are getting older, and they deserve to relax and enjoy these years. On the trip home from San Francisco, your dad talked about retiring. He said he'd come to the point where he'd like to give up working so hard and start enjoying his time with Eleanor. How can he do that with us living here and a baby crawling around the house?"

Templeton looked down and said nothing.

"And what about your poor mom? She's cooking for a family again. If we weren't here, don't you think she and your dad would be going out to dinner more often like we did in San Francisco? You know they would. They've already raised their family; now it's time for us to raise ours."

Templeton gave an almost imperceptible shrug and sat there with her shoulders slumped and her chin dropped down on her chest. Several seconds ticked by before she said, "Maybe there is a grain of truth in what you say, but have you thought about what's best for Lizzy?"

"I'm absolutely thinking of Lizzy. She needs a room of her own. A house to grow up in, a yard where she can play; if we stay here, she won't have that."

"You're right. We are crowded in here and I know Lizzy will need a room of her own, but why does it have to be now? Can't we wait a year or two? You said yourself, San Francisco is only starting to rebuild. Do you want our baby's tiny little lungs breathing in all that dust and—"

A smile slid across John's face.

"Oh, now I understand," he said and chuckled. "You think I'm talking about moving back to San Francisco, don't you?"

"Well, aren't you?"

"No. My business is flourishing here, and you're happy. I thought we'd give it a few more years. When Lizzy is ready to start school, then we'll decide whether we want to stay or go back to San Francisco."

"But you said we needed to move…"

"We do. That's why I put a deposit on a house over on Clark Street. It's bigger than we need right now, but it's less than a twenty-minute walk from here and closer to the park—"

"So we're staying in Philadelphia?"

John nodded but before he could say anything more, Templeton's mouth came down on his. The kiss was long, sweet, and passionate. When she finally drew back, she whispered, "I love you, John Morehouse; love you with my whole heart. The luckiest day of my life was the day you stepped onto that streetcar."

"Mine too," he echoed.

IN SEPTEMBER THEY MOVED INTO the house. As John had indicated, it was way bigger than what they needed. A two-story brick Victorian with a corner turret, five bedrooms, and a front porch that stretched the full width of the house. Templeton's eyes were wide as she looked up at the building.

"It's huge. What on earth are we going to do with five bedrooms?"

John grinned. "I figured you'd want room enough for a studio, and then there's the chance that our little family will keep on growing."

"But *five* bedrooms?"

At first the house seemed overwhelming with its front and back staircase, empty rooms, and echoes that bounced from one wall to another. With having made such a quick decision, they'd moved in with only the barest necessities: a hurriedly ordered bedroom set, a rocking chair and bassinette for the nursery, and a kitchen table with four chairs which would do until the dining room furniture arrived.

Little by little Templeton filled the rooms: a velvet divan for the living room, a settee and two side chairs for the sitting room. Some lamps and carpets, a painting to hang over the fireplace. With each trip to the furniture shops on Chestnut Street, she allowed a bit of extra time to stop into the department stores and specialty shops to ask about children's wear. There was very little selection and almost nothing she thought fashionable.

The idea that popped into her head when she was afraid of losing the baby refused to go away. Early on she'd decided not to do any more design work. She hadn't lost her love for it, but the cost was simply too high. She could be a designer and risk losing everything else, or she could find contentment in creating dresses for Lizzy and enjoy a full life with her husband and family.

She made her decision and stuck to it. When thoughts of designing called to her, she forced herself to remember how it was back in San Francisco—the endless arguments over production, the late delivery of supplies, the almost impossible deadlines, constant pressure with never enough time to enjoy her life. She definitely did not want to do that again. Things were different now. She had to consider Lizzy and John. It was impossible to be a full-fledged designer and a wife and mother. She'd learned that the hard way.

Remembering strengthened her resolve to steer clear of the fashion industry, but it didn't lessen her desire to design. She might well have continued along that troubling path were it not for a luncheon meeting with her friend, Lucille Bransfield, the women's wear buyer at Wanamaker's.

After lunch they'd lingered over a second glass of wine, and Lucille said, "You were always so good at fashion design, I'm surprised you don't miss doing it."

"Actually, I do miss it," Templeton replied, "but after what I went through with the production problems in San Francisco, I've decided not to let myself get involved again."

"You gave up designing just because of production problems?"

Templeton nodded. "It may sound like a small thing, but it's not. I felt as though I was living it twenty-four hours a day. It really got to be too much..." There was a melancholy echo woven through her words.

BETTE LEE CROSBY

"So why don't you focus on design and not get involved in the production?"

"Easier said than done."

"No, it's not. Instead of selling a design to the department store, you sell it to the manufacturer and let them take it from there. You make less money that way, but there's a lot less headaches."

"Doesn't the department store expect the designer to run interference with production even if it's contracted out?"

Lucille shook her head. "It's not contracted out. If you sell your design to the manufacturer, they own it and they're the one working with the department store. Once you deliver the patterns, everything else is their responsibility."

"Really?" Templeton pushed her glass aside and leaned in. "Do you know of anyone doing it that way?"

"Abraham Westley is doing it with his men's wear waistcoats and cravats. I also work with a designer named Rosetta Kramer. She does nightwear and undergarments. She comes in with the salesman from Milady. They show me the designs, note whatever changes I want, and from there on in I work with Sam, the production manager at Milady."

"Who is your purchasing agreement with?"

"The manufacturer, Milady's Under Fashions."

"I've never thought of doing it that way. I wonder if I could find a manufacturer interested in producing a line of children's wear."

Lucille laughed. "Honey, if you've got a department store buyer who likes your designs, you don't have to look far to find a manufacturing company chomping at the bit to take you on."

She went on to say that while Wanamaker's did not have a children's wear department, developing one for the store would definitely be a feather in her bonnet.

"Show me some children's wear sketches that are comparable to your other stuff, and I'll take it from there."

Templeton had thought that creating one-of-a-kind outfits for Lizzy would be enough to satisfy her need to design, except that it wasn't. The thought of working again set her brain buzzing. In the back of her mind, she could already imagine the bedroom at the far end of the hallway turned into a studio. The wall would be covered with tacked-up drawings. She could feel a pebbly sketch pad in her hand and see a row of pastel chalks sitting on the windowsill and ink stains on her fingers.

LATE THAT NIGHT, WITH JOHN asleep and Lizzy growing drowsy in her arms, Templeton pushed back and forth in the rocker. Looking up into the clear night sky, she could see the moon, fat and full, surrounded by a million stars. There'd been other nights when the sky was little more than a blanket of dark shadows and the moon a whisper thin crescent. All that beauty ebbing and flowing as it did somehow seemed a reflection of life.

In the four short years she and John had been married, they'd seen dark days and days bright with beauty and wonder. They'd traveled from one end of the country to the other, survived an earthquake, experienced the loss of a baby, the loss of their home and everything they owned, but here they were, right back where they started, happier than ever.

When Lizzy was fast asleep, Templeton placed her back in the bassinette then turned and stood looking out the window. Reflected in the glass was the shadowy image of her face and, beyond that, a moon bright with promise.

Over the past four years Templeton had come to accept that life was full of uncertainties. In the blink of an eye, the best of times could disappear and what seemed like an ordinary day could suddenly burst open with a near-blinding brightness.

She'd once thought her career would mean she'd never know the joy of having a child. Then when Lizzy came along, she'd believed that loving her family meant turning her back on her career. Both times she'd been wrong.

Yes, life was full of uncertainties, but Templeton now realized the one thing she could always trust was her heart. Going forward, that's exactly what she would do.

Epilogue

IN THE SPRING OF 1908 Wanamaker's introduced the Little T collection of children's clothing. It was a quiet affair, supported by a handful of newspaper ads, with none of the pomp and circumstance that surrounded the fashion shows at the Emporium. The collection sold out in just a few weeks and was reordered immediately. There was no exclusivity contract, so before the summer was out Little T children's wear was being sold in Arnold Constable, Macy's, and, yes, even the Emporium.

This time Templeton had gone into the business knowing the pitfalls, and she'd successfully avoided them. After months of talking to different manufacturers, she'd selected the Butterworth Company. She picked the company not because it was the largest or most impressive but because of Tom Butterworth himself. On her first visit, he'd given her a tour of the factory and introduced several employees. Unlike Charlie at Acorn, the workers seemed glad to see Tom. He'd called them by name and frequently made mention of their family or how long they'd been with the company. There was no yelling, no drama, and none of the dreariness that she'd seen at Acorn. She'd left Butterworth feeling good about the company, but it wasn't until later in the evening that she realized how much he reminded her of George and that was a very good thing.

ONCE THEY'D SETTLED IN THE house, there was no further mention of moving back to San Francisco. From time to time, John traveled back and forth on business trips but was never gone longer than three weeks. He often returned with stories of change and pictures of the rebuilt city, a new row of houses, or one of the many pubs where they'd drank wine and shared a pot of ragout.

After each trip they'd reminisce for a while, talking of friends they'd known and places they'd favored, but in time the conversation always segued into something about Lizzy, a design Templeton was working on, or one of the deals John was financing. The present never lingered in the past. It moved on, and before long their years in San Francisco became little more than fond memories.

Almost two years rolled by before there was word of May Ling. John was on one of his trips and spotted her as he hurried along Market Street. He'd caught a sideways glance of her profile and called out her name at the very last moment. The photograph he'd brought back showed May Ling surrounded by four sons, two daughters, her husband, and a white-haired elderly father. The smile on her face told of her happiness, and Templeton couldn't help but notice how the oldest of her boys had his arm protectively snugged around his mother's shoulder. The group stood in front of Ling's Souvenirs, a tiny shop with silk kimonos and paper umbrellas hanging in the window.

Like so many others, May Ling and her family had taken refuge in the Chinese section of the Presidio camp then gone to Oakland.

IN THE SUMMER OF 1915, Templeton returned to San Francisco one last time. By then she and John had three girls: Lizzy who was almost nine and growing like a weed, seven-year-old Ella who was named for her grandmother, and five-year-old Bertie, who if she'd been a boy would have been called Albert.

The trip came about because John had arranged financing for several exhibits at the Panama-Pacific International Exposition. At first Templeton was hesitant; she wanted to remember San Francisco as it had been when they lived there. But after months of listening to John talk about the Tower of Jewels, International Pavilions, and Palace of Fine Arts, she could no longer resist.

That August she packed up the three girls, several coloring books, and a well-worn copy of *Grimm's Fairy Tales*. The family climbed aboard the Intercontinental Express and headed for San Francisco where they checked in at the brand-new Chancellor Hotel on Union Square.

They spent five glorious days at the fair. Starting in the morning they went from one pavilion to the next, feasting on treats like cotton candy, sourdough bread, and enchiladas, then staying until long after dark. Templeton could not believe the marvels she saw. Gardens and floral displays so beautiful they made her eyes tear, a mechanized assembly line that churned out automobiles, flying machines doing loop-de-loops overhead, pagodas from distant lands, pageants, parades, and shows that filled the air with the oomph-pa-pa of the Sousa band.

On their last evening in San Francisco, John hired a nursemaid to stay with the children and took Templeton for a carriage ride around the city. As they settled into the leather seat, he slid his arm around her shoulder and said, "Do you remember…"

Many of the places she remembered were gone. Places where they had lingered over glasses of wine, listened to music, or laughed at the antics of a vaudeville performer were now little more than a distant memory. When they neared the Emporium, John leaned forward and spoke to the driver. The horse slowed and kept an easy clip-clop as they rode along Market Street.

Many of the quaint little shops Templeton frequented had been replaced by stores with large plate glass windows and dazzling displays. The fabric shop where she'd met Denise was now a charcuterie with cheeses and meats hanging in the window. The stationer where she'd ordered her first business cards was now a tavern. When they crossed over and turned down Jones Street, she gave a nostalgic sigh as she saw the office buildings and shops that stood where once there had been a row of houses. The street no longer had the feel of a neighborhood, and for a moment she resented the change.

It was just as everyone had predicted; the city had been rebuilt, the streets repaved, the landmarks restored. In many ways it was a city grander than before, but it would never again be the same as it was. Back then San Francisco had been like Templeton herself, young and wildly enthusiastic, full of innocence and gaiety; now that was gone. It was a city reborn, stronger and wiser perhaps, but never quite the same.

Her sadness lingered for a moment then disappeared as quickly as it came. Taking John's hand in hers, she snuggled closer and lowered her head onto his shoulder.

Later that evening when they returned to the hotel, she tiptoed into the second bedroom and stood watching as the girls slept. She imagined them someday married with children of their own. In time, there would be grandchildren and then great grandchildren. Tucking the coverlet around Bertie's shoulder, she smiled.

Templeton knew that like the city she'd loved, she too had changed. She was wiser and stronger now. She'd rebuilt her life into one with a solid foundation, something that would last a lifetime and beyond. This was not the future she'd dreamed of, but it was more beautiful than anything she could have ever imagined.

Acknowledgments

When a reader holds a finished book in hand, they see only the face of the author, but in truth, many people contribute to the successful making of a novel. Even the most skilled storyteller is only as good as the people who support her. There are an endless number of tasks to be done before the story I've written becomes a book and I couldn't do it without the wonderful team I have helping me.

First and foremost, I'd like to thank our daughter Trisanne Vricella, who stepped into the business to help out and has now become someone I could not do without. She handles a million and one tasks, does so graciously, and rises to meet every challenge. I could not ask for a better daughter or a more dedicated partner.

As a story grows and takes shape, I am fortunate to have an advisory team that willingly reads through every draft, unflinchingly tells me where I have gone wrong, and then shows up with wine and a homemade cake to help me find my way to a new and more beautiful storyline. No words could ever express how grateful I am for my Port St. Lucie Posse, Joanne Bliven, Kathy Foslien, Lynn Ontiveros, and Trudy Southe. Such amazing friends are a blessing beyond belief.

The right editor can make a story shine and I am extremely grateful to be working with Ekta Garg, who is a talented author in her own right. She somehow manages to catch my mistakes without ever losing sight of my voice, and pushes me to go deeper into the story. Without a doubt, I am a better writer because of Ekta and for this I am most grateful. I am also blessed in having Cecile Van Tyne as an early reader for she truly has the eye of an eagle and spots even the tiniest word that has somehow managed to make it through the scrutinization of our proofreading efforts.

To Amy Atwell and the team at Author E.M.S. I say thank you for turning my manuscripts into beautifully formatted pages and for being so wonderfully organized and dependable. I shudder to think of how I will manage without you.

I am also grateful for my Blue Sky Book Chat Author friends and very proud to call these wonderful ladies my colleagues. When the publishing world feels it is spinning out of control, they are always there with wisdom, understanding, support and advice. My heartfelt thanks to my fellow authors: Marilyn, Simon Rothstein, Patricia Sands, Barbara Davis, Soraya Lane, Lanie Cameron, Peggy Lampman, Alison Ragsdale, Kerry Anne King, Lisa Braxton, Loretta Nyhan, and Jane Healy. Such friendships are hard to come by and greatly treasured.

A very special note of thanks goes to the members of my BFF Clubhouse (Bette's Friends & Fans), they are the true followers who buy my books, share them with friends and take time to write reviews. Without such fans my stories might grow dusty on the shelf. Along with those in my BFF Group, I owe a tremendous debt of gratitude to the many Bloggers, Tour Organizers, fans and followers who share my work out and introduce me to new readers. I would be lost without supporters such as Linda Zagon of Linda's Book Obsession, Kristy Barrett of A Novel Bee, Susan Peterson of Sue's Reading Neighborhood, Annie McDonnell of The Write Review, Kathy Murphy of the Pulpwood Queens, Suzanne Weinstein Leopole of Suzy Approved Book Tours, and the many Facebook groups such as Novels & Latte, High Society Book Club, Reading is My Passion, Books, Nooks and Reviews, and the W.E.A.R. Book Club.

Lastly, I am, and forever will be, thankful that I met and married my husband Dick. He has given me the time and place to pursue my dreams. If you look closely your will see a trace of him in every lover, father, and hero that I create. He has been my inspiration for all of those characters. He is my soft spot to land in troubled times, my sun on a gloomy day, and my partner for life. I could not be who I am without him for he truly is my greatest blessing.

AWARD-WINNING NOVELIST BETTE LEE CROSBY is the USA Today bestselling author of twenty-five novels and recipient of over forty literary awards. Often hailed as a masterful storyteller, her 2016 novel, *Baby Girl*, was named Best Chick Lit of the Year by *Huffington Post*. Her 2018 novel *The Summer of New Beginnings*, published by Lake Union, took First Place in the Royal Palm Literary Award for Women's Fiction and was a runner-up for book of the year. Her 2019 release, *Emily, Gone* was a winner of the Benjamin Franklin Literary Award and received the International Book of the Year Award for Women's Fiction. Her most recent release *When I Last Saw You* is a historical novel based on a true story.

Crosby, a lover of small dogs and all things Southern, laughingly admits to being a night owl and a workaholic and claims her guilty pleasure is late-night chats with fans and friends on Facebook. She brings the wit and wisdom of her Southern mama to works of fiction, and the result is a delightful blend of humor, mystery and romance. "Storytelling is in my blood", Crosby laughingly admits, "My mom was not a writer, but she was a captivating storyteller, so I find myself using bits and pieces of her voice in almost everything I write."

Crosby currently lives on the East Coast of Florida with her husband and a feisty Bichon Frise who is supposedly her muse.

To learn more about Bette Lee, visit her website at:
https://betteleecrosby.com

CPSIA information can be obtained
at www.ICGtesting.com
Printed in the USA
BVHW070557290821
615169BV00003B/18